C01 069

D1141172

Seasonal Work

ALSO BY LAURA LIPPMAN

Collections

My Life as a Villainess

Hardly Knew Her

Stand-Alone Novels

Dream Girl

Lady in the Lake

Sunburn

Wilde Lake

After I'm Gone

And When She Was Good

The Most Dangerous Thing

I'd Know You Anywhere

Life Sentences

What the Dead Know

To the Power of Three

Every Secret Thing

Tess Monaghan Series

Baltimore Blues

Charm City

Butchers Hill

In Big Trouble

The Sugar House

In a Strange City

The Last Place

By a Spider's Thread

No Good Deeds

Another Thing to Fall

The Girl in the Green Raincoat

Hush Hush

For Molli Simonsen, without whom nothing would get done.

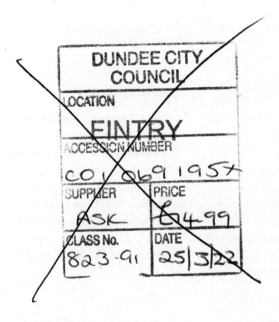

First published in the UK in 2022
by Faber & Faber Ltd
Bloomsbury House
74–77 Great Russell Street
London WC1B 3DA

First published in the USA in 2022
by HarperCollins Publishers
195 Broadway
New York NY 10007

Designed by Nancy Singer
Printed in the UK by CPI Group (UK) Ltd, Croydon CR0 4YY

ISBN 978-0–571–36102–1

A CIP record for this book is available from the British Library

10 9 8 7 6 5 4 3 2 1

Seasonal Work

and Other Killer Stories

Laura Lippman

faber

CONTENTS

PART 1

Good morning, Baltimore!

—*Scott Wittman and Marc Shaiman*

SEASONAL WORK

The photographer said she needed everyone to stand next to the minivan. I tried to get out of it. I'm fourteen now, although I look younger, and I didn't want my picture in the paper. I was wearing a T-shirt that was tight on me. My bangs were uneven because I cut them out of sheer boredom the other day. And I had a zit between my brows that looked like a third eye.

Gary gave me a stern look. He's big on manners, cooperating; it's part of how he's kept this family together. So I stood at the far end, hoping that if I closed my eyes or looked to the side, they might end up cutting me out. They don't need me. I don't fit. One of these things is not like the others. The littles are enough. They're still cute and they still care. This is the only life they've known. I'm old enough to remember staying in one place—a house with a yard and the possibility of a dog. Never an actual dog, but the promise hung in the air—when you're older, if you show responsibility. I was six when those promises were made. And, if you ask me, I've shown a lot of responsibility, but there's just no way we'll ever have a dog.

You see, my real dad died when I was six and then my mom married Gary and they had Lenny, Wade, and Barrett. Boom,

boom, boom. Barrett's a girl, by the way. She was supposed to be a boy and Mama had the name Rhett picked out. I guess Barrett's okay for a girl's name, especially given how pretty she is. Otherwise, it's not fun having a name that's like a boy's name, let me tell you. She's only five, but people can't stop looking at her. "My little angel," Gary says, and I want to tell him to cut it out, but he's right. She looks like something you'd see on a Christmas card, not that we get Christmas cards. It's hard when you have to move every December.

Sure enough, when the photographer, a lady, rearranged us, Barrett was in the middle of the photograph, the boys on either side of her. The photographer had to remind Barrett three times not to smile. Barrett can't help it. She just lights up. For cameras, for any flicker of attention.

The reporter, a man, asked Gary: "Can you tell me again what was in the minivan?"

Gary looked at the littles. "Well, it was supposed to be a surprise."

"Oh, but—" The reporter seemed really young, even to me. He was thin and kind of sullen, like he didn't want to be here. Maybe he was one of those people who thought that bad luck was contagious. If it is, then I have to admit you'd want to stay as far away as possible from my family.

"Daddy," Barrett said, "is Santa still coming?"

No one knew what to say to that. Gary gave me a look and I said, "Dad, is it okay if we go in and watch cartoons?"

"That would be great, Kathy." Gary smiled at me, grateful. This would give him a chance to tell the full story without the littles hearing every detail, which would include a full list of all the things they were never going to get. He got a disability check and decided to splurge on a big Christmas for us, despite being out of work. He would tell the reporter how he hit Best Buy and the mall, the one not too far from the motel where we're staying, the one with an Apple Store and a Claire's and a Build-A-Bear. He paid to have everything gift-wrapped because how could he wrap 'em in secret, the five of us living in just the one room? Well, two if you count the kitchenette, but it's in full view.

Anyway, Gary knew better than to leave the gifts in plain sight when he stopped at Target. Even here in the suburbs, you don't take those kinds of chances. But he drives a minivan—what else would you drive with four kids?—and you can't really hide stuff in the cargo section. We have a blanket to put over things, but maybe the paper peeked out or maybe if you put a blanket over the stuff in your trunk, people know it's worth stealing. Maybe having Texas plates is enough? People in the north really seem to hate Texas. Anyway, as Gary was probably telling the reporter, someone jimmied the lock and Christmas was gone, just that fast.

While we were watching television, the kids got hungry—all those damn commercials, how could they not get hungry, how could they not want things all the time? Some people call TV the "idiot box," Gary said, but he liked to call it the "cravin' box." He was very proud of that turn of phrase, although I didn't quite get it. When Gary likes a phrase, he can't let go of it. Anyway, I went outside to see if Gary had any change for the vending machines, although I knew he would not be happy to be interrupted.

I waited as patiently as I could while he and the reporter talked at the tables where the motel's smokers congregate. Gary used to smoke, but he gave up cigarettes when he realized how much money he was spending. "I did it for you," he said to me and the other kids, but mostly me. I'm really sensitive to smells and his breath was something horrible.

I stood over to the side, stamping my feet, exhaling as if I were having my own cig break. It wasn't that cold, for December. I've known colder and I've known warmer. Last year this time, we were up in Cooperstown, but Gary decided that was too small. A year before that, it was Phoenix, but that was too big. He's like Goldilocks, I guess. He said Baltimore looked to be just right. He said Baltimore would be our best place yet.

He says that every year, wherever we are.

Gary was saying: "I pick up odd jobs where I can. I was a long-haul trucker, but obviously I can't do that anymore. It's hard—I'm a man, I have pride—but I need to live somewhere we can get benefits. We started the school year in Texas, but there's just no help there. Someone told me Maryland was a nice place, so we decided to try it out. It was supposed to be a new start for the new year. Well, it's still a new start. We're starting from rock bottom, but that doesn't mean we can't climb to the top of the rock pile."

The reporter was writing everything down, his eyes on his pad. I coughed to get Gary's attention.

"I'm sorry, Dad, but it's the kids," I said. "They're hungry and I thought if I could just get some stuff from the vending machine to tide us over until dinner—"

"Don't you have a kitchenette here?" the reporter asked. "How do you feed these kids, anyway?"

"We do have a little kitchen," Gary said. "But I'm not ashamed to say that we go to soup kitchens, food pantries, wherever we can get a little help."

He began digging through his pockets, but I knew he wasn't going to come up with anything. The reporter just kept scribbling in his pad and my face burned at the thought of the words he was writing there. *He searched his pockets but couldn't even find enough spare change for a bag of chips.*

The photographer lady handed me five one-dollar bills.

"You shouldn't do that," the reporter man said to her. "You're becoming part of the story. That's unethical."

She ignored him. "What's the thing you'd most like to see under the tree on Christmas Day?"

"Books," I said. "I love to read. And maybe a locket."

Her kindness was hard. The kindness was always the hardest part. I gulped and took her money.

"Where are your manners, Kathy?" As I said, Gary was particular about manners.

"Sorry, Dad." I mumbled "Thank you" to the lady, scared I would burst into tears if I tried to say much more.

WE WENT TO THE FOOD court at the mall, had Chick-fil-A for dinner, looked at all the happy people with packages. Gary let us window-shop for fifteen minutes each. The boys picked the toy store, Barrett wanted to pretend she was going to buy diamonds, and I went to the bookstore, to the children's section, although I'm too big for kids' books. Back in Texas, I had the whole series of Oz books and the Betsy-Tacy books and the Harry Potter books and some old books of my mom's, about kids who kept finding magic things—a coin, a lake, a book, a well. Once upon a time, as they say. A long time ago, in a place far, far away.

"Tomorrow will be better," Gary said. What else could he say? He had to believe that, he had to say that. We went to bed. All four of us kids slept in one bed when we stayed in motels and I didn't mind, actually. They huddled against me like puppies. It was one of the few times I felt happy, when my brothers and my sister were curled up next to me. I would fall asleep running my fingers through Barrett's hair, her breath hot and wet on my shoulder. I didn't pray, not exactly. But I looked up at the ceiling and promised God that I would always take care of them best that I could.

Tomorrow wasn't better, not at first. We picked up a newspaper and there we were on page three. I was in the photograph and they said the thing I said, about wanting books and a locket. I looked awful, but not awful enough for them to cut me out. The littles were adorable, though, even with their sad faces. I keep thinking that someone's going to see Barrett one day and say, "She should be a model." Or an actress, or something. She's cuter than any kid I've ever seen in a commercial.

But that sort of thing probably couldn't happen in Baltimore. I guess we would have to be in California or New York and we're never going to try those places. Too big, too expensive.

The paper didn't say exactly where we were staying, just that it was a motel in Towson, which I guess is part of Baltimore. We passed the morning feeling glum. It was Christmas Eve and we were out of step with the world. Everyone else seemed excited and happy, full of anticipation. The temperature had dropped overnight and there was snow in the forecast. We'd never seen a white Christmas, not even in Cooperstown. But what does snow matter if you don't have a sled? Heck, we didn't even have mittens. Gary had said to leave those behind in Cooperstown. He said he would never make that mistake again, picking a place so cold. "Cold town, cold hearts," he said.

Then, about eleven A.M., things finally began to go crazy. It turned out that the reporter didn't start work until ten A.M. and when he did, his voicemail was full of people wanting to help us. A television station came and talked to Gary live for the noon news. After that, people started calling the motel and stuff just began arriving like magic. Food and presents and gift cards, lots and lots of gift cards. Also some checks, but those were never as exciting, and even some cash, which was Gary's favorite. People couldn't give us enough. There were four tablets, one for each kid. Not iPads, but still pretty nice. An Xbox, although we couldn't figure out how to hook it up to the motel television, not that we got around to taking it out of the box. There was just so much to look at. A huge box of books from a store called Women and Children First, which I thought was a funny name. We went back to the mall, got some new clothes, and the photographer returned, took a photo of us in our new clothes, sitting down to the Christmas Eve dinner Dad had managed to fix in the little kitchenette. The chicken and sides were from Boston Market, but he put them on plates and made sure we said grace. We always said grace on Christmas Eve.

"What do you think, kids? Our worst Christmas has turned into our best Christmas. As Anne Frank said, 'People are fundamentally good at heart.'"

I wasn't sure it was our best Christmas. I thought Baton Rouge was better. And I had memories of Christmas when it was just Mama and me and my real dad. But there was no point in arguing with Gary. Barrett raised her fork high, a piece of chicken stuck on its tines, looking for all the world like Cindy-Lou Who. That's another book I had in Texas, the one about the Grinch.

As soon as the photographer left, Gary told us to go through the gifts. We knew the drill. We could each pick one thing to keep, but not the electronics because they were too valuable. It was hard to say goodbye to those tablets and the Xbox, but he was right, they were worth too much money. Anyway, Barrett picked a doll that was almost as pretty as she was, while Wade and Lenny chose toy trucks. It was hard to pick between the books and the locket, but the locket was forever, whereas a book would get used up after a while. I was worried Gary was going to say that the locket was too valuable to keep, but he inspected it, nodding, and said: "Filigree." I didn't know what that meant, but I knew it was something that wasn't quite good enough. I could imagine him looking at me one day and saying just that. "Filigree." I was filigree and Barrett was pure gold. I didn't mind. She was his real daughter, after all. I wanted him to treat her good, to think of her as something far more precious than me.

ALTHOUGH THE SCHOOLS WERE CLOSED for the holidays, someone from the local district called Gary the day after Christmas to make sure he would register us when they reopened on January 2. I was surprised how long he stayed on the phone, going over every little detail. There must have been something about the woman who called that made him want to talk. He said the things he liked to say, about the rocks and the rock pile, about how whoever stole from us needed it more than we did. He talked about Anne Frank, said he knew we were better off than her, but living in motels like we did gave him an appreciation for what it was like to be cooped up someplace with your entire family. He told the person on the phone that he was my legal guardian, but he didn't have the papers he needed to prove it. What should he do? He listened intently, even took notes. He explained at great length that my mother left us five years ago, "just up and left." He said it had happened right before Christmas and that he always hated December because of it, but the good people of Baltimore made him dare to think our luck had changed.

LAURA LIPPMAN

I guess everything he said was more or less true. My mom was hit by a car five years ago. She died. That's a kind of leaving.

We lived in Waco then, although I noticed that Gary didn't say "Waco" anymore when he told the story. He said "Central Texas" or "Lacy-Lakeview," a nearby town. Since that show about renovating homes in Waco became a big hit, people think Waco is kind of fancy and filled with nothing but love and fuzzy feelings and cupcakes. We didn't live in that Waco. For a couple of weeks after Mom died, people were extra-nice to us and brought us casseroles and things and some ladies clearly were taking a shine to Gary, but he didn't care. It was Christmastime. He started telling people that Mom had a big bag of presents for us kids when she died and maybe she did, I don't know. The car that hit her knocked her out of her shoes, I do know that, so if there were presents, they were probably scattered all over Waco Drive. It was dusk; she was wearing dark clothes. She crossed against the light to get a burrito. My mom loved burritos.

The thing was, Mom was the one with a job. Breadwinner, Gary called it, although that seemed like a funny thing to say about earning money. Bread. Winner. That's not much of a prize, is it? Maybe she should have been called the burrito-winner. (Believe me, Mom would laugh at that if she heard. She had a sense of humor about herself.) She had gone to work at Hillcrest Baptist Hospital before she married my dad, and she liked it, she was good at what she did. She said she was the sheepdog and the doctors in the practice, smart as they might

12

be, were her sheep. Gary liked staying at home, taking care of the kids. If he was ever a long-haul trucker, it was before we knew him. Mom met him at the HEB when he asked her something about brownie mix. He was actually a little younger than Mom and so handsome. And it wasn't like a lot of men tried to date my mom. She was plump, her clothes were plain, she had a kid. "I'm not exactly catnip," she would say. But Gary said he liked the fact that we would be a ready-made family. They got married, had the three littles. Boom, boom, boom. We were normal. Then Mom died and nothing was ever normal again.

Around the first anniversary of Mom's death, Gary got restless. He called the newspaper and asked if anyone wanted to write an update about us, how we were doing. We were okay for money. All us kids got social security because my mom had been working for fifteen years. I think Gary even got a little, as her widower. It would sound like a lot if I told you, but four kids need more money than you might think.

And nobody cared. Gary decided that Waco was a hard town. He said our neighbors were hypocrites, people who talked about God's love and charity but didn't practice it. He sold most of our stuff and moved us to Baton Rouge. Three days before Christmas he went shopping, came home looking all disheveled and excited. Someone had broken into the car and taken all the presents, he said. He didn't call the police, but he told our pastor and the pastor called the newspaper and next thing we knew, we had more stuff than we could handle. I think Gary was telling the truth, that time. Maybe. I'm not sure.

But every town after that—those were lies, definitely.

Here's what he does: We move every January, start school somewhere in Texas. That way, we can keep the registration up on the minivan without too much trouble. And Texas is big, bigger than some countries. Then, right after Thanksgiving, Gary picks a new town in a different state. "You'll only miss three weeks of school." We check into some sad-sack place, like this motel we're in now. We go to food pantries and soup kitchens, Gary chats people up, makes friends. We find a church to attend. On December 22 or 23, he goes "shopping." He never calls the police because that would be breaking the law. If someone presses him to file a report, he says, "I just have to believe that the desperate soul who did this needs those things more than we do." He never gives his name the same way twice and he changes our names just a little. This year, we were Kathy, Leonard, Wayne, and Barbara. Our surnames so far have been Carey, Carr, Carter, and Carson, all variations on our real name, Carpenter. Gary did adopt me when he married Mom. And when she died, he took me aside and said he would be able to keep me as long as I behaved. So I behaved, did what he told me to do, kept my mouth shut because lies didn't come easy to me.

The hardest part was when they came back, the reporter and the photographer. Because we're expected to be so happy, so grateful. The littles are genuinely happy and Gary is in heaven. I think he loves the attention more than the money. He goes to the library, uses the computer to read the story online. Then he begins planning our next move.

As January first approached that week in Baltimore, we sat down as a family and talked about where we would go next, which Gary decreed had to be at least three hundred miles from our last place in Amarillo. We decided to try a town somewhere on the highway between San Antonio and Houston. Everything was happening as it always happened, as it always will happen.

Then the lady from the school district came to visit.

She knocked on the door at eight A.M. Friday. The boys were in their underwear still. Gary didn't have a shirt on. I was the only one who was presentable, so I answered, thinking it was the motel maid, maybe the owner. He had been a lot more attentive since we were on TV—wanted to make sure we were happy.

The lady in front of me was just a normal-looking lady. She wore black leggings tucked into boots, really nice suede ones. Her green coat was baggy, kind of a weird shape, but she had a cool old pin on the lapel. And she wore earmuffs, which made me like her. You don't see a lot of grown-up ladies wearing red earmuffs.

She kind of reminded me of my mom.

"They belong to my kid," she said, smiling. "She'll be mad when she finds out I took them. But I like earmuffs better than hats. They do the job just as well and there's less static."

She sailed into our room without asking permission. Maybe that should have been the first clue. Most people wouldn't do that. Gary dove into the bathroom, while Wade and Lenny squealed and hid under the covers. Barrett, who was wearing a new nightgown, part of the Christmas haul, just stood in the center of the room smiling. Barrett knew how pretty she was, with her fluff of blond hair and blue eyes. In the background, the television was yelling and I turned it off. The lady's eyes were sweeping the room like she had X-ray vision. I was so worried that she was a social worker. Gary always said social workers were a bigger threat than the police, we had to keep them away no matter what. The place was a mess. Cereal bowls, empty soda bottles, pizza boxes. The only thing that was neat was the little desk, which Gary had claimed for his own. There was a stack of checks there, an envelope that I knew was full of cash and gift cards.

"I'm Ms. Smith from the Baltimore County school district," she said. "I spoke to your father on the phone the other day?"

Gary came out of the bathroom, tucking his shirt in. He had taken time to brush his teeth, run a razor over his face.

"What's this, a surprise inspection?"

"Oh, no," she said. "I just want to make sure you have everything you need to enroll the children. Is this going to be your permanent address? Or are you going to relocate within the county?"

She wasn't a woman you'd call pretty, not exactly, but she had a way about her that just made you want to look at her, talk to her. I could see why Gary had spent so much time with her, even on the phone. If you had a problem, this woman could solve it—that was clear.

"What do I need again?" Gary asked.

"Birth certificates, of course. But also some proof of residency, that's why it matters what address you plan to use. Have you found a new place?"

"Not yet." Gary was slick, you have to give him that. I could see a dozen things that exposed our lies. His lies. Suitcases half-filled, only a handful of toys where a few days ago there had been mountains of boxes. The pile of checks, which he would trash because he couldn't deposit a check made out to a man who didn't exist. But the thing about Gary was that he could believe what he needed to believe when he needed to believe it. So, technically, he never lied.

"It's not going to be easy," the lady said. "You'll need at least three bedrooms."

"We can make do with two," Gary said.

"I don't see how—unless you give the kids the master bedroom, have them sleep in two doubles? There are some nice apartments nearby, but nothing's going to be large enough for four kids. But there's a place not far from here, the Versailles. Don't worry, it's not as grand as it sounds. You could do a three-bedroom for about $2,000 a month."

"Ma'am, I can't afford that. Not for long."

"Even with a Section 8 voucher, I don't think you can do much better than $1,500 a month. What kind of job are you looking for? You'd be surprised at the connections I have. I've lived in Baltimore all my life and I know people everywhere. State and city government, some retail businesses—my aunt owns a bookstore, my father has a restaurant. I even know some cops and lawyers."

She laughed, as if knowing cops and lawyers was hilarious.

"In fact, my aunt could use help right now. Can you run a cash register? Stock shelves?"

"I was a long-haul trucker, but I had to give it up when my wife left. I do odd jobs. But I can't work when the kids aren't in school."

"She's really family friendly. She'll tailor it to your needs—maybe just ten hours a week to start, but it's something, right?"

"I worry about my back—I injured it on a job a few weeks ago."

"Then maybe I should hook you up with a law firm that does disability work? With a solid work history, you'd be eligible for disability insurance. And it occurs to me—their mother could be accountable for child support. I know a PI who does that kind of work. Let me take you to a friend's office," the lady wheedled. "Get some basic info, it won't take long."

"Basic info?"

"Your ex's name, her Social."

"I appreciate your interest, ma'am, but I promised the kids we'd go to a movie today." First we'd heard of it. "I don't like to disappoint them. They've been through so much."

"We could drop them at the movies, then come back for them. The oldest—what's your name, sweetheart?"

"Ka-Kathy." I stuttered a bit, but I got it right.

"Kathy could look after the children at the movies while we're looking at apartments."

"Do I look like a man who would let a girl as young as Kathy be in charge of these three? I'm pretty sure I'd be in trouble with the law if I did that."

Very high and mighty for someone who did that all the time, but like I said, he believes every word when he's saying it.

The lady's smile never faded. She wrote her number on a piece of paper, urged Gary to call her when he was ready to start looking for a place, showed him on a map where the elementary and middle schools were, then said goodbye. At the door, she turned around as if she had forgotten something, then looked at Barrett. But her eyes didn't stay on Barrett as most people's do. She looked at the boys, too, then caught my eyes. I felt as if she could see inside my soul.

I didn't like it.

Gary decided to make his lie true, take us all to the movies, but I said I didn't want to see a little-kid movie, not another one with those dumb yellow people. He said I could stay and pack for the littles. He didn't have to tell me that we would be leaving the next day. That lady had spooked him, for sure.

About twenty minutes after he left, there was a knock on the door. I figured it was the maid, she usually came when she saw our car missing from the parking lot. But it was that lady, Ms. Smith.

"Ga—Dad's gone," I said.

"I know," she said. "I've been watching the room. He took the younger ones out to the movies."

"You followed him?"

"It's what I do," she said.

She handed me a card. Tess Monaghan, private investigator. Shit. Gary deserved to be caught, I know, but it made me angry. I had liked the nice lady, Ms. Smith, who wanted to do things for us. I wanted her to be real. I didn't want to know this Tess Monaghan.

"Let's take a little drive," she said. I was terrified to get into her car with her, but I was more terrified to say no. If she took me to the cops, I'd figure out what to say. If I didn't go with her, she might go straight to them anyway. Going with her would buy me some time.

"You said in the newspaper that you like books. I thought you might like to visit the store that sent your family that big box of kids' books."

That big box of books that Gary had tried to return for credit, but he couldn't persuade the people at the Barnes & Noble to give him a Starbucks card in exchange for them. I think he sold them to some half-price store.

The bookstore was downtown, near where the city meets the water. It had big windows and an old soda fountain where you could get coffee and milkshakes and it was pretty much what I imagine heaven would look like.

"Why is this place called Women and Children First?" I asked the lady who wasn't Ms. Smith. "Does it have something to do with the *Titanic*?"

"When it started, it was only books by women or for children. A few years ago, my aunt decided it had to be more general interest, so she added two sections—Dead White Men and Live Hot Boys. I always tell her that the crime section should be called Pretty Dead Girls and the Men Who Love Them."

She seemed to think this was funny, but I didn't get it. She brought me a muffin, but I didn't need to eat. She brought me a book called *Judy's Journey*.

"That's too babyish for me," I said.

"I know," she agreed. "But it reminds me of your family. It's about migrant workers who have to move from place to place. How many times has your dad pulled this scam, Kathy?" She said my name like it was a story she didn't believe. It wasn't my real name. I'm actually Kyle. But how could she know that?

"It's not a scam," I said. "We were robbed."

"Yes, I read the story. What did he say? It was a very distinct turn of phrase—*We're starting from rock bottom but that doesn't mean we can't climb to the top of the rock pile.* You know what's interesting? A man named Barry Carr said that to the paper in Phoenix two years ago. And in Cooperstown, New York, last Christmas, only he was named Harry Carson. Both of them mentioned Anne Frank, too, and said the person who stole the gifts probably needed them more than he did."

She pulled some computer printouts from her bag. I recognized the stories. I wondered why she hadn't found Baton Rouge or Chattanooga, but maybe he hadn't figured out his clever little sayings by then, or maybe the reporter hadn't used them.

"He never uses the same names. Not for him, and not for you kids. That was smart. If you Google the names, you don't come up with anything. Run a criminal record check on any of these Harrys or Barrys and that comes back empty, too. Even if someone thought to run the license plates, all you'd get is a registration, which is currently attached to an apartment in Amarillo, Texas. But there were two constants—the make of the minivan and those quotes. Three car break-ins in three different towns. That is a lot of bad luck for one family."

I wanted to say, *Lady, you don't know the half of it.* But I just kept looking at the book she had given me. She wasn't a cop. She couldn't prove anything. She couldn't do anything.

"Filing a false report is serious stuff—what's your real name?" She waited, but I wasn't dumb enough to step into silences. "Your dad is risking prison. And with that, he's risking the family."

"He never makes a police report," I said. "He tells someone—some busybody. That person calls the police. The police come, Gary—Dad—says he doesn't want to file a report, that gone is gone and he's never going to get it back." I didn't mention how Gary is the one who calls the newspaper, claims to be a store clerk or a pastor, or maybe even the cop who tried to convince him to take the report. "People give us stuff. We don't make them do it. And they don't do it for us, anyway."

"What do you mean? Of course they do."

"They do it for themselves. It's a cheap way to feel good. They give some toys to the poor kids and figure they've done their bit. You were the first person who ever followed up, who tried to do more for us. And you were a liar, so it doesn't count. Why do you even care? What's it to you? Are you upset because your aunt sent us a bunch of books we didn't even want?" Although I did want them. I wanted them so bad. When I read books, I felt safe.

The woman—Tess Monaghan, she had used a fake name, too, so who was she to judge us?—looked upset. Good. "I have friends at the newspaper. An editor. He thought your story seemed suspicious, but he didn't want to hurt the reporter's reputation. He's a kid, he made some dumb mistakes. But it turns out he's not the first person to be taken in by your father."

"So you're worried about the newspaper."

"I'm concerned about you and your siblings. You can't keep going on like this."

"How do we stop?" I prayed, really prayed, that she had an answer, that she could right us.

"I could talk to your father—"

And just like that, I knew she didn't have a solution. Nobody does. That's the problem. I've been thinking on this for four years and I don't have an answer yet. How could some stranger figure it out in one day?

"No," I said. "It won't work. He'll pretend to feel bad. He'll be all apologetic. Maybe he'll cry. Maybe he'll even admit that my mom is dead, not 'gone.' He'll cry and he'll ask for your help and you'll come back here the next day and we'll be gone. We're leaving tomorrow. You can't stop us."

"I can tell my friends at the newspaper what I've found. They'll write a follow-up story."

"Great. Then they'll come in and bust up my family and we'll go to foster care. You think anyone wants all four of us? Maybe, just maybe, they'll keep the three littles together, because they have the same mom and dad. Nobody's going to want me, ever."

"That sounds like something you've been told, to keep you in line."

By now, every muscle in my body was tight from the effort of not crying. She wasn't wrong. He had told me that. He told me that all the time. Except in slightly different words. *No one is ever going to love you. No one is ever going to want you. Except me, Kyle. Only me. I'm all you've got now.*

"That doesn't make it untrue," I said. I risked looking straight at her. To my amazement, she was the one who was crying. For one crazy minute, I thought I should comfort her. And then I was angry. Who was she to come into my family and learn all our secrets and cry like that? If you want to pity me, you better give me something. That's how the game is played. Give me money, give me a gift, then go home and bawl your eyes out. No gift, no tears.

"I'm obligated to go to Social Services. To do something."

"You do what you have to do," I said. There's no way I could give her permission.

"How about if I give you a night to think about it? You can choose if I talk to your dad or call Social Services. You can call me tomorrow, okay? I won't do anything until I hear from you."

I looked at the number on her card. "It's hard for me to make a call without being heard."

"There's actually a pay phone near your motel, just around the corner on Joppa. Might be the last pay phone in all of North Baltimore. You can call me collect. Do you think you can get away for even five minutes? I promise I won't do anything until I hear from you."

We used to have a Monopoly set, back in Waco. It was an old one, it had belonged to my mom when she was a kid. It had those cards, orange and yellow, some good and some bad. One deck, I never remember which one, was called Community Chest, it was like one of those charity funds that gave my family food and clothing. Holding on to that woman's card, it was like that moment in the game before you turn the card over, the feeling of wondering if you were going to get a good card or a bad card. GET OUT OF JAIL FREE. ADVANCE TO GO.

Or maybe it was just one of the silly ones, like twenty-five dollars for second place in a beauty contest.

"I'll call," I promised her.

She bought me a book, *The Diary of Anne Frank*. "Your dad doesn't have the quote quite right," she said with a crooked smile as she let me out at the motel. "Now you see the phone booth over there? That's my cell number on the card, so you can call anytime. You can't call too late or too early."

"I'll call," I said.

WE WERE ON THE ROAD by midnight. Gary was upset, but he thought I handled it well. I told him about the newspaper clippings, told him where he had screwed up. He was going to have to give up Anne Frank and the rock pile line. I could tell that bugged him. He was proud of that saying, which was all his own. As for the minivan, he decided he could risk it for the trip back, but we'd trade it in once in Texas. We'll have a lot of cash when he finishes selling the gift cards.

We're a team. That's what that lady didn't get. We're a

25

family. We're in this together. I couldn't risk the littles not being with me.

Besides, in four more years, I'm going to be eighteen and I'll be old enough to take care of the littles, who won't be so little anymore. I'll be old enough to protect Barrett, who gets prettier every day, not that pretty has anything to do with it. I'm not that pretty.

Then maybe I'll cut Gary's throat in the middle of the night and we'll all be free. I'll say there was a break-in or something, I don't know. By then, I'll have had four more years of practice lying to people. I'm already pretty good at it. "Someone broke in and killed our dad." People will feel sorry for us.

I bet they'll even give us money.

THE BOOK THING

Tess Monaghan wanted to love the funky little children's book-shop that had opened just two years ago among the used book-stores that lined Twenty-Fifth Street in North Baltimore. There was so much to admire about it—the brightly painted miniature rockers and chairs on the converted sun porch, the mynah bird who said "Hi, hon!" and "Hark, who goes there!" and—best of all—"Nevermore."

She coveted the huge Arnold Lobel poster posted opposite the front door, the one that showed a bearded man-beast hap-pily ensconced in a tiny cottage that was being overtaken by ramshackle towers of books. She appreciated the fact that ancil-lary merchandise was truly a sideline here; this shop's business was books, with only a few stuffed animals and Fancy Nancy boas thrown into the mix. Tess was grateful that gift-wrapping was free year-round and that the store did out-of-print book searches. She couldn't wait until her own two-year-old daugh-ter, Carla Scout, was old enough to sit quietly through the Saturday story hour, although Tess was beginning to fear that might not be until Carla Scout was a freshman in college. Most of all, she admired the counterintuitive decision to open a bookstore when so many people seemed to assume that books were doomed.

She just thought it would be nice if the owner of The Children's Bookstore actually *liked* children.

"Be careful," the raven-haired owner hissed on this unseasonably chilly October day, as Carla Scout did her Frankenstein stagger toward a low shelf of picture books. To be fair, Carla Scout's hands weren't exactly clean, as mother and daughter had just indulged in one of mother's favorite vices, dark chocolate peanut clusters from Eddie's grocery. Tess swooped in with a napkin and smiled apologetically at the owner.

"Sorry," she said. "She loves books to pieces. Literally, sometimes."

"Do you need help?" the owner asked, as if she had never seen Tess before. Tess's credit card begged to differ.

"Oh—no, we're looking for a birthday gift, but I have some ideas. My aunt was a children's librarian with the city school system."

Tess did not add that her aunt ran her own bookstore in another part of town and would happily order any book that Tess needed—at cost. But Tess wanted this bookstore, so much closer to her own neighborhood, to thrive. She wanted all local businesses to thrive, but it was a tricky principle to live by, as most principles were. At night, her daughter asleep, the house quiet, she couldn't help it if her mouse clicked its way to online sellers who made everything so easy. Could she?

"You're one of those, I suppose," the woman said.

"One of—?"

The owner pointed to the iPad sticking out of Tess's tote.

"Oh—no. I mean, sure, I buy some digital books, mainly things I don't care about owning, but I use the reading app on this primarily for big documents. My work involves a lot of paper and it's great to be able to import the documents and carry them with me—"

The owner rolled her eyes. "Sure." She pushed through the flowery chintz curtains that screened her work area from the store and retreated as if she found Tess too tiresome to talk to.

Sorry, mouthed the store's only employee, a young woman with bright red hair, multiple piercings, and a tattoo of what appeared to be Jemima Puddle-Duck on her left upper arm.

The owner swished back through the curtains, purse under her arm. "I'm going for coffee, Mona, then to the bank." Tess waited to see if she boarded a bicycle, possibly one with a basket for errant nipping dogs. But she walked down Twenty-Fifth Street, head down against the gusty wind.

"She's having a rough time," said the girl with the duck tattoo. Mona, the owner had called her. "You can imagine. And the thing that drives her mad are the people who come in with digital readers—no offense—just to pick her brain and then download the e-versions or buy cheaper ones online."

"I wouldn't think that people wanted children's books in digital."

"You'd be surprised. There are some interactive Dr. Seuss books—they're actually quite good. But I'm not sure about the read-to-yourself functions. I think it's still important for parents to read to their kids."

Tess blushed guiltily. She did have *Hop on Pop* on her iPad, along with several games, although Carla Scout so far seemed to prefer opening—and then deleting—her mother's email.

"Anyway," Mona continued, "it's the sudden shrinkage that's making her cranky. Because it's the most expensive, most beautiful books. *Hugo*, things like that. A lot of the Caldecott books, but never the Newberys, and we keep them in the same section. Someone's clearly targeting the illustrated books. Yet not the truly rare ones, which are kept under lock and key." She indicated the case that ran along the front of the counter, filled with old books in mint condition. *Eloise in Moscow*. Various Maurice Sendak titles. *Emily of Deep Valley*, Eleanor Estes's *The Hundred Dresses*. A book unknown to Tess, *Epaminondas and His Auntie*, whose cover illustration was deeply un-PC.

Tess found herself switching personas, from harried mom to professional private investigator who provided security consultations. She studied her surroundings. "All these little rooms—it's cozy, but a shoplifter's paradise. An alarm, and a bell on the door to alert you to the door's movement, but no cameras. Have you thought about making people check totes and knapsacks?"

"We tried, but Octavia got the numbers confused and when she gets harried—let's just say it doesn't bring out her best."

"Octavia?"

"The owner."

As if her name conjured her up, she appeared just like that, slamming back through the door, coffee in hand. "I always forget that the bank closes at three every day but Friday. Oh well. It's not like I had that much to deposit." She glanced at Mona, her face softer, kinder. She was younger than Tess had realized, possibly not even forty. It was her stern manner and dyed black hair that aged her. "I can write you a check today, but if you could wait until Friday—"

"Sure, Octavia. And it's almost Halloween. People will be doing holiday shopping before you know it."

Octavia sighed. "More people in the store. More distractions. More opportunity." She glanced at Carla Scout, who was sitting on the floor with a Mo Willems book, "reading" it to herself. Tess thought Octavia would have to be charmed in spite of herself. What could be more adorable than a little girl reading, especially this little girl, who had the good sense to favor her father, with thick dark hair that was already down to her shoulders and fair skin. Plus, she was wearing a miniature leather bomber jacket from the Gap, red jeans, and a Clash T-shirt. Tess had heard "She's so adorable" at least forty times today. She waited for the forty-first such pronouncement.

Octavia said: "She got chocolate on the book."

So she had. And they already owned *Don't Let the Pigeon Drive the Bus!*, but Tess would have to eat this damaged copy. "I'll add it to my other purchases when I check out," Tess said, knowing it was folly to try to separate Carla Scout from any object that was keeping her quiet and contented. "I understand you've been having some problems with theft?"

"Mona!" Owner glared at employee. Tess would have cowered under such a glance, but the younger woman shrugged it off.

"It's not shameful, Octavia. People don't steal from us because we're bad people. Or even because we're bad at what we do. They do it because they're opportunistic."

"A camera would go far in solving your problems," Tess offered.

Octavia sniffed. "I don't do gadgets." She shot another baleful look at Tess's iPad, then added, with slightly less edge: "Besides, I can't afford the outlay just now."

Her honesty softened Tess. "Understood. Have you noticed a pattern?"

"It's not like I can do inventory every week," Octavia began, even as Mona said: "It's Saturdays. I'm almost certain it's Saturdays. It gets busy here, what with the story time and more browsers than usual—often divorced dads, picking up a last-minute gift or just trying desperately to entertain their kids."

"I might be able to help—"

Octavia held up a hand. "I don't have money for that, either."

"I'd do it for free," Tess said, surprising herself.

"Why?" Octavia's voice was edged with suspicion. She wasn't used to kindness, Tess realized, except, perhaps, from Mona, the rare employee who would sit on a check for a few days.

"Because I think your store is good for North Baltimore and I want my daughter to grow up coming here. To be a true city kid, to ride her bike or take the bus here, pick out books on her own. Betsy-Tacy, Mrs. Piggle-Wiggle, *The Witch of Blackbird Pond*. Edward Eager and E. Nesbit. All the books I loved."

"Everyone wants to pass their childhood favorites on to their children," Octavia said. "But if I've learned anything in this business, it's that kids have to make their own discoveries if you want them to be true readers."

"Okay, fine. But if I want her to discover books there's nothing like browsing in a store or a library. There are moments of serendipity that you can't equal." She turned to her daughter just in time to see—but not stop—Carla Scout reaching for another book with her dirty hands. "We'll take that one, too."

BACK ON TWENTY-FIFTH STREET, CARLA Scout strapped in her stroller, Tess was trying to steer with one hand while she held her phone with the other, checking emails. Inevitably, she ran up on the heels of a man well-known to her, at least by sight. She and Crow, Carla Scout's father, called him the Walking Man and often wondered about his life, why he had the time and means to walk miles across North Baltimore every day, in every kind of weather, as if on some kind of mission. He might have been handsome if he smiled and stood up straight, but he never smiled and there was a curve to his body that suggested he couldn't stand up straight. When Tess bumped him, he swung sharply away from her, the knapsack he always wore rising and falling with such force that he grunted as if he had been punched. Tess wondered if he weighed it down to help correct his unfortunate posture.

"Sorry," Tess said, but the Walking Man didn't even acknowledge their collision. He just kept walking with his distinctive, flat-footed style, his body curving forward like a C. There was no bounce, no spring, in the Walking Man's stride, only a grim need to put one foot in front of the other, over and over again. He was, Tess thought, like someone under a curse in a fairy tale or myth, sentenced to walk until a spell was broken.

BEFORE HER FIRST SATURDAY SHIFT at the bookstore, Tess consulted her aunt, figuring that she must also see a lot of "shrinkage" at her store.

"Not really," Kitty said. "Books are hard to shoplift, harder to resell. It happens, of course, but I've never seen an organized ongoing plan, with certain books targeted the way you're describing. This sounds almost like a vendetta against the owner."

Tess thought about Octavia's brusque ways, Mona's stories about how cranky she could get. Still, it was hard to imagine a disgruntled customer going to these lengths. Most people would satisfy themselves by writing a mean review on Yelp.

"I will tell you this," Kitty said. "Years ago—and it was on Twenty-Fifth Street, when it had even more used bookstores—there was a rash of thefts; the owners couldn't believe how much inventory they were losing, and how random it was. But then it stopped, just like that."

"What happened then? I mean, why did it stop? Did they arrest someone?"

"Not to my knowledge."

"I should probably check with the other sellers on the street, see if they're noticing anything," Tess said. "But I wonder why it's happening *now*."

"Maybe someone's worried that there won't be books much longer, that they're going to be extinct."

It was clearly a joke on Kitty's part, but Tess couldn't help asking: "Are they?"

The pause on the other end of the phone line was so long that Tess began to wonder if her cell had dropped the call. When Kitty spoke again, her voice was low, without its usual mirth.

"I don't dare predict the future. After all, I didn't think newspapers could go away. Still, I believe that there will be a market for physical books, I just don't how large it will be. All I know is that I'm okay—for now. I own my building, I have a strong core of loyal customers, and I have a good walk-in trade from tourists. In the end, it comes down to what people value. Do they value bookstores? Do they value books? I don't know, Tess. Books have been free in libraries for years and that didn't devalue them. The Book Thing here in Baltimore gives books away to anyone who wants them. Free, no strings. Doesn't hurt me at all. For decades, people have bought used books everywhere—from flea markets to the Smith College Book Sale. But there's something about pressing a button on your computer and buying something so ephemeral for ninety-nine cents, having it whooshed instantly to you—remember *Charlie and the Chocolate Factory*?"

"Of course." Tess, like most children, had been drawn to

Roald Dahl's dark stories. He was another one on her list of writers she wanted Carla Scout to read.

"Well, what if you could do what Willy Wonka—Dahl—fantasized, reach into your television and pull out a candy bar? What if everything you wanted was always available to you, all the time, on a twenty-four/seven basis? It damn near is. Life has become so à la carte. We get what we want when we want it. But if you ask me, that means it's that much harder to identify what we really want."

"That's not a problem in Baltimore," Tess said. "All I can get delivered is pizza and Chinese—and not even my favorite pizza or Chinese."

"You're joking to get me off this morbid train of thought."

"Not exactly." She wasn't joking. The state of food delivery in Baltimore was depressing. But she also wasn't used to hearing her ebullient aunt in such a somber mood and she was trying to distract her, the way she might play switcheroo with Carla Scout. And it worked. It turned out that dealing with a toddler day in and day out was actually good practice for dealing with the world at large.

THE CHILDREN'S BOOKSTORE WAS HECTIC on Saturdays as promised, although Tess quickly realized that there was a disproportionate relationship between the bustle in the aisles and the activity at the cash register.

She also noticed the phenomenon that Mona had described, people using the store as a real-life shopping center for their virtual needs. She couldn't decide which was more obnoxious—the people who pulled out their various devices and made purchases while standing in the store, or those who waited until they were on the sidewalk again, hunching over their phones and e-readers almost furtively, as if committing a kind of crime. They were and they weren't, Tess decided. It was legal, but they were ripping off Mona's space and time, using her as a curator of sorts.

At the height of the hubbub, a deliveryman arrived with boxes of books, wheeling his hand truck through the narrow aisles. He was exceedingly handsome in a preppy way—and exceedingly clumsy. As he tried to work his way to the back of the store, his boxes fell off one, two, three times. Once, the top box burst open, spilling a few books onto the floor.

"Sorry," he said with a bright smile as he knelt to collect them. Except—did Tess see him sweep several books off a shelf and into a box? Why would he do that? After all, the boxes were being delivered; it's not as if he could take them with him.

"Tate is the clumsiest guy in the world," Mona said with affection after he left. "A sweetheart, but a mess."

"You mean, he drops stuff all the time?"

"Drops things, mixes up orders, you name it. But Octavia dotes on him. Those dimples."

Tess had not picked up on the dimples, but she had a chance to see how they affected Octavia when the deliveryman returned fifteen minutes later, looking sheepish.

"Tate!" Octavia said with genuine delight.

"I feel so stupid. One of those boxes I left—it's for Royal Books up the block."

"No problem," Octavia said. "You know I never get around to unpacking the Saturday deliveries until the store clears out late in the day."

He looked through the stack of boxes he had left, showed Octavia that one was addressed to Royal Books, and hoisted it on his shoulder. Tess couldn't help noticing that there wasn't any tape on the box; the top had been folded with the overlapping flaps that people used when boxing their own possessions for a move. She ambled out in the street behind him, saw him put the box on his truck, then drive away, west and then north on Howard Street—completely bypassing Royal Books.

He looks like someone, Tess thought. *Someone I know, yet don't know. Someone famous?* He probably resembled some actor on television.

Back inside the bookstore, she didn't have the heart to tell Octavia what she suspected. Octavia had practically glowed when she saw Tate. Besides, Tess had no proof. Yet.

"So, did you see anything?" Octavia asked at day's end.

"Maybe. If there was anything taken today, it was from this shelf." Tess pointed to the low one next to where the box had fallen, spilling its contents. Mona crouched on her haunches and poked at the titles. "I can't be sure until I check our computer, but the shelf was full yesterday. I mean—there's no Seuss and we always have Seuss."

"If you saw it, why didn't you say something?" Octavia demanded, as peevish as any paying customer. "Or *do* something, for god's sake."

"I wasn't sure I saw anything and I didn't want to offend . . .

a potential customer. I'll be back next Saturday. This is a two-person job."

LIFE IS UNFAIR. TESS MONAGHAN, toting her toddler daughter in a baby carrier, was invisible to most of the world, except for leering men who eyed the baby's chest-level position and said things like "Best seat in the house."

But when Crow put on the Ergo and shouldered their baby to *his* chest, the world melted, or at least the female half did. So he stood in the bookstore the next Saturday morning, trying to be polite to the cooing women around him, even as he waited to see if he would observe something similar to what Tess had seen the week before. Once again, Tate arrived when story hour was in full swing, six boxes on his hand truck.

No dropped box, Crow reported via text.

Damn, Tess thought. Maybe he was smart enough to vary the days, despite Mona's conviction that the thefts had been concentrated on Saturdays. Maybe she was deluded, maybe—

Her phone pinged again. Taking one box with him. Says it was on cart by mistake. I didn't see anything, tho. He's good.

Tess was on her bike, which she had decided was her best bet for following someone in North Baltimore on a Saturday. A delivery guy, even an off-brand one working the weekends, had to make frequent stops, right? She counted on being able to keep up with him. And she did, as he moved through his route, although she almost ran down the Walking Man near the Baltimore Museum of Art. Still, she was flying along, watching him unload boxes at stop after stop until she realized the flaw in her plan: How could she know which box was the box from The Children's Bookstore?

She sighed, resigned to donating yet another Saturday to a story-hour stakeout.

AND ANOTHER AND ANOTHER AND another. The next four Saturdays went by without any incidents. Tate showed up, delivered his boxes, made no mistakes, dropped nothing. Yet, throughout the week, customer requests would point up missing volumes—books listed as in stock in the computer yet nowhere to be found in the store.

By the fifth Saturday, the Christmas rush appeared to be on and the store was even more chaotic when Tate arrived—and dropped a box in one of the store's remote corners, one that could never be seen from the cash register or the story-time alcove on the converted sun porch. Tess, out on the street on her bike, ready to ride, watched it unfold via FaceTime on Crow's phone, which he was holding at hip level. The action suddenly blurred—Mona, taken into Tess's confidence, had rushed forward to try to help Tate. Tate brushed her away, but not before Carla Scout's sippy cup somehow fell on the box, the lid bouncing off and releasing a torrent of red juice, enough to leave a visible splotch on the box's side, an image that Crow captured and forwarded in a text. Tess, across the street, watched as he loaded it, noted the placement of the large stain.

It was a long, cold afternoon, with no respite for Tess as she followed the truck. No time to grab so much as a cup of coffee, and she wouldn't have risked drinking anything because that could have forced her to search out a bathroom.

It was coming up on four o'clock, the wintry light beginning to weaken, when Tate headed up one of the most notorious hills in the residential neighborhood of Roland Park, not far from where Tess lived. She would have loved to wait at the bottom, but how could she know where he made the delivery? She gave him a five-minute head start, hoping that Tate, like most Baltimore drivers, simply didn't see cyclists.

His truck was parked outside a rambling Victorian, perhaps one of the old summer houses built when people would travel a mere five to fifteen miles to escape the closed-in heat of downtown Baltimore. Yet this house, on a street full of million-dollar houses, did not appear to be holding its end up. Cedar shingles had dropped off as if the house were molting; the roof was inexpertly patched in places, the chimney looked like a liability suit waiting to happen. The delivery truck idled in the driveway, Tate still in the driver's seat. Tess crouched by her wheel in a driveway three houses down, pretending to be engaged in a repair. Eventually, a man came out, but not from the house. He had been inside the stable at the head of the driveway. Most such outbuildings in the neighborhood had been converted to new uses or torn down, but this one appeared to have been untouched. A light burned inside, but that was all Tess could glimpse before the doors rolled shut again.

That man looks familiar, she thought, as she had about Tate the first time she saw him. *Is he famous or do I know him?*

The man who met Tate at the end of the driveway was the Walking Man. No knapsack, but it was clearly him, his shoulders rounding even farther forward without their usual counterweight. He shook the driver's hand and Tess realized why she thought she had seen Tate before—he was a handsomer, younger version of the Walking Man.

Tate handed the Walking Man the box with the red stain. No money changed hands. Nothing else changed hands. But even in the dim light, the stain was evident. The man took the box into the old stable and muscled the doors back into place.

Tess was faced with a choice, one she hadn't anticipated. She could follow Tate and confront him, figuring that he had the most to lose. His job was on the line. But she couldn't prove he was guilty of theft until she looked inside the box. If she followed Tate, the books could be gone before she returned and she wouldn't be able to prove anything. She had to see what was inside that box.

She texted Crow, told him what she was going to do, and walked up the driveway without waiting for his reply, which she supposed would urge caution, or tell her to call the police. But it was only a box of books from a children's bookstore. How high could the stakes be?

SHE KNOCKED ON THE STABLE door. Minutes passed. She knocked again.

"I saw you," she said to the dusk, to herself, possibly to the man inside. "I know you're in there."

Another minute or so passed, a very long time to stand outside as darkness encroached and the cold deepened. But, eventually, the door was rolled open.

"I don't know you," the Walking Man said with the flat affect of a child.

"My name is Tess Monaghan and I sort of know you. You're the—" She stopped herself just in time. The Walking Man didn't know he was the Walking Man. She realized, somewhat belatedly, that *he* had not boiled his existence down to one quirk. Whoever he was, he didn't define himself as the Walking Man. He had a life, a history. Perhaps a sad and gloomy one, based on these surroundings and his compulsive, constant hiking, but he was not, in his head or mirror, a man who did nothing but walk around North Baltimore.

Or was he?

"I've seen you around. I don't live far from here. We're practically neighbors."

He stared at her oddly, said nothing. His arm was braced against the frame of the door—she could not enter without pushing past him. She sensed he wouldn't like that kind of contact, that he was not used to being touched. She remembered how quickly he had whirled around the day she rolled her stroller up on his heels.

"May I come in?"

He dropped his arm and she took that as an invitation—and also as a sign that he believed himself to have nothing to fear. He wasn't acting like someone who felt guilty, or in the wrong. Then again, he didn't know that she had followed the books here.

The juice-stained box sat on a worktable, illuminated by an overhead light strung from the ceiling on a long cable. Tess walked over to the box, careful not to turn her back to the Walking Man, wishing she had a name for him other than the Walking Man. But he had not offered his name when she gave hers.

"May I?" she said, indicating the box, picking up a box cutter next to it, but only because she didn't want him to be able to pick it up.

"It's mine," he said.

She looked at the label. The address was for this house. Cover, should the ruse be discovered? "William Kemper. Is that you?"

"Yes." His manner was odd, off. Then again, she was the one who had shown up at his home and demanded to inspect a box addressed to him. Perhaps he thought she was just another quirky Baltimorean. Perhaps he had a reductive name for her, too. The Nosy Woman.

"Why don't you open it?"

He stepped forward and did. There were at least a dozen books, all picture books, all clearly new. He inspected them carefully.

"These are pretty good," he said.

"Good for what?"

He looked at her as if she were quite daft. "My work."

"What do you do?"

"Create."

"The man who brought you the books—"

"My younger brother, Tate. He brings me books. He says he knows a place that gives them away free."

"These look brand-new."

He shrugged, uninterested in the observation.

Tess tried again. "Why does your brother bring you books?"

"He said it was better for him to bring them than for me to get them myself."

Tess again remembered bumping into the Walking Man on Twenty-Fifth Street, his grunt as his knapsack rose and fell.

"But you still sometimes get them for yourself, don't you?"

It took him a while to formulate a reply. A dishonest person would have been thinking up a lie all along. An average person would have been considering the pros and cons of lying. William Kemper was simply deliberate with his words.

"Sometimes. Only when they need me."

"Books need you?"

"Books need to breathe after a while. They wait so long. They wait and they wait, closed in. You can tell that no one has read them in a very long time. Or even opened them."

"So you 'liberate' them? Is that your work?"

The Walking Man—William—turned away from her and began sorting the books his brother had brought. He was through with her, or wanted to be.

"These books weren't being neglected. Or ignored."

"No, but they're the only kind of books that Tate knows how to get. He thinks it's all about pictures. I don't want to tell him they're not quite right. I make do with what he brings, and supplement when I have to." He sighed, the sigh of an older brother used to a sibling's screwups. Tess had to think that Tate had done his share of sighing, too.

"William—were you away for a while?"

"Yes," he said, flipping the pages, studying the pictures, his mind not really on her or their conversation.

"Did you go to prison?"

"They said it wasn't." Flip, flip, flip. "Any rate, I got to come home. Eventually."

"When?"

"Two winters ago." It seemed an odd way to phrase it, a little affected. But for a walking man, the seasons probably mattered more.

"And this is your house?"

"Mine and Tate's. As long as we can pay the taxes. Which is about all we can do. Pay the taxes."

Tess didn't doubt that. Even a ramshackle pile in this neighborhood would have a tax bill of at least $15,000, maybe $20,000 per year. But did he actually live in the house? Her eyes now accustomed to the gloom, she realized the stable had been converted to an apartment of sorts. There was a cot, a makeshift kitchen with a hot plate, a minifridge, a radio. A bathroom wasn't evident, but William's appearance seemed to indicate that he had a way to keep himself and his clothes clean.

Then she noticed what was missing: *books*. Except for the ones that had just arrived, there were no books in evidence.

"Where are the books, William?"

"There," he said, after a moment of confusion. Whatever his official condition, he was very literal.

"No, I mean the others. There are others, right?"

"In the house."

"May I see them?"

"It's almost dark."

"So?"

"That means turning on the lights."

"Doesn't the house have lights?"

"We have an account. Tate said we should keep the utilities, because otherwise the neighbors will complain, say it's dangerous. Water, gas, and electric. But we don't use them, except for the washer-dryer and for showers. If it gets really cold, I can stay in the house, but even with the heat on, it's still cold. It's so big. The main thing is to keep it nice enough so no one can complain."

He looked exhausted from such a relatively long speech. Tess could tell that her mere presence was stressful to him. But it didn't seem to be the stress of *discovery*. He wasn't fearful. Other people made him anxious in general. Perhaps that was another reason the Walking Man kept walking. No one could catch up to him and start a conversation.

"I'd like to see the books, William."

"Why?"

"Because I—represent some of the people who used to own them."

"They didn't love them."

"Perhaps." There didn't seem to be any point in arguing with William. "I'd like to see them."

FROM THE OUTSIDE, TESS HAD not appreciated how large the house was, how deep into the lot it was built. Even by the standards of the neighborhood, it was enormous, taking up almost every inch of level land on the lot. There was more land still, but it was a long, precipitous slope. They were high here, with a commanding view of the city and the nearby highway. William took her through the rear door, which led into an ordinary, somewhat old-fashioned laundry room, with appliances that appeared to be ten to fifteen years old.

"The neighbors might call the police," William said, his tone fretful. "Just seeing a light."

"Because they think the house is vacant?"

"Because they would do anything to get us out. Any excuse to call attention to us. Tate says it's important not to let them do that."

He led her through the kitchen, the lights still off. Again, out-of-date, but ordinary and clean, if a bit dusty from disuse. Now they were in a long shadowy hall closed off by French doors. William opened these and they entered a huge, multi-windowed room, still dark, but not as dark as the hallway.

"The ballroom. Although we never had any balls that I know of," he said.

A ballroom. This was truly one of the grand old mansions of Roland Park.

"But where are the books, William?" Tess asked.

He blinked, surprised. "Oh, I guess you need more light. I thought the lights from the other houses would be enough." He flipped a switch and the light from overhead chandeliers filled the room. Yet the room was quite empty.

"The books, William. Where are they?"

"All around you."

And it was only then that Tess realized that what appeared to be an unusual slapdash wallpaper was made from pages—pages and pages and pages of books. Some were only text, but at some point during the massive project—the ceilings had to be at least twenty, possibly thirty feet—the children's books began to appear. Tess stepped closer to inspect what he had done. She didn't have a crafty bone in her body, but it appeared to be similar to some kind of decoupage—there was definitely a sealant over the pages. But it wasn't UV protected because there were sun streaks on the south-facing wall.

She looked down and realized he had done the same thing with the floor, or started to; part of the original parquet floor was still in evidence.

"Is the whole house like this?"

"Not yet," he said. "It's a big house."

"But William—these books, they're not yours. You've destroyed them."

"How?" he said. "You can still read them. The pages are in order. I'm letting them live. They were dying, inside their covers, on shelves. No one was looking at them. Now they're open forever, always ready to be read."

"But no one can see them here, either," she said.

"I can. You can."

"WILLIAM IS MY HALF BROTHER," Tate Kemper told Tess a few days later, over lunch in the Papermoon Diner, a North Baltimore spot that was a shrine to old toys. "He's fifteen years older than I am. He was institutionalized for a while. Then our grandfather, our father's father, agreed to pay for his care, set him up with an aide, in a little apartment not far from here. He left us the house in his will and his third wife got everything else. My mom and I never had money, so it's not a big deal to me. But our dad was still rich when William was young, so no one worried about how he would take care of himself when he was an adult."

"If you sold the house, you could easily pay for William's care, at least for a time."

"Yes, even in a bad market, even with the antiquated systems and old appliances, it probably would go for almost a million. But William begged me to keep it, to let him try living alone. He said Grandfather was the only person who was ever nice to him and he was right. His mother is dead and our father is a shit, gone from both of our lives, disinherited by his own father. So I let William move into the stable. It was several months before I realized what he was doing."

"But he'd done it before, no?"

Tate nodded. "Yes, he was caught stealing books years ago.

Several times. We began to worry he was going to run afoul of some repeat-offenders law, so Grandfather offered to pay for psychiatric care as part of a plea bargain. Then, when William got out, the aide watched him, kept him out of trouble. But once he had access to Grandfather's house . . ." He shook his head, sighing in the same way William had sighed.

"How many books have you stolen for him?"

"Fifty, a hundred. I tried to spread it out to several places, but the other owners are, well, a little sharper than Octavia."

No, they're just not smitten with you, Tess wanted to say.

"Could you make restitution?"

"Over time. But what good would it do? William will steal more. I'm stuck. Besides—" Tate looked defiant, proud. "I think what he's doing is kind of beautiful."

Tess didn't disagree. "The thing is, if something happens to you—if you get caught, or lose your job—you're both screwed. You can't go on like this. And you have to make restitution to Octavia. Do it anonymously, through me, whatever you can afford. Then I'll show you how William can get all the books he needs, for free."

"I don't see—"

"Trust me," Tess said. "And one other thing?"

"Sure."

"Would it kill you to ask Octavia out for coffee or something? Just once?"

"Octavia! If I were going to ask someone there out, it would be—"

"Mona, I know. But you know what, Tate? Not everyone can get the girl with the duck tattoo."

THE NEXT SATURDAY, TESS MET William outside his house. He wore his knapsack on the back, she wore hers on the front, where Carla Scout nestled with a sippy cup. She was small for her age, not even twenty-five pounds, but it was still quite the cargo to carry on a hike.

"Are you ready for our walk?"

"I usually walk alone," William said. He was unhappy with this arrangement and had agreed to it only after Tate had all but ordered him to do it.

"After today, you can go back to walking alone. But I want to take you someplace today. It's almost three miles."

"That's nothing," William said.

"Your pack might be heavier on the return trip."

"It often is," he said.

I bet, Tess thought. He had probably never given up stealing books, despite what Tate thought.

They walked south through the neighborhood, lovely even with the trees bare and the sky overcast. William, to Tess's surprise, preferred the main thoroughfares. Given his aversion to people, she thought he would want to duck down less-trafficked side streets, make use of Stony Run Park's green expanse, which ran parallel to much of their route. But William stuck to the busiest streets. She wondered if drivers glanced out their windows and thought: *Oh, the Walking Man now has a Walking Woman and a Walking Baby.*

He did not speak, and he shut down any attempt Tess made at conversation. He walked as if he were alone. His face was set, his gait steady. She could tell it made him anxious, having to follow her path, so she began to narrate the route, turn by turn, which let him walk a few steps ahead. "We'll take Roland Avenue to University Parkway, all the way to Barclay, where we'll go left." His pace was slow by Tess's standards, but William didn't walk to get places. He walked to walk. He walked to fill his days. Tate said his official diagnosis was bipolar with OCD, which made finding the right mix of medications difficult. His work, as William termed it, seemed to keep him more grounded than anything else, which was why Tate indulged it.

Finally, about an hour later, they stood outside a building of blue and pink cinderblocks.

"This is it," Tess said.

"This is what?"

"Go in."

They entered a warehouse stuffed with books. And not just any books—these were all unloved books, as William would have it, books donated to this unique Baltimore institution, The Book Thing, which accepted any and all books on one condition: they would then be offered free to anyone who wanted them.

"Tens of thousands of books," Tess said. "All free, every weekend."

"Is there a limit?"

"Yes," Tess said. "Only ten at a time. But you probably couldn't carry much more, right?" Actually, the limit, according to The Book Thing's rather whimsical website, was 150,000. But Tess had decided her aunt was right about people according more value to things they could not have so readily. If William thought he could have only ten, every week, it would be more meaningful to him.

He walked through the aisles, his eyes strafing the spines. "How will I save them all?" William said.

"One week at a time," Tess said. "But you have to promise that this will be your only, um, supplier from now on. If you get books from anywhere else, you won't be allowed to come here anymore. Do you understand, William? Can you agree to that?"

"I'll manage," William said. "These books really need me."

It took him forty-five minutes to pick his first book, *Manifold Destiny*, a guide to cooking on one's car engine.

"Really?" Tess said. "That's a book that needs to be liberated?"

William looked at her with pity, as if she were a hopeless philistine.

"HE SPENT FIVE HOURS THERE, selecting his books," Tess told Crow that evening, over an early supper. Crow worked Saturday evenings, so they ate by five o'clock in order to spend more time together.

"Did you feel guilty at all? He's just going to tear them apart and destroy them."

"Is he? Destroying them, I mean. Or is he making something beautiful, as his brother would have it? I go back and forth."

Crow shook his head. "An emotionally disturbed man with scissors, cutting up books inside his home, taking a walk with you and our daughter, whose middle name is Scout. And you didn't make one Boo Radley joke the entire time?"

"Not a one," Tess said. "You do the bath. I'll clean up."

But she didn't clean up, not right away. She went into her own library, a cozy sunroom lined with bookshelves. She had spent much of her pregnancy here, reading away, but even in three months of confinement she'd barely made a dent in the unread books. She had always thought of it as being rich, having so many books she had yet to read. But in William's view, she was keeping them caged. And no one else, other than Crow, had access to them. Was her library that different from William's?

Of course, she had paid for her books—most of them. Like almost every other bibliophile on the planet, Tess had books borrowed from friends that she had never returned, even as some of her favorite titles lingered in friends' homes, never to be seen again.

She picked up her iPad. Only seventy books loaded onto it. *Only*. Mainly things for work, but also the occasional self-help guide that promised to unlock the mysteries of toddlers. Forty of the seventy titles were virtually untouched. She wandered into Carla Scout's room, where there was now a poster of a man-beast living in a pile of books, the Arnold Lobel print from The Children's Bookstore. A payment/gift from a giddy Octavia, who didn't know how Tess had stopped her books from disappearing, and certainly didn't know that her crush had anything to do with it. During Carla Scout's bedtime routine, Tess now stopped in front of the poster, read the verse printed there, then added her own couplet. "It's just as much fun as it looks / To live in a house made of books."

It's what's in the book that matters. Standing in her daughter's room, which also had shelves and shelves filled with books, Tess remembered a character in a favorite story saying that to someone who objected to using the Bible as a fan on a hot summer day. But she could no longer remember which story it was. Did that mean the book had ceased to live for her? The title she was trying to recall could be in this very room, along with all of Tess's childhood favorites, waiting for Carla Scout to discover them one day. But what if she rejected them all, insisting on her own myths and legends, as Octavia had prophesied? How many of these books would be out of print in five, ten years? What did it mean to be out of print in a world where books could live inside devices, glowing like captured genies, desperate to get back out in the world and grant people's wishes?

Carla Scout burst into the room, wet hair gleaming, cheeks pink.

"Buh," she said, which was her word for *book*, unless it was her word for *ball* or, possibly, *balloon*. "Buh, p'ease." She wasn't even in her pajamas yet, only her diaper and hooded towel. Tess would have to use the promise of books to coax her through putting on her footed sleeper and gathering up her playthings. How long would she be able to bribe her daughter with books? Would they be shunted aside like the Velveteen Rabbit as other newer, shinier toys gained favor? Would her daughter even read *The Velveteen Rabbit*? William Kemper suddenly seemed less crazy to Tess than the people who managed to live their lives in houses that had no books at all.

"Three tonight," Tess said. "Pick out three. Only three, Carla Scout. One, two, three. You may have three."

They read five.

• • •

AUTHOR'S NOTE: The Book Thing was a very real thing, but was temporarily closed when this collection went to press. The Children's Bookstore on Twenty-Fifth Street is my invention, along with all characters.

THE EVERYDAY HOUSEWIFE

The summer that she was a newlywed, Judith Monaghan watched *The Newlywed Game* almost every day, except when it was preempted by the hearings. She watched those, too, marveling at Senator Ervin's eyebrows and Maureen "Mo" Dean's outfits, but she preferred *The Newlywed Game*, despite the fact that she had once been vitally interested in politics. Actually, maybe that was why she preferred the game show to the hearings; it seemed more real to her.

The Newlywed Game came on at two P.M. on Channel 13 and Judith set aside the next two hours to accomplish whatever could be done while seated in the living room—darning socks, shelling peas, whipping in hems, teaching herself to knit. She was sure that she and Patrick could answer every question correctly, as they had known each other for six years before they married. But how would they get to California from Baltimore? Would her mother be upset about the inevitable "making whoopee" questions? And was it possible to angle to be on the show when the top prize was a washer-dryer? Judith didn't like the look of the furniture sets given away as prizes—too shiny new for her tastes—and the Monaghans already had a perfectly good television, a wedding gift from her second-oldest brother, who owned two electronics stores.

The Newlywed Game was followed by a show called *The Girl in My Life*, about women who had made a difference to others. She didn't care for it as much. She usually switched to *The Edge of Night*, which led right into *The Price Is Right*, where she won almost everything. Or would have, if she had been in the studio audience. Judith was a very focused shopper, paying attention to prices, calculating the per-unit cost among different brands.

Judith did have a washer, but no dryer, a problem during that clammy, damp summer, when the sun rose every day only to disappear until four P.M.—the time that Judith tied an immaculate apron over one of her pretty, hand-tailored dresses and began to prepare dinner for her husband, who arrived home at five thirty P.M. and expected his food at six. (He spent the intervening half hour with a beer and the evening paper, the Orioles pregame show on WBAL.) She liked making Patrick dinner. She liked doing things in general. Judith was as restless as a hummingbird and the small brick duplex required so little of her. She cleaned the woodwork with a Q-tip, vacuumed the venetian blinds, scrubbed the long-discolored grout with a toothbrush, and still she ended up with time on her hands. She even started ironing the sheets when she changed the linens on Fridays and she might have washed them more often, but they took so long to dry on these strangely overcast summer days. She tried to bake her own bread, once. The loaves were flat and dense; Patrick said he preferred store bread, anyway. But Patrick liked Wonder Bread and Judith liked Maranto's, the fresh, paper-wrapped Italian loaves.

"Those only taste good the day you buy them," Patrick said. "Wonder Bread tastes good all week long."

They had only one car and of course Patrick took that every day; the bus stop was four blocks away and he would have been required to change buses on Route 40. Besides, he needed the car for his job, which involved driving from bar to bar, doing inspections. Judith didn't mind. She did a big grocery shop on weekends and could do any daily marketing on foot—vegetables, last-minute items—at the High's Dairy Store on Ingleside, or even the grocery stores on Route 40 if it came to that. She knew if she shopped efficiently, she wouldn't have to do these daily runs to High's, but the walk down Newfield Road was another way to fill the long days.

Married life was lonely, which seemed strange to her. Shouldn't marriage be the end of loneliness? She tried to find a neutral way to express this thought to her mother, who called every day at nine A.M., despite the fact that Judith told her repeatedly that was when she cleaned the kitchen.

"The days seem so long that I find myself cleaning even more than you did."

"I," her mother said, "had four sons. No one could clean more than I did."

"I cook a lot, too. I'm getting pretty good." Judith was proud of her cooking, the meals she put together for Patrick. She would never be like the woman in the Alka-Seltzer commercial, the one who made heart-shaped meatloaf. "Sometimes I wonder if I should have kept my job until I got pregnant."

A quick laugh at her own expense, as if what she was saying was silly. But she did miss work, the intrigues of an office, being around others. She had lived at home until she married. She had wanted to take an apartment with another girl after she finished college, but her parents wouldn't hear of it.

"Marry in haste, repent in leisure."

Judith adjusted the phone, which she had cradled between her ear and shoulder, thinking she must have misheard. For one thing, no one could call Patrick Monaghan's courtship hasty.

"I didn't catch that," she said. "I'm washing the breakfast dishes." Patrick liked to start the day with eggs, bacon, toast, and juice. She had made the juice fresh until he told her he preferred Minute Maid concentrate. That was okay, she used the empty containers to set her hair after he left in the mornings, the best way to get the smooth look that he liked.

"Mrs. Levitan died that way. She was washing the dishes and the phone slipped in the sink and she was electrocuted."

"I don't think that's what happened," Judith ventured.

"You're right. Mrs. Levitan is the one who died while talking on the phone in a thunderstorm. It was Irene Sandowski who dropped the phone. Although I think it was in the bathtub."

"Oh, Mother, how could someone drop the phone in the bathtub? The Sandowskis aren't the type of people to have a phone in the bathroom."

"She thought she was so clever, that one. And grand. She had her husband find an extra-long cord—I think he had to call Bell Atlantic special—and she hooked it up to a princess phone, pink, a birthday gift, and she would take it into the bathroom and prop it up on the toilet and take bubble baths like she was Doris Day or somebody, talking the whole while. Well, one day, the whole thing fell in." A pause. "I just realized—I never did understand why she got a pink phone, when her bedroom was all gold and white, but the bathroom was pink."

"Irene Sandowski is alive," Judith said.

"Are you sure?"

"She was alive as of last week when I got the invitation to Rachel's wedding. Irving *and* Irene Sandowski request your pleasure, et cetera, et cetera."

"I didn't say she *died*. But that's why she has that white streak in her hair and now she has to be careful when she gets her teeth cleaned because her heartbeat is irregular. So Rachel is getting married? Someone nice, I hope."

Nice meant Jewish. *Nice* meant rich, or at least someone who might be rich, someday. It also meant: Not like your husband, the Irishman, the Mick, who took you to the far side of town where I suspect you are eating *ham* every day. Yet the Weinsteins didn't keep kosher and ate pork when they had Chinese carryout, while crabs were okay as long as they were eaten outside on newspaper. Her mother had never tasted lobster, however, a fact of which she was strangely proud.

"It's nice over here," Judith said. Sometimes, saying a thing could make it true. It wasn't *not* nice. It just wasn't where she had expected to live.

"It's tacky, sharing a wall with another house," her mother said.

"You grew up in a rowhouse."

"*You* didn't," her mother said. "I'll talk to you tomorrow."

"You don't have to call every—" But her mother had already hung up.

Judith thought maybe she should spend less time talking to her mother and more time with her brother Donald, the one closest to her in age. A bachelor who worked for a state senator, Donald was used to listening to people. Plus, he liked Patrick, had helped get him the job with the liquor board. Donald had lots of connections, lots of pull.

"Maybe you should get a job, Judith," Donald said. "I can help you if that's what you want."

"Oh, no," she protested. "I'm a married woman now. And the babies will start coming any day. I'd end up quitting."

Those wished-for babies were the reason for the house on Newfield Road, which Patrick had rented without consulting her. "With three bedrooms, a yard, and a washing machine—no dryer, but it has one of those umbrella-like things to hang the clothes on and the yard gets good sunlight, I made sure to check that. And a garbage disposal, Judith. Plus an unfinished basement, which we could make into a rec room, the landlord said improvements were fine. Of course, we probably won't be there long enough to care. I mean, it's okay for one kid, but once we get past that—"

Patrick had never said so many words at one time in all the years Judith had known him.

"Newfield Road? I don't even know where that is," she had said.

"Edmondson Heights. Over by Social Security, but closer to Route 40. You know Mr. G's, where I used to take you for soft ice cream when we started dating? And the drive-in where we saw that movie together the night we met? Sort of between those two places."

Judith had fond memories of both Mr. G's and the drive-in. But Judith had considered those exotic adventures, akin to going on an African safari. *Observe the Baltimore Irish Catholic in his natural environment, eating "soft" ice cream and onion rings after a movie.* The boys Judith knew congregated at diners, after dropping their dates at home. Edmondson Heights was seven exits away on the Beltway from where she grew up in Pikesville. It might as well have been seven hundred miles.

"I don't know people who live over there."

"You'll meet some. I have lots of cousins in the neighborhood, if it comes to that."

"I mean, I mean—" But she could not say: *I don't mean* people *people. I mean* my *people. Your people are not my people.* How could she point out that there wasn't a single temple along the Route 40 corridor? Patrick thought she wasn't going to go to synagogue anymore. They had thrown in their lot together, Romeo and Juliet, vowing to disown their disapproving families and live their own lives, by their rules. Only it turned out their families would not be disowned so easily and what were supposed to be their rules, Patrick and Judith's, were turning out to be Patrick's rules. He chose where they lived. He chose how they spent their weekend hours. She suspected, come December, he would choose to have a tree in the living room. At which point, should Judith's mother visit, she would drop dead on the spot.

But, so far, her mother had inspected the rowhouse only once. She had walked through it without comment, unless sniffs could be counted as comments. In which case, she had made roughly forty, fifty comments, five to ten per room. The thing that seemed to bother her the most was the umbrella-like drying line in the backyard that Patrick considered such an asset. She had placed a hand over her heart and shook her head ever so slightly, the way she did when she watched the war coverage on TV.

Certainly, her mother could not be surprised that Judith didn't have an automatic dryer, and she had to admit the duplex was a step up from the Bonnie Brae Apartments. Louise Weinstein, as a newlywed, had pinned clothes to a line strung behind a Butchers Hill rowhouse, not that far from where the Monaghans lived in Fell's Point. Both families had moved up and out, of course, but the Weinsteins had headed northwest, while the Monaghans marched due west. Judith and Patrick might never have met if they hadn't ended up on a double date together, and it wasn't even with each other. Judith's date, Harold, asked to find a boy for her friend Thelma, had suggested Patrick Monaghan, an enthusiastic volunteer in the governor's race. Thelma was a pretty girl, but Judith could feel Patrick's eyes on her neck throughout the entire film, *What a Way to Go!* The next day, Patrick called and asked if she was really as interested in politics as she had claimed over soft ice cream at Mr. G's, because the Stonewall Democratic Club was always looking for volunteers. Oh, she was *interested*. She was interested in politics and interested in this stoic Irish redhead. Go figure—the man was trustworthy, but politics broke her heart. Patrick's, too, if it came to that. They never quite got over what happened in that governor's race. The Watergate hearings, as far as Judith was concerned, were just an opportunity for the rest of the nation to learn what they already knew. It was all a shuck, a game, business as usual. Patrick and Judith had presented their youth and idealism like a burnt offering to pagan gods, then comforted each other when it came to naught. At least they had a marriage to show for it. Lots of young couples were marrying early, if only because of the lottery numbers the boys had been assigned. But Patrick had a high number. Judith knew he really loved her.

Besides, whatever the pace of their courtship, she was not *repenting*. She didn't regret her marriage. The house was fine, just fine, especially for a place to pass through. The neighborhood was—

There, her resilience failed her. She hated Edmondson Heights, the blocks and blocks of brick rowhouses exactly like her own, thrown up in the '50s to address the shortages after the war. She could and did walk for miles, but the scene seldom changed. Sometimes, she walked all the way to the Westview Mall, but it was a dark, jerry-rigged place, an open-air shopping center that had closed itself in to keep up with the times. Besides, she had no money to buy the things she really wanted, clothes and shoes and books, so she ended up at Silber's bakery, eating those abominations known as pizza rolls, hunks of white bread with tomato sauce and cheese smeared on top. She would probably weigh an extra ten pounds if it weren't for all the walking.

Over the summer, she gradually began to see the small distinctions from block to block along Newfield Road, which had initially looked all of a piece to her. She could tell, for example, where the neighborhood changed over from renters to owners. The tiny front lawns were better-kept and often had shrubberies, the ones hung with bright red berries that Judith had always heard were poisonous, but perhaps that was a story told to scare children. The doors and shutters were painted in glossier colors and the houses had storm doors. Renters kept iridescent globes on pedestals in their yards. Owners nailed ceramic cats to their brick facades. Some even had those hitching posts that looked like jockeys, although the faces had all been whitewashed. There were more children, too, in these blocks. Judith's block was almost childless. Two blocks over, the Lord Baltimore diaper truck was a daily presence. Go another five blocks and it was the Good Humor man.

Walking as she did, day in and day out, Judith felt like a spy in her own life. She looked like the other women she saw, she lived a life like theirs, and yet she was not one of them, she was sure of that. Was it merely being Jewish in a neighborhood where almost everyone else seemed to be Catholic? Her face burned with the memory of her humiliation when she served pot roast to one pair of neighbors on a Friday night, only to have Mrs. Delaney say quietly: "We go meatless on Fridays."

"Oh, who gives a crap, Frances?" said Mr. Delaney, who took seconds. It was a good pot roast; Judith couldn't help preening a bit. Mrs. Delaney limited herself to potatoes and the Jell-O salad, said she was considering giving up red meat anyway.

"Frances would be a hippie if I let her," Mr. Delaney said. "But I'm not going to be married to a hippie. And I'm not going to live on rabbit food. She even wants to grow her own vegetables, like a peasant."

Judith's face had burned at that, too, thinking of the plot that Patrick had planted in their backyard.

Frances Delaney was young, younger than Judith, yet Judith still thought of her as Mrs. Delaney, perhaps because Mr. Delaney was so much older, in his forties, closer to her parents' generation than hers. He had been career military until a year or so ago, and Judith was unclear where he had met his bride. His attitudes, too, made him seem old. Gruff, bossy. He worked at the Social Security Administration, as did many in the neighborhood. At the dinner table that night, he placed his large hand over Mrs. Delaney's and said: "No hippies and no women's libbers for us, right, Pat? Our wives stay home and take care of us, as it should be."

"Judith worked at her father's variety store before it went bust," Patrick said, missing, as he often did, the point beneath the actual words, words not being something he used very much. "She also worked at her brother's jewelry store, then got a job as a secretary at Procter and Gamble."

"*Before* you married," Mr. Delaney said.

"Yes."

"That's okay. Frances here was a nurse."

"And you met—" Judith began.

"Oh, it's such a boring story," Frances Delaney said. "Don't bore them with it, Jack. Where did you two meet?"

"The movies," Pat said. No one would ever accuse Patrick Monaghan of telling long stories. At night, when Judith tried to share her observations about their neighborhood, he would say: "I'm not much of one for gossip, Judith."

But Judith didn't mind that Patrick was the strong, silent type. She had come from a family of big talkers. Patrick was her Quiet Man. She loved his silences. Except when she didn't and then she locked herself in the bathroom, wishing she had a phone cord that stretched all the way in there. Only whom would she call? Her mother, who would repeat the line about marrying in haste? Her girlfriends, who had married proper Jewish boys and were living proper Jewish lives in the northwest suburbs? Judith might be able to find a cord long enough to stretch into the bathroom, but she wasn't sure that there was any phone line long enough to take her back to the life she had known. She was a spy. A spy in what her mother called the land of Mackerel Snappers and Shanty Irish.

She did not look that different from the other women. Her hair had a reddish cast and she was given to freckles, even in this sunless summer. She was often asked, in fact, what parish she had grown up in, a question she eventually realized was meant to suss out whether she preferred St. William of York or St. Lawrence. There was some confusion in the neighborhood about which parish to join, and the choice was considered a tip to one's ambitions. Would you be moving southeast, to the larger houses in Ten Hills and Hunting Ridge, or west, closer to Social Security, where Jack Delaney worked? It was all very complex, a mathematical equation made up of the husband's ambitions and prospects, the pace at which the children arrived. Even if Judith managed to sidestep that first question, the other questions were still lying in wait. Patrick had a good job as an inspector for the city liquor board. Safe, solid. But how high would they rise? How many children would they have? And when those children arrived, how would they be raised? All very well to say love was all one needed when it was only the two of you, but baby makes three and some very difficult questions, as Judith was now realizing. Who was she? Who would her children be?

So while others might call what she did on her walks snooping or spying, Judith believed she was simply trying to find a way to be. Would she move toward Ten Hills or Woodlawn? Would she have an iridescent globe on a pedestal in her yard? (Probably not, they struck her as tacky.) She definitely would not have one of those hitching posts. And she didn't know what to make of the people who affixed those pairs of kittens to their brick-fronts, always a white one and black one. What was that about? Who were they? Who was she?

The summer continued cool and damp. Good for sleeping and good for walking, but not for much else. Judith imagined this was like summer in London, not that she had been there, or San Francisco, not that she had been there, or—well, she really hadn't been anywhere. She had grown up in Northwest Baltimore, the youngest of five, the only daughter. Spoiled, she saw in retrospect, but does anyone ever realize they're spoiled until the spoiling ends? Yet spoiled as she might have been, she could put her little house shipshape by eleven A.M. and then what? She could have stayed in and watched soap operas, but she was more interested in the soap operas playing out in the neighborhood. In plain sight, once one knew where to look. The battling Donovans. The literally bursting-at-the-seams Katie O'Connell, who had just given birth to her fifth child in five years. The Horton hooligans, as they were known, a brood of terrifying brothers. Judith took to walking down the narrow lane that led to the carports behind the houses of Newfield Road. This was where real life could be glimpsed. Almost no one here had a proper garage and some didn't even have carports, only concrete pads. She saw Betty Donovan sitting on her back steps, which could use a coat of paint, smoking a cigarette and holding a frozen package of succotash to a swollen eye. She saw the Horton boys trying to burn ants with a magnifying glass, which made her glad that the sun was weak and fitful. She saw Katie O'Connell tie one of her children to the useless umbrella drying rack in her backyard.

"He tried to run away," Katie said when she saw Judith looking. "What else can I do?"

And Judith saw the Lord Baltimore diaper service truck parked in the carport behind the Delaney house, despite the fact that the Delaneys had no children.

"They do shirts," Frances Delaney said one July morning as Judith headed out again for a walk, thinking she might do a little marketing, or even have an ice cream cone at High's for lunch. She always left by way of the street, then returned via the alley, her bag of groceries a cover of sorts, a legitimate reason for being in the alley. It would be natural, with a bag of groceries, to want to enter the house through the kitchen door.

"Excuse me?"

Frances Delaney was on her knees in her front yard, tending to a small flower bed. The men did the lawns, the women did the flowers. Judith did not have a green thumb, perhaps because her own mother did not.

"Lord Baltimore diaper service," Frances said, rising to her feet, brushing off her knees. She was wearing short shorts and a halter that left a strip of her midriff bare. A good outfit for tanning if the sun ever came out again. Judith didn't feel comfortable in such clothes since she married. She thought the whole point of being a wife was to look polished, grown-up. To look as if you had someplace to go, even if it was only High's Dairy Store. *She* was wearing Bernardo sandals and a hot-pink shift that she had made from a remnant at Jo-Ann Fabrics, a coordinating scarf over her hair, which she would wash and set later today in the loose straight style that Patrick liked. "They do shirts, too."

"You send your husband's shirts out?"

"Jack's fussy in his way."

Judith thought about Mr. Delaney. *Jack.* He had come to her home for Friday night supper in a Banlon shirt. He wore his hair very short, even shorter than Patrick's, practically a crew cut. He had picked his teeth at the table and touched his wife a lot, stroking her, patting her. He reminded Judith of the fairy tale in which a Chinese emperor kept a nightingale to sing for him.

"His work shirts," Frances Delaney continued. "They're particular at Social Security. Always looking for something to hold against a man, Jack says. He liked the army better, he says. The rules were clear. He even liked Germany when we were stationed there."

"Is that where you met? Germany?"

Frances laughed as if the idea were absurd, meeting someone in Germany. "Anyway, he likes his shirts just so and I like Jack to be happy."

"Isn't that expensive? Sending out shirts?"

"Jack doesn't know I send his shirts out. He only knows that they're ironed and starched to his standards, which are very high." She smiled shyly. She looked like a gypsy to Judith, but Patrick said Frances Delaney was pure black Irish—dark hair, blue eyes so pale that they were barely there. But there was something in her voice, a suggestion of an accent that had been vanquished, or was being kept in place through strict discipline.

"Where did you go to high school?" she asked Frances. It was usually the first thing Baltimoreans asked of one another.

"All over," she said.

"Army brat?"

"Of a sort. My father's work took us to Asia and Europe."

That probably explained her accent, although it wasn't so much an accent as a complete absence of accent, unusual here in Edmondson Heights, where almost everyone, except Judith, spoke with the exaggerated *O*'s and extra *R*'s that marked what people called a Baltimore accent.

Judith knew she shouldn't ask more questions, that part of being a good neighbor was to respect all the little boundaries—the cheap white pickets that people placed down the middle of their shared lawns, the invisible lines dividing the parking pads, the shouts and sounds heard through the paper-thin walls late at night.

Yet she pressed, curious: "Don't you get an allowance? Doesn't he go over the checkbook?"

"I'm clever with money. I economize on the groceries—I'm a good cook, if I do say so myself. No one's ever left my table unhappy." Was Frances Delaney suggesting that she had left Judith's table unhappy? That was so unfair. It wasn't Judith's fault that she forgot most Catholics didn't eat meat on Fridays. "And I use what's left over for the laundry. What he doesn't know won't hurt me." She clapped a hand to her mouth. "I mean what he doesn't know won't hurt *him*. I always get that wrong. Would you like to come in for a Tab?"

"Sure," Judith said.

Over the next two weeks, she stopped at Frances Delaney's house almost daily, enjoying Tab or Fresca and, sometimes, a white wine that was quite unlike anything Judith had ever tasted. They talked about everything and nothing. They complained, in the self-deprecating code that was allowed, about their husbands' foibles. Silent, oblivious Pat. Gabby, grabby Jack. They watched the Watergate hearings and made fun of Sam Ervin's eyebrows, talked about Mo Dean's style, which Judith admired but Frances thought drab.

"If my husband had that kind of job, I'd look better than that," said Frances, who almost always wore cutoffs and halter tops. "She looks dowdy to me."

"I worked in politics," Judith confided in Frances. "I thought I was going to change the world."

"The world never changes," Frances said, smoking a Virginia Slim. Judith yearned to join her, but she had worked too hard to give it up.

"That's what I found out."

Inside the Delaney house, she saw enough evidence of money to believe that Frances Delaney did have a household budget with considerable fat in it. The appliances were new, unusual in this block of renters. The dining room set could have come straight from the grand prize package on *The Newlywed Game*. Mahogany, shiny. Tacky, but expensive, and Frances seemed to loathe it, too, neglecting to use coasters beneath their sweating glasses. The television set was color and huge, a Magnavox with a stereo built in.

"Do you own or rent?" Judith asked one day.

"Own." Frances made a face. "It was his mother's house. She died, left it to us, so we moved here. We could afford something nicer, but he says there's no point in moving until we outgrow it."

"So you're going to have a family?"

"Of course." She looked—insulted, that was it. As if Judith had given offense. "Why wouldn't we? Jack's only forty-two."

"My oldest brother is forty," Judith said, a peace offering. "I'm the youngest of five, the only girl. I grew up in Pikesville."

"Pikesville. Isn't that all Jews?"

"Yes," Judith said, thinking it the most tactful way to reply. If she knew anything about her new friend, it was that she was delicate and sensitive, not at all like her coarse, belligerent husband. She would not want to think she had hurt Judith's feelings.

"Wow. How did you stand it?"

Judith thought very hard about what to say next.

"Hasn't it been the worst summer?"

"Yes, but it's a blessing in a way," Frances said. "These houses get so hot, don't you think? The second floor is usually unbearable during the day." Frances stuck out her bottom lip and blew a few errant tendrils from her face. "You know, I suppose we should have you over to dinner, in return. I should have thought of that sooner."

"Oh, please—don't worry about that."

A rumbling noise from the carport. From where they sat, in the dining room, Judith could see a white truck pulling to a stop. The Lord Baltimore diaper truck.

"I should go."

Frances didn't protest. "Friday night," she said, not rising from her chair. She dangled a hand between her thighs absentmindedly, then across her collarbone, caressing herself. Judith left behind a half-full can of Tab, desperate to be out of the house before the Lord Baltimore diaper service driver crossed the threshold.

When she returned from High's forty minutes later, the truck was still there.

The next day was Thursday. It rained all day and Judith decided not to walk anywhere, but to stay inside and watch the hearings.

Friday night Judith and Patrick walked down their front walk, traveled perhaps fifteen yards and then up the Delaneys' front walk. Judith carried a loaf of zucchini bread, although the Delaneys had come to her dinner empty-handed. But proper people, truly mannerly people, did not visit empty-handed, in her experience.

"I wonder what they'll serve us," she said.

"Probably fish sticks," Patrick said mournfully. "I thought I was leaving this behind when I married you."

They were both surprised—Patrick happily, Judith ambivalently—to learn that Frances Delaney was an outstanding cook. Yes, dinner was fish, but poached salmon, served with little potatoes unlike anything Judith had ever tasted, something called "fingerlings." The salad was served *after* the main course, which Frances said was how the French ate.

Her husband rolled his eyes. "Judith studied cooking in France. I promised not to bitch about her predentions as long as her grub is good."

"Predentions?" Judith couldn't help asking. "France?"

"You know," Jack said. "Putting on airs. Predentions."

"Oh, pretensions," she said, then hated herself for it. She was trying to show Frances Delaney, by example, how a well-mannered person behaved, but Frances Delaney seemed to be one step ahead of her. She was even better dressed than Judith tonight, in a modest knee-length lace shift that exposed only her arms. As she moved back and forth between the dining room and the kitchen, serving dinner with an ease that Judith had yet to master, Frances seemed not to notice Jack Delaney's proprietary pats on her rear end. Judith did, though. She also noticed, with a sinking heart, Patrick's approving looks at the house, the furniture. He probably thought this dining room set was classy.

"What the fuck is in my salad?" Jack Delaney held up a fork with a yellow blossom on the tines.

Judith had wondered the same thing, but would never have questioned it and would certainly never have used *that* word, which she did not remember ever hearing spoken aloud before, except through the walls late at night, when the Mulcahys were fighting. At least, they started out fighting. Where they ended up was more shocking still.

"Nasturtiums," Frances said. "They're edible."

"They're flowers," her husband sputtered. Patrick looked

hopeful, as if his host's temper tantrum might get him off the hook.

"Don't forget your promise to me, Jack," France said, her tone even and polite. "To try anything once."

"And don't forget yours to me," he said. "Try *everything* once."

Frances seemed paler than usual, but she said nothing, not even when he patted her rear end again, leaving a grease stain on the white lace that she had managed to keep spotless while preparing and serving this meal.

"Hey, Pat, do you know what they call the alley behind our houses?" Jack Delaney did not wait for an answer. "Bonk Alley! Could there be a better place to live? *Bonk Alley*."

"I don't get it," Judith said. She didn't. She looked at Patrick. Patrick busied himself, making a little pile of flowers on the side of his plate. He was a polite man, but he had his limits.

"Bonk—it's slang for screwing." In some ways, Judith found Jack's use of that word even more shocking. "Something I picked up from the Brits."

"Brits?"

"You know, when I was in London. God, that city is a shithole. They're preverted, too, the Brits. Think they're so superior to us. But they're the preverts."

"Perverts," Frances said quietly. "The word is 'pervert.'"

"Well, you would know, honey. You would know."

Jack fondled his wife's rear end again as she collected the salad plates, making way for dessert. "Coffee?" she asked brightly. She made it in a Chemex, Judith observed. Judith and Patrick normally drank Nescafé. Patrick said he preferred it, yet he had seconds on Frances's coffee.

Frances did not serve Judith's zucchini bread for dessert. Judith could not fault her for this lapse, as Frances had prepared something called tiramisu. "Could you get the recipe for this?" Patrick asked Judith.

"I'm not sure I could make something like this," Judith said. She couldn't even spell it.

"It's not so hard," Frances said, "if you use store-bought lady fingers."

"Do you?" Judith asked.

A slight pause. "Sometimes I do, sometimes I don't. I made these. But then, I like to bake. It fills the long afternoons."

Judith felt she had lost a contest, although she wasn't sure what it was, or who she was playing. She was almost tempted to make a crack about long afternoons, but she knew the women were in this together.

At least Judith could help clean the kitchen. She scraped the plates into the trash—the Delaney house did not have a garbage disposal, score one for her—and tried not to think about the white Silber's bakery box she saw in the can, a box that clearly had held something nowhere in evidence. Lady fingers?

They parted, promising to do it again, knowing they never would.

The next time Judith walked to High's, she did not return via what she now knew was Bonk Alley. She did not want to see the white Lord Baltimore truck coming and going, did not want to risk being taken into Frances Delaney's confidences, confidences she sensed would be too heavy for her to bear. August passed. The gavel came down on the hearings and the country went on, as Judith knew it would. Everything goes on. The weather turned glorious around Labor Day, just in time to mock the children returning to school. The days were shorter, technically, although they still felt long to Judith. The vice president resigned and while some Marylanders felt ashamed of their native son, Judith and Patrick, Stonewall Democrats, toasted the news, he with a beer, she with vermouth, which she had bought under the mistaken belief it would taste like the white wine that Frances Delaney had served. But the two couples, the Monaghans and the Delaneys, did not socialize again. Nor did the two women. Judith kept to the street, eyes straight ahead, trying not to see or hear the secrets all around her.

But it was impossible to miss, ten days before Halloween, the ambulance parked outside the Delaney house, lights twirling, Jack Delaney being carried out in a gurney, face covered. All the women of the neighborhood gathered to watch, somber yet excited in some horrible way. At least something was happening.

"Is he okay?" Judith asked Katie O'Connell, who may or may not have been pregnant with number six under her shapeless coat. Probably better not to ask.

"He's dead," she said. "They don't pull the sheet up over your face unless you're dead, Judith."

"But how?"

"Who knows? Heart attack, probably. That's what a man gets, taking up with a younger woman."

"You mean they—in the afternoon?" The O'Connells shared a wall with the Delaneys. She shrugged.

The news would not make its way up and down the street for several days. Frances Delaney, in her quest for culinary sophistication, had harvested the yew berry bushes at a neighbor's house a block over, asking permission before she did so. She had researched the berries carefully at the Catonsville library—or so she thought. It turned out the berries themselves were not poisonous if prepared properly. But everything else about the plant was so toxic that any preparation was risky. She had made her husband a tart. The only reason she hadn't eaten any was because she had given up desserts, worried about her weight. He had awakened with a stomachache and called in sick to work, but Frances hadn't thought it could be that serious. He was dead by the time the ambulance arrived.

Within a week, a for-sale sign went up in the yard. Within a month, the sign was gone and the neighbors, who had felt sympathy for the young widow, were incensed: Frances Delaney had sold to the first Black family in Edmondson Heights. The gossip flew up and down the street. Who did she think she was? Where was she from, anyway? Not here. She hadn't even gone to high school in Baltimore.

A week after that, Judith saw a moving truck pull into Bonk Alley. Not a regular moving truck, a Hampden Van Lines or a Mayflower. It was just a U-Haul. No, not even a U-Haul, but a gray, no-name thing.

And it was driven by the dark-haired man who used to drive the Lord Baltimore diaper service truck. Frances Delaney came out with a box of things, caught Judith watching, gave her a cheery wave.

"I'm moving to San Francisco," she said. "Isn't it exciting?"

"Is that where you're from?"

"I'm not really from anywhere."

"Army brat, right?"

"Something like that."

A week after that, the men in black suits came to Newfield Road. They walked up and down, up and down, knocking on doors. They said they were insurance investigators. They asked questions about the Delaneys. Nice people? Friendly people? Did Jack Delaney talk much about his work? Where had Frances Delaney said she was going? These conversations were reported along the back fences and the sidewalks of Newfield Road. More gossip, Patrick sighed, when Frances tried to talk to him at night, when all he wanted to do was watch *Kojak*. Katie O'Connell had the most to share and tell.

Until the day the men in the black suits knocked on Judith's door.

"Did Mr. Delaney talk about his work much?"

"Only that he worked for Social Security."

"Doing what?" There were two men, one named Simon, the other Arthur.

"Oh, goodness, what does anyone do at Social Security? Make sure all the checks go out, I suppose."

"But did he ever say what he did?" pressed Simon. Or Art.

"No. I remember his wife said he liked it better in the army. That the rules were clearer."

"He said he was in the army."

"Yes, in Germany, I think. Although he also said he spent time in London. I guess things are awfully close over there."

"And the wife, Frances—she cooked with plants a lot?"

"I wouldn't say a lot," Judith said. "There were nasturtiums in the salad, the one time we ate over there. She was a good cook. Still, I would have known she wasn't from here, once I heard about the yew berries. No one who grew up in Baltimore would ever touch a yew berry."

"Anything else?" The two men, Simon and Art, looked at her with so much hope that she felt obliged to try.

"She said she made her own lady fingers from scratch. But she didn't."

They left, clearly unimpressed by this intelligence, but Judith thought it meaningful. Why had Frances lied about the lady fingers? Later, when Judith relayed the story to her brother Donald, who liked to talk in the way that women did, he asked what insurance company they represented. She went to look for the card, only to realize she didn't have one. But she had seen one, surely. Something State? State something? Something State Something?

"Jesus, Judith, don't you even know who you let into your house?"

"Don't be so paranoid," she told her brother.

"Everyone's paranoid," Donald said. "It's in style, like sideburns."

A few days later, her brother dropped by, looking serious. "That neighbor of yours. What did you say his name was?"

"Jack Delaney."

"And he worked at Social Security? That's what he told you? Do you know what he did there?"

Hadn't Simon and Art asked the same thing? Judith gave the same answer. "What does anyone do there?"

Donald's question turned out to be rhetorical. "He was developing computer programs, Judith. Computer programs that don't have anything to do with senior citizens getting their checks every month. Yeah, he went to Woodlawn every day, parked his car in the lot. He worked at Social Security, but not for them."

"I don't understand."

"Judith, have you ever heard of a guy named Oleg Lyalin?" He didn't wait for her answer. "KGB. Defected two years ago in England, in part because he fell in love with his secretary. The Russians don't like that, in-house adultery. They think it makes you vulnerable. So he defected, got to be with the love of his life, in return for whatever information he had."

"I guess it sounds familiar." Judith used to be so up on things. What had happened to her? A summer of *The Newlywed Game*, walks on Newfield Road, ice cream cones from High's Dairy Store, Frances Delaney's brief and baffling friendship.

"You don't get it, do you, Judith?"

"Get what?"

"The Delaneys—I have an old friend working for Mac Mathias. This guy, your neighbor. He's a computer whiz. He was married to someone else. He wanted to be with his secretary. Someone made it happen. Not officially, not like Lyalin. But Jack Delaney—or Boris Badunov, or whatever his real name was, and maybe he worked for the East Germans, not the Russians—this guy, he came in from the cold on the condition that his girlfriend could come, too."

"The house belonged to his mother. Frances told me that."

"Yeah, *she* told you that. Did she tell you where they met?"

It's such a boring story. "No."

"Did she tell you where she was from?"

All over. Asia. Europe. An army brat? *Something like that.* "No."

"They brought her over, thinking they were going to make him happy. Wanting their computer whiz to be happy. But I guess the KGB, having lost one agent to his secret love, had a better plan. She killed him. Killed him and took off."

"Took off with the Lord Baltimore diaper truck driver."

Donald laughed. "Where did you hear that? He was her handler. CIA. And he was found dead in St. Louis three weeks ago."

"He used to be parked in her driveway. For long stretches. I thought—"

"That's probably what they wanted all you gossipy housewives to think, Judith."

They were sitting at the little built-in breakfast nook in Judith's kitchen, drinking coffee from the Chemex she had bought a few weeks ago. It really did make better coffee. She looked at the clouds forming in her half-empty cup, glanced up at the kitchen clock. Almost four P.M., time to fix Patrick's dinner. Then it would be time to clean up. Two hours of television after dinner. Tonight was a Wednesday, which meant *Adam-12* and the NBC Mystery Movie. She hoped it was *The Snoop Sisters* tonight and not *Banacek*, although George Peppard was very cute.

"Donald, how is what you do—talking to people, finding out stuff, then telling other people—how is that different from what housewives do? Isn't it all just gossip?"

"You have a point there, Judith. I guess it's a thin line between gossip and espionage."

"Do you think your boss could help me get a job, the way he did with Patrick? Given that he knows Mathias?"

"You want a job with the feds, not the city or the state? I suppose I could swing that. What are your qualifications? What type of job are you looking for?"

"I type eighty words per minute. And I see things. I want to work at the CIA."

"You didn't see two spies under your own nose."

"I will," she said. "You see what you look for. Once I start looking for spies, I'll see them."

She did not tell him everything else she had seen that summer, things that no one thought mattered. She saw Katie O'Connell, worn down by a baby a year and a husband who was never going to advance in his career. She saw Betty Donovan, smoking and weeping on her back steps. She saw the Horton boys, who had stopped trying to burn up things and moved on to suffocating cats in milk crates, cats that Judith freed. She saw ceramic cats nailed to walls, iridescent globes on pedestals, whitewashed lawn jockeys. She saw a laundry truck parked for hours behind the Delaneys' house. Donald was wrong. Judith wasn't just seeing what someone wanted her to see. The Lord Baltimore driver may have started out as Frances Delaney's handler, but Frances Delaney had learned how to handle him before long. He probably knew about the yew berries, thought they would end up together.

"You know I'll ace the civil service exam," Judith said. "And with two salaries, we can move up and out of here."

"Not sure you need to take a test," her brother said. "Anyway, I'll see what I can do."

The CIA meant a two-hour commute to Langley, so Judith settled for NSA, just down the parkway in Fort Meade. She accepted a clerical position, but even that demanded absolute nondisclosure on her part. When her neighbors, soon to be her old neighbors, asked what she did, Judith smiled and said: "I can't tell you. But I can assure you that we are not involved in *domestic* spying. NSA is forbidden by law to spy on our own citizens. So domestic spying is just my hobby."

Then she winked, as if it were all a big joke. The women of Newfield Road—talking over back fences, drinking Tab during the soap operas, running into each other at High's Dairy Store, tying their children to the clothesline, holding frozen vegetables to their eyes, pretending not to see the little boys who tortured living things—the women of Newfield Road said: "Did you hear? Judith Monaghan claims she's a spy. A spy in Edmondson Heights. Did you ever hear of anything so ridiculous?"

PART 2

For the female of the species is
more deadly than the male.

—Rudyard Kipling

COUGAR

"Sorry," said the young man who bumped into her, knocking over the tray of glasses she was carrying, although he didn't sound particularly sorry. Almost the opposite, as if he were muffling a laugh at her expense. At least it was water, and she could change into her other blouse, the one she had worn on the walk here, assuming Mr. Lee didn't object. Surely Mr. Lee wouldn't make her work the rest of the shift in a soaked white blouse that was now all but transparent.

"Sean!" his girlfriend chided without conviction.

"Hey," said he-who-must-be-Sean. "It was an accident. I didn't even see her."

Of course, Lenore thought, going to the back to change. *A five-foot-ten blonde in a sushi bar is hard to spot.* Yet she knew he wasn't lying. He hadn't seen her. No one ever saw her. She was here every Friday and Saturday night—seating them at their tables, bringing them their drink orders when the waitstaff got backed up—but even the regulars didn't seem to recognize her from week to week. For young people who came here, the sushi dinner they gulped down was preamble, preparation for the long night of barhopping ahead. If she wasn't the same age as their mothers, she was close enough, forty-two. Fact was, she had her own twenty-one-year-old son at home, living in the basement with his nineteen-year-old girlfriend, and she was invisible to them, too.

Still, at least one young man seemed to register her presence as she walked to the back room to get her shirt. Well, he noticed her tits, given that the thin white blouse was now plastered to her front. "Nice," he said to his friend, not even bothering to lower his voice. "Check out the cougar."

So now she was presumed to be deaf as well as invisible. Deaf, or in some strange category where she was expected to tolerate whatever others said about her. Was it the job? Her age? But then, it was the same at home. Worse, actually.

"A KID AT WORK CALLED me a cougar last night," she said over breakfast the next morning, a Sunday. Not hers. Lenore had eaten breakfast at ten A.M., a respectable time for a woman whose shift ended at midnight. Now it was almost one P.M., but her son and his girlfriend had roused themselves a few minutes ago and were nodding over bowls of cereal, their heads hanging so low that their chins almost grazed the milky ponds of Trix.

"Was he nearsighted? I can't imagine anyone thinking you was hot." That was Marie, the girlfriend, and the insult was so automatic that it carried no sting. As far as Lenore could tell, it was the reason that Frankie kept Marie around, to insult his mother. Otherwise, he would have to do it himself and that was too much effort.

"I think it's because my shirt was soaked through. Another kid bammed into me when I was carrying a tray of water glasses."

"Big thrill," Marie said.

"Well," Lenore said, "pretty big." She had a showgirl's figure and she didn't care what the magazines deemed fashionable—an hourglass would always be in style. Marie was flat-chested and soft with baby fat. Which made sense, because Marie was still a baby—lolling in bed all day, watching cartoons, eating all the sugar she could find.

"Shut up," Frankie said tonelessly. They did as he said. They always did as he said.

If Marie was a baby, then Frankie was a six-foot-two toddler, perpetually on the edge of a tantrum. He had returned home unexpectedly six months ago, with no explanation for where he had been or what he had been doing in the two years since Lenore had last seen him. She had offered him his childhood room, but he sneered at that, claiming the basement that she had just renovated into a television room. She had planned the room as a retreat, a place to watch movies late at night, maybe work on her various craft projects. But now it belonged to Frankie and she had to knock if she wanted to enter, even if it was to do his laundry in the utility room in the back. Once, just once, she had walked in without knocking and she wasn't sure what scared her more—the drugs on the coffee table or the look on Frankie's face.

I could lose my house, she thought as she backed out of the room, laundry basket clutched to her middle. Until that moment, she had—what was it called?—plausible deniability. She had suspected but not known what went on in her basement. But now she knew and if Frankie got caught, the government could take her house. That very thing had happened to Mrs. Bitterman up on Jackson, and there were rumors that it was why the house on Byrd Street was going to auction at the end of the month. Lenore lived every day torn between wishing her son would get busted, and knowing that his arrest would probably destroy her life instead of saving it.

Kicking him out wasn't an option. She was scared of Frankie. *She was scared of her son.* It was such an awful thought, she hadn't dared to let it form, not for a long time. She had even daydreamed that the man in her basement wasn't Frankie at all, but some audacious imposter. Certainly, he bore no resemblance to the boy she remembered, a serious but sweet child who never stopped puzzling over his father's disappearance when he was still such a little thing. And he was so much bigger than the fourteen-year-old they had taken away from her, put in the Hickey school, then that weird place out in western Maryland, where they taught them to cut down trees or something. He didn't even resemble the nineteen-year-old who had moved out in disgust two years ago, when she had said he had to live by her rules if he wanted to stay under her roof. She had been shocked when he actually went, because she had no idea how to make him do anything—pick up his clothes, rinse a plate. If he had refused to leave, she would have been powerless.

In the two years since then, Frankie must have figured that

out. And now he was in her basement, dealing drugs, running up her electricity bills, leaving crusty bowls strewn about, eating everything in sight and contributing nothing. Once, she had steeled herself to ask him if he might kick in for food or utilities. "Marie don't eat much" was all he said. His meaning was clear. She owed him room and board for the rest of his life, however long that might be. She owed him everything he wanted to take from her. She owed him for the big mistakes—not being able to hold on to his father—and the small ones, such as not getting him the right kind of sneakers when he was at Thomas Johnson. Sometimes, late at night, when she heard police cars hurtling down Fort Avenue, she wondered where Frankie was, if he was dead, and she wouldn't have minded too much if that were so.

And then she thought how unnatural she was, how a mother should always love her child no matter what.

FRANKIE HAD COME HOME IN March and now it was August, the end of a miserable, fretful summer. Working two jobs—the sushi place on weekends, Sparkle-and-Shine cleaning service Mondays through Thursdays—she should have been able to save on her A/C bill, but Frankie and Marie ran it full force, forgetting to turn it down when they headed out, which was usually four in the afternoon. Every day, Lenore came home to a chilled catastrophe of a house. She tried to remind herself how lonely she had been over the past two years, how empty her free evenings had seemed. That's when she had taken up various crafts in the first place, teaching herself crocheting and knitting, figuring out what her computer could do, where it could take her. But the computer was in the basement, along with the television, and it made her heart sore to see what the once-pretty room had become since Frankie took it over. She was stuck in the kitchen, listening to the Orioles on the radio, or sitting out in the living room with the newspaper, which she never had time to read in the mornings.

Only on this particular August afternoon, there was a man on her sofa. A young man, Frankie's age, dressed like Frankie— T-shirt, baseball cap, jogging pants, as Lenore still thought of them, although Frankie insisted that she say *tracksuit*. Dozing, he looked harmless, but Frankie probably looked smooth and sweet, too, when he was sleeping.

She cleared her throat. The stranger jumped, and his feet— huge, puppyish feet, as if he hadn't gotten his full growth yet, although he was already pretty big—barely missed the porcelain lamp on the end table. As it was, he had already left vague scuff marks on the peach leather.

"Who are you?" he asked.

"Frankie's mother," she said. It took her a second to remember that she had a right to know who he was.

"Aaron," he said. "Frankie said I could crash here for a while."

Beaten down as she was, she had to ask: "Here, as in the house? Or here, as in on my sofa? Because that's a nice piece, and your shoes have already—"

Aaron jumped to his feet and Lenore thought, *This is it, this is where I get hit for standing up for myself in my own home.* She feared Frankie. Not just the drugs and the consequences of his business being discovered. And not just the physicality of a slap or a punch, but the meaning of such a blow. She hadn't been a good mother, or a good-enough mother, and Frankie, ruined as he was, had returned home to remind her of that fact for every day of the rest of her life and maybe his, depending on how things worked.

But this boy, this Aaron, actually felt bad. He knelt to examine the mark. "That was stupid of me," he said. "But I know a trick my aunt taught me. She had six boys, so believe you me, she knew how to get any kind of stain out of anything. You got any talcum powder?"

She did, a rose-scented talc that she hadn't thought to use for months, years. He sprinkled it on the arm of the sofa, his fingers as light and gentle as the priest who had baptized Frankie, then said: "Now we let it sit overnight. The powder will draw out the grease."

"Like salt on a red wine stain," she said.

"Exactly. The main thing is, you don't want to use water, this being leather and all. It's an awfully nice sofa. I feel bad about not taking my shoes off. But Frankie and Marie were downstairs and wanted to be alone—" He actually blushed, as if Frankie's mother might not know why her son and his girlfriend preferred to be alone in the basement. "He told me to come up here, and I got so sleepy. I coulda gone upstairs, I guess, but that seemed forward."

He looked at her strangely and then Lenore realized the only thing strange about the look was that it was direct. He felt bad, he cared what she thought of him, at least for this moment. If he hung around, he would soon absorb Frankie's attitude toward her. But, for now, he was the kind of boy she always wished Frankie would be. She cast around in her memory. What did you do with your son's friends when they came to visit?

"Hey," she said. "You want a snack? Or a beer?"

UNLIKE MARIE, AARON DIDN'T MOVE in, but he was there more nights than not, and Frankie offered him the guest room on the second floor. "Is that okay?" Aaron asked Lenore. Frankie didn't give her a chance to answer.

"Of course it's okay."

She was the one who gave Aaron a key, however. It was over breakfast. Although he came in at three or four A.M. with Frankie and Marie, he would get up when she rose at seven for her cleaning job and share a cup of coffee with her. He said he couldn't sleep once he heard her moving about, and she believed him because she had found she couldn't really fall asleep until she heard the trio come home.

"You don't have to—" he began.

"It's no big deal," she said. "And this way, if you want to come home earlier than the others, you don't have to wait around with them." Then, after a moment's hesitation, she asked what she had never dared to ask Frankie. "Where do you go? I mean, all the places close down at two, don't they?"

"Most of them. But there are some. And—well, the corner,

there's usually some late-night business. Although . . ." Now it was his turn to hesitate. He got up, rinsed his coffee cup out in the sink, placed it in the dishwasher. He was considerate that way. Sometimes, he even brought Frankie and Marie's dirty dishes up from the basement and rinsed them.

"What, Aaron? Is he taking chances? You can tell me. You know I don't judge."

"There've been some . . . disputes. Guys moving in. But meth isn't as territorial as crack, so you don't have to worry."

Meth. Right, she had nothing to worry about. If Frankie didn't get her arrested, he would blow her sky-high. "Is he—?"

"Yeah," Aaron admitted.

So not only selling it and storing it, but making it in her house.

"I don't like it," she said, catching Aaron's eye. "I wish I could make him stop."

"It's hard for anyone to tell Frankie anything."

"Yeah. I'm scared of him, you know." She had never said that out loud to anyone. It didn't sound so bad.

"He wouldn't hurt you."

"He might."

"No, I wouldn't let him."

And that was as far as she let it go, that time. Lenore resolved not to discuss Frankie again with Aaron, not unless Aaron brought up the subject.

SHE STARTED TAKING A LITTLE more care with her appearance. Small things, like lipstick in the morning, before she came downstairs to put the coffee on. A new peach robe, modestly cut, both secure and more close-fitting than the old terry cloth one, and a matching nightie. She got a pedicure, although now fall was coming on and the kitchen floor was cool beneath her feet as she padded about. Marie asked Lenore why she had bothered. "Pink toenails on an old lady like you? Who cares? Who sees your feet?"

"I'm only forty-two," Lenore said. "I'm not on the shelf. Some women have babies at my age."

"Gross," Marie said, and Frankie nodded. Aaron didn't say anything. Lenore poured him a glass of juice and passed him the plate of muffins—from a box mix, but still fresh and hot. "What about me?" Frankie asked, and she slid the plate across the table to him—but only after Aaron made his choice.

AND THIS WAS HOW THE days went by, fall fading into winter, Aaron sleeping in the spare bedroom more often than not, Lenore taking ever more care with her appearance—looking younger day by day, even as she behaved far more maternally than she ever had. She cut back on drinking and joined the local Curves. She splurged on lotions and moisturizers, choosing those with the most luxurious smells. Alone with Aaron, she confided in him, but always in a maternal way. How she worried about Frankie, how she wished he would just say no to drugs, how she was nervous about him getting busted. How she wished she could save him from himself, but wasn't sure that anything would work for Frankie, even the forced sobriety of prison.

The only problem was Marie, who was turning out to have sharp eyes in that pudgy little face.

"Flirting with a boy your son's age," she said one night, peeved because Lenore had forgotten to buy Lucky Charms, Marie and Frankie's new favorite, although she had remembered Aaron's Mueslix. "You're pathetic."

"I'm just being nice," Lenore said. "Besides, a young kid like that could never be interested in an old broad like me."

"Got that right," Marie said, stomping downstairs to the basement. Soon, Lenore heard her laughing with Frankie, and their laughter was as ugly and acrid as the smell that rose from the floor below. Aaron was down there, too, but he wasn't laughing with them. Lenore was sure of that much. She was also sure that she was going to have to sleep with him eventually. The only question in her mind was whether it would be before or after.

IT TURNED OUT TO BE after, and it was Frankie, in his way, who made it happen. The four of them had been sharing another late breakfast—this one was cinnamon rolls, the kind that you baked at home, then coated with sticky white frosting. There were eight in a carton, two apiece, but Lenore had decided she wanted only one and passed her extra to Aaron.

"I wanted that," Frankie objected.

"I'm sorry," Lenore said, not the least bit sorry.

"You act as if *he* was your son," Frankie said. "Or your boyfriend. Just like when I was younger."

"I never had boyfriends when you were a boy," Lenore said, upset by the unfairness of it all. She might not have been a good mother to Frankie, but she had never been a slutty one. "I was strict about that."

"Oh, you didn't let guys move in or have breakfast with us, but you still brought them home sometimes, did them up in your room and sent them on their way before I woke up. If I didn't have a stepdaddy, it wasn't for the lack of free samples. You just never could seal the deal."

"Who wants the cow when you already have the milk?" said Marie, clearly unaware of how much milk she had given away in her young life.

"I wasn't that way." Lenore realized her voice was trembling. "I did the best I could, under the circumstances."

"You were a shit mom. You chased away Dad, then you just sat back and let them take me to juvie, didn't even spring for a decent lawyer when I got in trouble."

"I did the best—"

"You didn't do shit." Frankie banged his fists on the table. "You were a shitty mom and you're a stupid cunt, mooning over some young guy. It's disgusting."

He stomped out of the kitchen, followed by Marie. Lenore began to clear the kitchen table, only to drop the dishes in the sink, her shoulders shaking with sobs that she didn't have to fake.

"He didn't mean that." Aaron came over and started patting her shoulder awkwardly.

"He did," she said. "And he was right. I wasn't a very good

mother. I should have found him a stepfather when his own father left, or at least put him in some program. Like Big Brother, or whatever it's called. I failed Frankie. I failed him over and over again."

"It will be okay," Aaron said, but it was more a question than a statement.

"How? He's either going to get arrested or killed. If he gets arrested—well, that will be even worse for me, once he tells the police he was dealing here. They'll take our house for that, Aaron. Even if you can prove you didn't know, or couldn't stop it, they take your house."

"Frankie's pretty careful—"

"You said there was some quarrel over his territory?"

"Not so much now." She turned then, and the hand that had patted her on the shoulder passed briefly over her breast, then dropped in embarrassment. "A little."

"He could be killed. Some guys who want his corner could just open fire one night, and the police wouldn't even care. You know how they do. You know."

"Naw—" He met her gaze. "I guess so. Maybe."

"Killed, and no one would care. No one."

Two nights later, Aaron woke her at three A.M. to tell her that Frankie had been shot on the corner. He was dead.

"Were you there?" she asked.

"I'd gone to the 7-Eleven to buy smokes," he said very convincingly. "When I started back, I saw the cop cars, the lights, and decided not to get too close. Marie was shot, too."

"So she's a witness."

"Maybe. I don't know. What should we do?"

"What should we do?" She hugged him in a perfectly appropriate way, a maternal way. Her son was dead, his friend was dead. It made sense to hold him, to comfort each other. It also made sense when he kissed her, and when he reached under the peach gown that matched her silk robe. It made even more sense to crawl on top of him and stay there for most of the night. Lenore had not been with a man for a long time, but that only increased her stamina and her longing. And, besides, she was very grateful to this young man, who had done what she needed him to do, and without her ever having to ask straight-out.

In the morning, after the police called to ask if they could swing by before she went to work—Frankie didn't have a current ID on him and so it had taken them a while to sort out where he lived, if he had next of kin—she told Aaron that he should probably move on, go somewhere else, maybe back home to Colorado.

"Marie is conscious," she told him. "She's saying she thinks it was a white guy who fired shots at them."

She could see Aaron thinking about that.

"She's also saying it was a robbery, that she and Frankie were just walking home from a club. Still . . ."

"I've got a friend in New Mexico," he said.

"That's supposed to be nice."

"But not much saved up," he said, a little sheepish. "Even with you giving me a free place to stay, I never did put much away."

"That's okay," she said, reaching deep into a cupboard behind layers of pots and pans, one place Frankie and Marie would never have meddled. "I have some."

She gave him all she had stashed away without admitting why she was saving it, $1,000 in all.

"I didn't—" he said.

"I know."

"I even thought—"

"Me, too. But I want you to be safe."

"I could come back. If things cool down."

"But they probably won't."

He looked confused, hurt even, but Lenore knew he would get over that. Perhaps he felt used, but he could over that, too.

The police were on their way. She would have to get ready for that, be prepared to cry for the loss of her boy. She would think about Frankie as a child, the boy she had in fact lost all those years ago. She would think about the man she was losing now. Somehow, she would manage to cry.

And then, when the police were gone, leaving her to the business of burying her own boy—she would go down in the basement and begin the business of reclaiming her house, washing sheets and throwing open the tiny windows in spite of the wintry chill. Her house was hers again, and no one would ever take it from her.

SNOWFLAKE TIME

I don't remember the date. Later, lawyers tried to make hay out of that fact, as if it proved my behavior was "chronic," indicating a "pattern of abuse." But it was the opposite.

I couldn't remember the date precisely because nothing extraordinary happened that day. I didn't do what they said I did, it's that simple, and a man can't remember the things he didn't do. After everything that has happened to me, I think that's what I find most galling. I was an innocent man and I didn't get my day in court because I couldn't remember the exact day on which I said the thing I never said. It was cheaper to reward the women claiming offense, cheaper to punish me. Kill two birds with one stone. Follow the money. Those are clichés I wouldn't allow in my fiction, but real life trumps fiction every time.

It was August 2016, I am sure of that much. I had arrived at work, Gotham News Network, my place of employment for the last fifteen years, and was preparing for my evening show, *The Doyle Dossier*, which had been the king of its time slot for more than a decade. I was going through the New York papers, reading the *Washington Post* online, looking for a topic for my final segment, "Doyle's Dos and Don'ts." It looked simple, that closing segment, but finding a timely topic that can be broken down into a series of black-and-white quick takes is actually very difficult. There was a reason that no one else across the cable news landscape had enjoyed the kind of success I had.

And no one envied me more than my own network. To the world, GNN was a tribe, a cohesive unit. But when the camera was turned off, it was nothing but a pack of jackals, all looking for a chance to take down anyone who showed a sign of weakness.

So, August 2016. I asked my assistant to go get me lunch. That's what she was there for, right? To assist me. But she was one of those Ivy League millennials who thought she should be running the network, not running errands. She rolled her eyes as I rattled off what I wanted—turkey sub, extra hots, a cream soda, I'm not some Nobu-eating fancy pants—and then she asked if it was okay if she ran a personal errand while picking up my lunch.

"Can I go to Duane Reade and get some Advil?" she said. "I have the worst menstrual cramps. I almost called in sick today, the pain is so bad."

Now, in my opinion, that was unprofessional and typical of this generation, which finds every moment of its existence worth documenting and broadcasting. *Here's my lunch, I just checked in at a concert, I have a headache.* If I had started talking about my prostate or asked her to go fill my Cialis prescription—I don't have a Cialis prescription or anything like that, that's just a hypothetical—I'd have been hauled on the carpet faster than you can say "trigger warning." But I was trying to write my segment, I just wanted my lunch, my blood sugar was spiking, so all I said was: "I don't need to know anything about your body unless it affects my body."

She brought me my lunch. I wrote a "Dos and Don'ts" about a woman who was trying to keep park police from rounding up feral cats living in Central Park. I love animals—okay, I like dogs—but this woman was one of those whack jobs who thrives on publicity. In college, she had lived in a tree for several months, or something like that. A dilettante, flitting from so-called cause to so-called cause. In my day, you would have called her a dirty hippie, I don't know what you call such a person now. The park police and animal welfare people were actually trying to rescue the cats, get them to a shelter on Long Island, where they would be spayed and neutered. There was no argument to be made for feral cats in Central Park. When Peter Minuit arrived in Manhattan in 1626, there were no feral cats on the island. (Cougars don't count.)

Do honor the natural order.

Don't forget who's at the top of this food chain, Kitty Con Artist.

It was a great bit, if I do say so myself. We got a lot of mail on both sides, which is the best feedback possible. The only thing I never wanted was a neutral response.

What made people nuts about my show was that no one could stick a partisan label on me. I'm not even that interested in politics, except when it threatens our civil liberties. I'm not registered as a Republican or a Democrat. Some people try to hang the libertarian mantle on me, but that's not right, either. I'm for common sense. If there was a political party with an IQ test, I might join that. For example, I don't vote in presidential elections in my state, or in any election where the outcome is a foregone conclusion. End the Electoral College and I might change my mind. But, for now, my vote and, more importantly, my time are wasted by standing in line on Election Day.

Furthermore, I believe that we should have a flat income tax rate, with no deductions whatsoever. Deductions are for fat cats and they encourage waste. Eliminate deductions and you'd eliminate more than half of the lobbyists in Washington, which would help end gridlock, although I'm not sure that's a positive. I am a First Amendment absolutist. You're free to say whatever you want to say, but—here's the catch—so is the other guy. If you want to say "Happy holidays," say "Happy holidays," but I'm sticking to "Merry Christmas." That was one of my most popular "Dos and Don'ts" segments of all time.

Do offer whatever seasonal greeting you prefer.

Don't deny other people the right to do the same.

A couple of weeks went by. As you might recall, 2016 was a busy year in news, or so we thought until 2017 came along. Then a week before Christmas, I was summoned to a meeting with legal. My former assistant—she had chosen to go work on another show because she claimed she had Lyme disease and needed a less demanding schedule—was there. And she was telling quite a tall tale about what happened the day she volunteered to me the state of her uterus. According to her, what I said was: "I'm not interested in your body unless it's *touching* my body." It was a subtle but shrewd distinction. I couldn't claim I hadn't said anything at all, and absent a tape recorder, I couldn't prove my version over hers. By the time it was all over, she was claiming that I had told her to pick up some condoms and added that, if she were lucky, she'd find out if the ribbing really did add to her pleasure. That never happened and I wanted my day in court to prove it.

Then other women started coming forward.

Turned out the bosses had done a little witch hunt, calling women in and asking if they had "unsettling" experiences with me. They all but *incentivized* lying about me. "Look, here's the little pot of money, underwritten by our liability insurance, would you like some? All you have to say is that John Doyle said something untoward." There were five women altogether and, believe me, not a one that I would have made a pass at. But there was blood in the water and other people began showing up to nibble on my entrails. All of a sudden there were women everywhere, claiming that this was a pattern, that I had been doing this for years. One lawyer said he had tapes, but I sure never heard them. In the end, it was the insurance company that pushed for the settlements, based on nothing but the cost-benefit analysis of the price of taking each case to trial. To the network, a not-guilty verdict was worthless if it cost them millions to get there. To me, it meant everything. He who steals my purse, etc., etc. Yes, I can quote Shakespeare. He's not for snobs, you know. He wrote for the people, the common man.

Years ago, I reported on a story from Baltimore, about how

the public buses had to have cameras installed because when there was a minor accident, people tried to get on the bus after the fact and claim injury. *(Do get your day in court. Don't try to take someone else's.)* So I was the Baltimore bus and these "ladies" jumped on and took me for a ride. But they were supposed to stay quiet and at least one of them didn't honor that part of the settlement. Oh, they were smart enough to say "no comment" when reporters began snooping around, but how did the reporters even know to start asking questions? Someone violated the confidentiality agreement. Someone, maybe several someones, should have given that money back to the insurers, but shakedown artists aren't exactly principled, are they?

There was a bigger picture. Isn't there always? Whenever anything happens, anything, ask yourself: Who benefits financially from this? I was making—well, let's call it a hefty sum. My program was popular, my ratings weren't affected at all after the story about the settlement was leaked. The advertisers who pulled their commercials were scared, but there was never an organized boycott. Plenty of advertisers would have increased their sales by standing by me.

Instead, I was told by the brass that I had to make a public show of penance. Apologize on camera, then go into some sort of rehab. But I couldn't apologize for things I didn't do, not even for expediency's sake, and I wasn't going to go to some bogus "rehab" for speaking my mind, the only thing of which I'm guilty. I said no. They fired me with only three months' severance. No one else wanted to hire me. I was too conservative for MSNBC and CNN, not enough of a loyalist for Fox. I had always been a maverick, a lone wolf, marching to my own tune. That's why I was expendable. I didn't belong to any of the tribes.

I knew my exile from television would end eventually; I was too good at what I did not to bounce back. I started a podcast from my house in Rye, but that didn't bring in much cash and I had a big nut. I have some savings, of course. I'm a responsible person. I'm not living the high life with a place in the Hamptons and a Florida mansion and season tickets to the Knicks and the Yankees. But between our rigged tax system and two ex-wives and child support and the Rye house and the apartment I kept in the city, my monthly expenses were high. It was only a matter of time before I got another gig, but in the meantime, I needed to be more liquid.

That was when I came up with the idea of writing a mystery series.

Do be nimble when you need to be. Don't cry in your beer.

Now over the years I had built up a nice sideline, writing about great men in history. (Only great men so far. Of course there are great women, but I hadn't found one who interested me enough to stick with her story for three hundred pages.) But those books took at least three months of research, plus they were already under contract. To get an infusion of cash, I decided I needed another publishing contract. People didn't realize this, but I used to write fiction. No fake news jokes, please. Almost twenty years ago, I wrote a crime novel when I was the anchor on *PM Chicago* back in the day. It was fun. I basically killed—in print—anyone who had ever irritated me. I have always lived by the Conan Code: You must crush your enemies, see them driven before you, and hear the lamentations of their women. My book had lots of murder, lots of sex, and a very neat variation on a locked-room mystery, if I do say so myself. Unfortunately, I didn't know much about the publishing business then and I worked with a subpar company run by my college roommate, so I never saw a dime after my initial advance. First editions of that book now sell for $125 a pop on the internet, but that doesn't help me.

Anyway, that kind of book, fun as it is, sort of James Bond meets Walter Cronkite—it wasn't right for me in my current circumstances, although I secretly believed my hero, Savoy Taylor, could knock Jack Reacher on his ass if they were ever to meet mano a mano. I might have said no to rehab, but I did understand that my image could use a little burnishing. My literary agent and I made a study of what was publishing. One obvious choice was a book about a woman who's not reliable (as if any women are reliable). The way it was explained to me—do you think I've had time to read fiction while doing five shows a week, forty-nine weeks a year for fifteen years?—the woman drinks or she lies or something, so you can't be sure if she's telling the truth. Do you want to know how you can tell if a woman is lying in my experience? She's breathing. Anyway, my agent and I agreed that's not the right kind of book for me to write right now.

So I thought about the times we live in, how much people

needed to believe in a place where good would always triumph. Those "girl" books spoke to our general paranoia, which was understandable. But these are raucous, out-of-control times. Values such as self-respect and hard work are under siege. We used to pride ourselves on being rugged individualists, now we cringe if people disagree with us. In times like this, people want comfort. They want to see order restored, they want good people to prosper and bad people to suffer. So I read a little Louise Penny, a little Jan Karon, and decided to combine the two into my own original series. I came up with *Murder Comes for Christmas*, the first book set in the fictional town of Christmas, Ohio, a place that embodies true American ideals.

I devised the basic outline, then we hired a guy to flesh out my ideas. A lot of the best novelists work that way now. The hero is the town sheriff, Doug Champion. He doesn't always do things by the book, but he reliably does the *right* thing, no matter how unpopular. In the first book, some unknown party is trying to disrupt the annual Christmas festival, which accounts for a big chunk of the town's annual revenue. The disturbances begin small—ugly graffiti at the Christmas bazaar, defaced signs, a cat in the microwave at the local coffee shop. (Coffee shop, not a coffeehouse. There is a Dairy Queen in Christmas, Ohio, but no Starbucks, a Taco Bell but no Chipotle. Real food for real people.) Christmas, Ohio, has four churches, one synagogue, and no atheists.

But when someone finds a body inside one of the ice sculptures in the town park, it's clear that whoever is doing this is much more than your average teen hooligan. It's a war against Christmas on multiple levels. I wanted to call the book *The War Against Christmas*, but the publisher pointed out that would look as if I'm taking sides in the culture wars, which I've always avoided. Like I said, you can say what you want, I'm sticking with "Merry Christmas." Free speech. What a misnomer. My free speech cost me millions. Well, not me, but Gotham News' insurance company.

The pace of publishing felt dirgelike after television—it took the ghostwriter ten weeks to finish the novel. But the book was done in time to go on sale in mid-November. Preorders were strong and while some early reviewers took the expected shots at me and my history, I didn't write it for reviewers. I wrote for my fans and it turned out I still had a pretty good fan base. My fans—older women, for the most part—were angry with Gotham News and they bought my book as a show of support. Even without the nightly exposure of my show, I still hit the *New York Times* bestseller list at No. 7. My publisher was ecstatic. They were talking to me about speeding up production. Could I finish another "Christmas" book by Easter? Not that they were all going to be holiday-themed. They just wanted a new one on the shelves in six to eight months. The working title for the next one was *Christmas in Summer*. There was going to be a shooting at the Fourth of July regatta, at the exact moment that they fired the cannon. And the romance between Sheriff Champion and Carlotta Mandible, the young widow who owned the coffee shop, was going to start heating up. Tastefully, of course.

No out-and-out sex scenes. It wasn't that kind of series. My tour was extended through December, with the last event scheduled for December 20 at the Mysterious Bookshop in New York, almost a year to the day since I was betrayed by Gotham News.

Then something weird happened: My Goodreads rankings, which had been a solid 3.8, began tanking. The online reviews, which had always been good once you controlled for personal vendettas that had nothing to do with the book, began diving, too. It had every appearance of a coordinated campaign. Turned out that the whole thing had started with a tweet from an Ohio woman who had thirty-seven followers:

Disappointed that @JDoyleDossier thinks it's
OK to kill cat in such a vile manner. #CatHater
#Unacceptable #BoycottChristmasOhio

It's true that @JDoyleDossier was my verified Twitter handle, but I never used it; when I was at the network, one of my assistants managed the account, mainly retweeting articles and promoting the show. I don't even have the password for it and my publisher had set up a different Twitter account to publicize the Christmas books (@ChristmasOhioIsReal). So I hadn't seen the tweet, nor realized it was gaining some kind of stealth traction on social media, with more and more outraged women—and they were all women—posting about how much they hated this one paragraph. It wasn't even gory! We had been very careful to avoid gratuitous violence or sex in the Christmas books.

But I had seen a television show where someone microwaved a hamster and I thought it was pretty cool. I was very clear with my writer, some literary novelist who's never sold more than two thousand books, that the scene should be left to the reader's imagination, that we have to cut away right before Carlotta Mandible opens the microwave and then, jump cut, she's being comforted by Sheriff Champion. That scene is pivotal because she hates him more for seeing her weak, while he finds his feelings for her are complicated now that he's seen the vulnerable woman beneath the tough, sassy exterior.

Don't respond, my publisher said. The whole outcry will die a natural death if you don't stoke it. The outrage machine requires oxygen in the form of attention, rebuttal. They can't make you respond.

But the comments kept coming. On Twitter, on Facebook, on Goodreads, on Amazon. Somehow, the damn cat in the microwave got linked to what happened at the network, which wasn't relevant at all. I seemed to have done the unthinkable, unite women—and it was all women, mostly old women, best I could tell—across the political spectrum. Apparently, you can grab a pussy, you can parade in your pussy hat, but you can't kill a kitty in a novel. That thought came to me late one night, when I was sitting up with a nightcap in my study, reading the latest comments on my laptop. *You can grab a pussy in real life, but you can't kill a kitty in a crime novel.*

So I tweeted just that.

Do say what you think. Don't say it when angry or irritable. Or drunk.

Within an hour, I had deleted the tweet, but someone had a screenshot. Two days later, when I showed up at a signing in a small Ohio town that claimed it was the model for Christmas (it's not) there were more people outside the store protesting than were inside the store waiting for their WELCOME TO CHRISTMAS mugs and cookies. The signs said things like CAT KILLER! and LEAVE MY PUSSY ALONE, which made no sense at all. Some PETA knockoff group was using the whole thing to boost its public profile. I'm pretty sure they were paying people to protest. But it was good optics, I guess, and it was a slow news day and somehow I became the story. Image Rehab 101 was not going as planned.

I got calls to appear on television, even from my old network, which wanted me to defend my God-given right as an American to write a scene in which someone puts a cat in the microwave. Someone evil! That was the point. Only a bad person would put a cat in the microwave. By the end of the book—spoiler alert, the killer trying to hurt Christmas is a bitter, unattractive spinster— the killer lunges for Sheriff Champion with a knife, but Carlotta foils the attack by throwing scalding coffee on her. I thought that was a good twist, the woman saving the man.

As the protests grew, some bookstores began canceling. It was bad for business. December is a big month for bookstores and the protesters made shoppers nervous. Easier to pull the plug on my appearances in order to appease all these crazy cat ladies than to stand up for the principle of free speech. I was disappointed, but that's what our country has become, a nation of craven *I've got mine* opportunists.

The Mysterious Bookshop was one of a handful of stores that stood by me. I was told they would not be intimidated by the protesters and that my event would go on as planned. As my tour limped into its final days, I found myself looking forward to that last reading. And it exceeded all expectations. For one thing, Mysterious Bookshop alerted the police when the protests started and, sure enough, those batty dames didn't have permits to protest. Technically, you don't need a permit to picket in New York City, but you do need one for amplified sound and the pickets have to keep moving. So goodbye, bullhorn, and without the bullhorn, twenty old ladies moving in lazy circles didn't attract much attention, nor did they intimidate the people who wanted to attend my signing. Half of them had decamped to Le Pain Quotidien down the street before I even arrived.

Once inside the store, I was gratified to find that I had a standing-room-only crowd of more than one hundred and another two hundred books to sign for mail orders. I had sprung for champagne for this final signing, along with the usual case of Coors to honor Sheriff Champion, but the store also had a nice spread. Crackers, cheese, but not brie, just good American cheeses like cheddar and Swiss. Turned out that when the controversy first started, lazy reporters, reluctant to leave Manhattan, had asked the store's staff to comment over and over again. People who hadn't realized that this gem of a store was in Tribeca had started showing up, leaving with armfuls of books.

One of the clerks explained to me what I had failed to understand: Killing a cat in a mystery is a cardinal sin. Kill a child. Kill two dozen prostitutes. Kill a bride on her wedding night. That's all fine. But to kill a cat in a so-called cozy mystery—apparently that's what I had written, a cozy, I'm not sure why it's called that—is simply never done. They told me there are even mysteries in which cats solve the crime. So: *Do kill as many people, brides, and children as you like. Don't kill cats or curse.*

At any rate, I drank champagne from a dark plastic cup and enjoyed myself enormously. I would have rated the night a grand success on any scale—and that was before I met Vivien.

I had noticed her earlier in the evening. She seemed a little younger than most of the crowd and didn't appear to know anyone else there. Slender yet curvy, with big brown eyes and dark hair worn in a messy bun on top of her head, little tendrils falling around her face. She looked familiar, but I thought that was because she had an Audrey Hepburn cast to her features. She couldn't stop looking at me. I thought it was my imagination, but when the crowd thinned at the end of the night, she came over to where I was signing stock for the store.

"Can I get one of those?" she asked, pointing to the stack of books.

"Is it for you, or is it a gift?"

"I consider it a gift to myself. How's that?"

"May I inscribe it?" Our eyes were locked on each other's.

"To Vivien Kocia," she said.

"That's a lovely name. Is it Italian?"

"No, Polish."

"I never realized Polish was so melodious."

I'm actually very shy around women. That's something that's easily overlooked, in all the stories about me. I'm shy. The man who went on television, speaking with confidence and certitude, he disappeared when a beautiful woman walked by. I could never have said the things they claimed I said at the network, not if I were attracted to those girls. And if I wasn't attracted to them, why would I say those things? They were young, inexperienced. They probably didn't shave under their arms, yet waxed their private parts bare, which I understand is how things are done these days. Young women are baffling.

But Vivien Kocia was my type. She was at least thirty-five, maybe forty, but a terrifically maintained forty. At first glance, her clothes were conservative—a sweater dress that hung below her knees, with a big cowl at the neck, suede boots. But the dress hugged every curve and the boots must have been over the knee because I couldn't see the tops.

I wanted to see the tops.

"Do you like mystery books?" I asked, desperate to prolong the encounter, tongue-tied as a boy at a dance.

"I just started reading them," she said. "I admit, I was always a snob, but now I feel foolish. They're so satisfying. Look at your book—a spinster, driven mad by the abortion she had as a young girl, unable to have children, wreaks havoc on a small town that opens its arms to her. When she tries to kill Sheriff Champion—"

"Spoiler alert," I said with a smile, although there was no

one listening to us at this point. The store had emptied; it was going on eight o'clock, closing time.

"I know it's wrong, but it's so satisfying when Carlotta throws hot coffee on her. The woman doesn't deserve to die— well she does, I believe in capital punishment, but that's for a court to determine, a fate for a jury to mete out. And yet, in the moment, how I gloried in it."

"People think of novelists as being disproportionately liberal," I told her. "Novelists and readers. But that's not true in my experience. The mystery form recognizes what a lot of us believe, in our guts. There is a right and a wrong, and there can be no wrong if it restores right. I think that's part of the reason our genre is the most commercially robust of all."

"I thought that was romance," she said, her eyes still locked on mine.

"Do you need a ride?" I asked. "I have a car outside."

"Alas," she said, "I drove into the city tonight." She pointed outside, to a panel van parked on Warren Street. "My work vehicle."

"What do you do?" I asked. "Why do you need a van?"

"Well," she said, "I'm a licensed massage therapist who uses essential oils." She reached out and kneaded my shoulder with her fingertips. "How many books have you signed in the last month? Five hundred? A thousand? I can tell you're off-balance. I bet there's a pinch right here—" She kneaded the side of my neck. "If you're not careful, you'll throw your back out before the new year."

"Do you know anyone who can help me?" I asked.

"I'm the best I know, honestly, but I'm booked up through the holidays. Although I have the night free if you'd like to try it—"

Five minutes later we were on the FDR, her van following my town car, heading to my place.

Once in my apartment, I didn't really care about the massage. I would have been happy to open a bottle of wine, segue to more of a date night vibe, take a rain check on the massage. But she was very serious and earnest, looking for the best place to set up her table. (She chose my bedroom, which made me optimistic, I'll admit.) She excused herself while I got ready, stripping down to my underwear and a towel, lying facedown on the table. She told me she needed to go back to her van and grab her supply of essential oils, but she turned on the radio channel with the kind of dreamy, nothing music you hear in spas. I'm a fifty-seven-year-old man, I've lived a full life, and I'm not embarrassed to say that. I've lived a man's life, a real man's life, shaped by my understanding that people aren't that different from animals. The way lions live makes more sense than the way people live. Polygamy is rooted in human behavior. I never advocated for it on the show because it was too loaded a topic. But if I had, I might have said:

Do understand men and women are fundamentally different.

Don't claim you can simultaneously believe in Darwin and monogamous men. Pick one.

I heard her come back into the apartment, huffing and puffing as if she was carrying something heavy. But when she entered my bedroom, she just had a small bottle of oil. "*Nepeta cataria*," she said, passing it under my nose. "Doesn't it smell wonderful?" It seemed pretty ordinary to me, like one of those herbs they started adding to everything. Not cilantro, but like cilantro. I hate cilantro.

"Nice," I said, wanting to be polite.

She oiled her hands and began working on me. Her touch was surprisingly light. I wasn't sure she really knew what she was doing. I didn't feel as if I were being rubbed so much as I was being coated. Every now and then she would stop and do those little karate chops, but mainly she seemed intent on rubbing the oil into my flesh, covering every inch.

"Roll over," she said huskily.

I did, making sure to keep the towel tight. I wanted whatever we did to be her decision.

"Now drink this herbal tea to help you relax."

"I don't—"

"Drink it," she said. She sounded very much in charge. It was kind of exciting. She propped up my head, held the mug to my lips.

The tea was foul, a mix of grass clippings and chalk, but she was now oiling my calves and, to my amazement, my face. I was glad, as I felt the oil seeping into my pores, that I didn't have to go to a television studio the next day and film. As much as I missed my job—and my paycheck—I didn't really miss being on television. Do you know the kinds of things people say about your appearance when you're a public figure? I tried not to read the comments and the hate mail, but so much of my face, my body had been dissected in public. They said I had a double chin. (I don't, that was just the unfortunate angle in the photographs.) They made fun of my skin, my hair, my complexion, which was prone to rosacea. Apparently, men were fair game, but if you even suggested a women had cankles, you could lose your job. That's what one of the women at the network said, that I had criticized her calves.

Do be kind.

Don't be a patsy. If someone criticizes you, feel free to criticize them. Sauce for the goose, baby.

She was pressing on my cheeks, that spot between my eyes, grooved from years of looking serious on television. It was heavenly. It was almost better than sex because nothing was expected of me. Women think men have it so easy. We don't. We don't. We don't.

"What did you say, John?"

I hadn't realized I was speaking out loud. My tongue felt thick in my mouth. I tried to tell her not to worry. I think I asked her how she felt about being the next ex–Mrs. John Doyle, trying to make a joke, lighten the mood. My lips couldn't make words. My eyes had been closed because it was awkward, looking at someone rubbing your face, but now I found I couldn't open them. My stomach rumbled.

"It's okay, John," she said. "It's okay."

And that was the last thing anyone said for a while.

I woke up in the bathroom, retching into my toilet. Could

have been minutes, hours, days later, I was that disoriented. There was nothing really in my stomach but that awful tea, which was probably the cause. My knees were weak, my legs rubbery, and I had to brace myself on the sink to stand.

There was a book on the sink. My book. Vivien's book, the one I had signed to her. It must have been a bummer to have your date get sick, but that seemed rude, leaving it behind.

There was a note inside:

Dear John,

I confess I told you a little white lie. I am not Vivien Kocia. I am the woman you so elegantly called the "Kitty Con Artist, the Krazy Kat Lady of Central Park." Despite your attempts to ruin me, I am still trying to protect natural feral cat sanctuaries wherever they may be, although it is sometimes necessary to remove some cats from the public, especially if they have become dangerous to themselves and others.

Three such cats are in your apartment right now. And that oil I applied to you is made of catnip. As for the tea, it was simply Lipton cut with ipecac and a roofie.

Until we meet again.

P.S. I didn't read your book, I just read the spoiler forums on Goodreads so I could fake it.

I tried to open the bathroom door, but she had somehow barricaded me in. I called her name. Nothing. I thought about screaming until the neighbors phoned downstairs to the door-man, who would come in and investigate, if only to quell their complaints. But he would find me nude, covered in catnip oil. He might gossip. I decided to shower first and it was only then that I realized the shower was running. Why was the shower running? Had I turned it on when I stumbled in here to throw up? I wrenched open the door and the last thing I saw was three sodden masses of fur, coming right at me. They were so desperate to escape that shower that they knocked me down and I was so slippery from the oil that I couldn't get to my feet again.

My last conscious thought, as they swarmed over me, nipping and clawing, tearing my flesh, treating me like the world's largest catnip mouse, was: *I bet I can use this in a book. This would make a great scene in the next book.*

And that's when I knew I really was a novelist.

TRICKS

He is aware of the glances they attract as they cross the lobby of the Hotel Monteleone, but doubts she notices. She is too busy looking at him. Her gaze is like a stray hair on his cheekbone—light yet irritating, hard to brush away. He's much too handsome for her. Everyone sees it. Even she sees it. She clearly cannot believe her good luck.

She shouldn't.

He, however, is flush with luck, the kind of luck that comes only with due diligence and hard work. You don't find a mark like this by accident. It takes weeks of moving patiently and slowly, building a rapport. It takes a little money, too, to appear as flush as he claims to be. This suit he's wearing, the Hermès tie, the Gucci loafers—those things cannot be faked. Stolen, on occasion, but never faked.

However, that's phase one. Moving on to phase two now, the honeymoon, literal and figurative, where everything will be on her. Also literally and figuratively.

They approach the registration desk and she is all fluttery, old-fashioned enough to think that the hotel cares whether they are husband and wife yet. "Darling, lots of women don't take their husbands' names," he assured her when he told her to make the reservation. "I would," she said. "I can't wait to take your name."

And I can't wait to take whatever you have to give. But there will be time enough. Time enough to settle in, to move into her house in the Pacific Palisades, the one in all the pictures she has sent him. Time, too, to persuade her to tap into the equity, which he will use for his can't-fail business venture. That part is true—it never fails, not where he's concerned. He makes a profit every time, no matter what's going on in the economy.

"Olive Dunne," she says to the clerk in her little mouse-like voice. God, if he really had to live with that voice until death did them part, he would soon be exhausted from leaning in, the better to hear her. She's a timid one. They run to timidity, his brides, but she's especially shy, irritatingly shy. The courtship was an unusually long one, almost three months since he sent his first email, and that doesn't include the start-up costs, the search process on various matchmaking sites. But once he gets her in bed, she will be his.

He hands the clerk his new credit card, the one Olive presented him with just this morning when they met face-to-face for the first time at Louis Armstrong International Airport. She was the one who offered to add him to her AmEx after he explained how the problems in the financial markets overseas were tying up all his accounts, threatening this long-planned rendezvous. The clerk takes them in. The clerk takes *him* in—his tailored suit, the Hermès tie, the Armani sunglasses. All the real thing, purchased with his own scarce dollars, the cost of doing business; he should be able to deduct them from his income tax. Not that he pays income taxes, but why should he, when the system is rigged against the working man? And make no mistake about it, he works hard for his money. He's like a soldier, or someone on an oil rig. When he gets a gig, it's 24/7, no time off for weeks. Sometimes the highlight of his day is his morning crap, the only time he gets to be himself, by himself.

The clerk upgrades them to the Tennessee Williams suite, but it's not quite as grand as he'd hoped. Nice enough, but he's seen better. Olive, however, is overwhelmed by the smallest things—the galley kitchen, which is nothing more than a noisy minifridge and a coffeemaker, the enormous glass box of a shower stall, the fact that there's a dining room table. "It's like an apartment," she says over and over. She flits from window to window, taking in the views of the French Quarter, exclaiming over everything.

"What do you want to do first?" she asks.

He thinks that's pretty obvious, although it's not what he wants to do first, but what he knows he *should* want to do first.

He takes her in his arms, closes his eyes, and thinks of . . . his mind scans several images, actresses and models, then settles on the literal girl next door, Betty. She used to anoint herself with baby oil and offer herself up to the sun, moving her ratty old lounge chair as the shadows crept over her, hour by hour. That was out in Metairie, barely ten miles from here, where he grew up. Betty was always on her back when he saw her, breasts pointing to the heavens, yet her tan was very even. She was five years older; he had no shot, the gulf between twelve and seventeen too huge. When he started out, the women were five years older, ten years older, fifteen years older. He likes older women. Olive is his first younger woman in a long time and she has a trim little figure beneath her dowdy suit. He caresses her promisingly firm rump and thinks of Betty, wonders if Viagra is going to be added to the list of his professional expenses, but, no, thank goodness, he's going to be able—

"Not now," she whispers, pulling away. "Not yet. Maybe I'm old-fashioned, but I want to wait until I'm your bride. Besides, didn't you say you wanted to call your bank, straighten out what's going on with your credit cards?"

"My bank is in London," he says, "and that's six hours ahead. They're closed for today."

The story, this time, is that he's a victim of identity theft and all his credit cards, even his ATM card, are "locked" until he can talk to his personal money manager. He discovered this problem when he and Olive began planning their trip a week ago, and she quickly agreed—volunteered, in fact—to add him to her credit card account, even procured an extra ATM card for him, which he used this morning to pull out the maximum amount. "Because a man needs to have cash," she said. "Walking-around money, my daddy called it."

Yes, indeed. A man does need money to walk around. And even more to walk out. How much will Olive be good for? Assuming she can get a second mortgage, the house in California must have at least a half million in it. He's looked up the property records and she's owned it for ten years.

"Do you want to walk around?" he asks her. "Go shopping? See if we can get a table at Galatoire's?"

"Could we"—she is blushing, furiously—"walk along Bourbon Street? When I was twelve, my church group came to New Orleans to compete in a chorale competition, but they kept us out near the airport, never let us get near the city proper."

"Of course we can, baby. I'll buy you a big ol' drink and we'll walk along Bourbon Street."

He's no stranger to Bourbon Street. His life tricking began here, almost twenty-five years ago, and that's how he always thought of it: *tricking.* Not hustling, but engaging in a fantasy with a consenting adult, and how was that any different from someone paying money to go see a magician? Almost too good-looking as a young man, he decided early on to find out what that commodity was really worth, to test how high the sky was, what one could procure with a pretty face and a great body. Back then he had sex with men and women alike, and while he found some good sugar daddies in his salad days, he also discovered that men were a little harder to control. He lived almost six months with an older man, Jacques, in a mansion in Uptown. They had an argument one night, and it had been shocking how quickly it escalated. The old queen had beat him up pretty bad—and *he* had ended up being charged with assault somehow, not that he stayed around to face the music. He had decided then and there to stick to women for business.

Besides, with women, there is the possibility of marriage in all fifty states. And with marriage, there is so much more access to whatever wealth they have, and no one in the world can call it a con, what happens between husbands and wives. Sure, some of them made him sign prenups, but prenups didn't matter when a man never bothered with the formality of divorce. He got whatever cash there was, he moved on. He's lost count of how many times he's been married by now. Twelve, thirteen? Yeah, he's pretty sure that little Olive is going to be number thirteen. And she hasn't breathed a word about wanting a prenup. She's a pliable one, a sheltered girl whose parents, before they died, had spent most of their time telling her that she had to beware fortune hunters, that no one would ever love her just for her.

The internet was both friend and foe in his business. A few ex-wives had set up blogs, tried to spread the word about him, but his name always changed just enough so that a Google search wouldn't kick him out. A background check under his original name—that's what he really lived in fear of, but no one knows his real name or Social Security number. *He* barely remembers his real name or Social Security number. Besides, the gals never run that kind of background check. They don't want to. They buy into the fantasy willingly. They know themselves, what their prospects really are. They don't want to question too closely why this handsome, rich man is on an internet dating site, much less why he is interested in them, writing them flowery emails.

Relatives, however, can be skeptical. That's why all-alone-in-the-world Olive, as he thinks of her, is such a prize. Several years back, he dated a woman whose daughter was clearly skeptical of him, based on the emails he began to get. "Jordan wants to know—" "Jordan asked me to ask you" "Jordan thinks I should see some kind of prospectus before I invest." That was one of the ones he didn't take to the end. He got some money from her but decided to skip out before marriage, mainly because of that pesky daughter. He's smarter now, makes sure his ladies are isolated. *All alone in the world*, as Olive described herself in her listing on the dating site. Although, come to think of it, who isn't alone in the world? He's been fending for himself all along, his father figuring the room and board to age eighteen were all he was owed, his mother barely lifting a hand to wave him good-bye. He was doing the best he could with what he had. People think it's an advantage to be born handsome, but that's just raw material. No, it's the Olives of the world who have it easy, being born with money. The things she takes for granted. She thinks everyone knows how to eat escargot, for example. Certainly, he does, but that was part of his training. He taught himself by watching *Pretty Woman*. Something else he should be able to deduct, buying his own copy of *Pretty Woman*, but it has paid off. He learned everything he needed to know from movies— the James Bond films, although only the early ones; *The Philadelphia Story*; *Bringing Up Baby*. He has better manners than most. Better than Olive, for example, who is openly gawking at the sights along Bourbon Street. She slips her sweaty little palm into his, and he can tell she is nervous but exhilarated.

"How about one of those?" he says, pointing to a stand where the drinks are served in large plastic cups that resemble grenades.

"Oh, I couldn't," she says, pressing her face into his armpit, which can't be that pleasant. He's a little damp. Who wouldn't be, wearing a suit on Bourbon Street in September? He forgot how long summer hangs on here, but Olive wouldn't be dissuaded. She had never been to New Orleans, she told him, first in emails, then in their Skype conversations. Besides, Louisiana makes it very easy for out-of-towners to marry here. That reminds him: They should wander over to the clerk's office in an hour or so, do the deed. Bless his laissez-faire hometown, where most of the rules can be waived by simple request—the waiting period, the requirement to show a birth certificate. Then on to the wedding night, but first a lovely meal, paid for with his new credit card. He would be needing some oysters, for sure.

But the drink has hit little Olive hard. Has she eaten anything today? Imagine how excited she was, how early she had to start to fly here from California. She starts to stagger, complains of feeling nauseous. The wedding will have to wait. He leads her back to the hotel, half carrying her the final blocks, puts her to bed, makes a cold compress for her head, runs his fingers gently across her arms and shoulder blades. "Giving chills," his mother had called it. "Come here, Gus, give me chills." She would stretch out across the sofa in the living room, the blinds drawn so the room was dark all the time, the television on but silent, two or three beer cans on the floor. Never more, because if you drank more than three beers in the afternoon, his mother explained, you were an alcoholic. But if you drank three between noon and five and then another three between five and bedtime, you were just honoring the packaging. "Why do you think they sell them six to a pack?" she would say. Did that mean one should eat a dozen eggs in two sittings? Once, he drank a six-pack of Coca-Cola in one sitting and she gave him a spanking for being greedy and wasteful. But he liked giving his mother chills, was happy to stand next to her and provide her a little pleasure. It was, he supposes, how he discovered his vocation.

He will marry Olive tomorrow. In fact, he will insist they spend the morning shopping, purchasing a new outfit for her to wear, as today's suit is now a little worse for wear, crumpled and hanging on a chair. She's sleeping in a full slip; he can't remember the last time he saw one of those. The shopping trip will distract her and she will probably forget about him calling his bank in London until, once again, it is too late. Once they are married, he will tell her—he sifts through the stories he has used over the years. His London-based business manager is a con man, a scoundrel. He made up the story about the attempted fraud, the locked accounts, and used the time to clean him out. Oh, he has other money, but it's complicated, tied up in a trust, he won't be able to get it right away. It might seem counterintuitive, telling a lie so close to the truth, allowing Olive to consider that there are people in the world who are not what they say, people who will pretend to be on your side but want nothing more than to fleece your pockets. But it works surprisingly well, he has found. Raise the specter of the very crime you are committing and no one suspects you of perpetrating the exact same fraud.

He is restless, though, a performer who had prepared himself only to find out at the last minute that the show has been canceled. The adrenaline has to go somewhere. He thinks about the clerk, the one who eyed him at check-in. Sometimes he likes a little something on the side, something rough and anonymous and nasty. It's tricky, though, finding someone who won't boomerang back, threaten one of his happy marriages. He can't just sit here in this suite all night as Olive sleeps off her one-bomb drunk. He runs a finger along her jawbone. "I'm going to go out for a meal, let you sleep, okay, precious? And then I'll sleep on the sofa when I get back, so you can have your rest. Big day tomorrow. Our wedding day."

He really does consider each marriage a big deal, no matter how many times he does it. The women are so happy at that moment, and who can put a price tag on that? To date, his marriages have netted him as little as fifteen thousand dollars and as much as two hundred thousand, and he's proud of the fact that each woman got the same quality job.

He's disciplined. He doesn't go too wild, stays out just late enough to find someone who wants to rid himself of energy as quickly and anonymously as he does. Then he creeps back in and, true to his word, stretches out along the sofa, doesn't even bother to pull out the foldaway bed. Olive will appreciate the gallantry, he thinks.

Could she really be a virgin? She has been coy about her age, which leads him to suspect that she's actually older than she looks. But even if she is ten years older than she appears, she's still on the young side, no more than her late thirties. He hasn't been with a woman that young since—well, ever. Even when he was young, the women tended to be over forty. It takes a woman a few years to amass a nest egg worth pursuing. But Olive is an heiress and an orphan. He has hit the exacta. He deserves it.

He awakens to a hard knock on the door—crap, he should have put the DO NOT DISTURB hanger on the knob—but before he can call out to warn the maid away, the door is thrown open and there is a sudden flurry that he can barely process in his sleep-dazed state. Voices, hard and emphatic, a trio of men circling him, calling him by his real name.

Calling him by his real name. The name that comes up on his rap sheet, from back in his hustler days in this very city. The name with a warrant or two, even a few of the earlier marriages. A name he hasn't used for years for that very reason. How do they know his real name?

They cuff him, then begin examining the contents of his wallet, sitting out on the dining room table that so impressed Olive. Olive. Where is she, how has she slept through this? Maybe she went out for breakfast or a café au lait. He will find a way to explain this to Olive. She will bail him out. But he needs to get out of here before she returns, talk to her without any cops around.

"This your credit card?" one of the cops asks, extracting the platinum card that Olive added to her account.

"Yes, and that's my real name, as you see from my ID. I have no idea who Gustave Meckelburg is." God, what a name. No matter his line of work, he would have dropped that handle.

"Really?" says the cop, a detective, probably fraud or larceny.

Whatever name he's ever used, he's never done anything vio-lent, after all, and he can't believe the New Orleans PD care about his old adventures in vice. "Weird thing is, credit card company says you applied for this online a week ago, but the Social you gave belongs to Gustave Meckelburg. And every-thing else you provided—your address, your income—turns out to be a straight-up lie. That's frowned upon, but it's so minor compared to the other stuff we have on you, we're not going to sweat it. Although you do owe for this hotel now that account has been closed."

"That's ridiculous. The primary account holder is my fian-cée and all she did was add me. When she returns, she'll clear this up."

"Olive Dunne? The one whose name was on the reserva-tion? She skipped, buddy. Doorman put her in a cab about six this morning. Told him her mother was ill."

"She doesn't have a mother."

"We've got a lot to sort out with you," the cop says, putting his hand on his shoulder. "And we'd like to go over the various infractions in our jurisdiction before we hand you over to the feds."

"The feds?"

"They've been advised that Gustave Meckelburg has never filed a tax return. They'd kinda like to talk to you about that."

SHE HAS A LONG LAYOVER in the Nashville airport, almost three hours. She changes into jeans and a T-shirt, dumps the suit in a trash can. It smells like him to her, although the odors really belong to Bourbon Street. He smelled okay. Not a surprise, given his line of work. She parks herself in a Starbucks, uses the wireless feed to empty the checking account she set up only a month ago, calls the bank to tell them what she's done. She bends the ATM card she extracted from his wallet early that morning, along with all the cash, and works it back and forth until it breaks in half. She kills out the photos of Olive Dunne's house in the Pacific Palisades, silently thanking the woman for the loan of her name and her home for these last few months, not that she will ever know. Then she makes another quick call.

"Hey, Mom."

"Jordan. Where are you?"

"Heading back to Providence. Ran down to New Orleans over the weekend for the hell of it."

"What prompted that?"

"Feeling restless."

Her mother is a sweet, trusting woman, despite all that happened, but she knows her daughter well enough to be skeptical. Jordan doesn't do much on impulse. "You're not still on that tear about Frankie, are you?"

"Frankie?"

"Thinking he's a con man, or whatever. He loved me, Jordan. You scared him off, making me ask all those questions. He thought I was too suspicious."

"He did take almost twenty thousand from you."

"For that hospital he's building in Brazil, Jordan. I don't mind that. It was a good cause."

"You're right, Mom." She is right. Twenty thousand is nothing in the grand scheme of things, and it had served a good cause if it kept her mother from marrying that creep. If her mother had married Gustave Meckelburg—then known as Frank Mercer—he would have taken her for much more. But twenty thousand was still too much to Jordan's way of thinking, and she had put a lot of time and effort into finding out who he was and getting him into a jurisdiction where that mattered. She had learned that bigamy may carry a social stigma, but it didn't fetch much in the way of criminal punishment. However, she knew how he had found her mother and she assumed he would find her that way, too, if she baited the hook just right. The hard part had been learning everything she could about him. But she has always been a patient young woman, the inevitable consequence of her father dying young and leaving behind her sweet but silly mother, who never bothers to read the fine print or question anything too closely.

Jordan says goodbye to her mother and takes a much-folded letter out of her purse, a printout of an email. "Dear Angel," it begins. "How can machinery match two souls so perfectly? How can this thing of wires and circuits know what is in my heart?" It is the letter that George Middleberg sent her three months ago. It is also, word for word, the letter he sent to her mother eight years ago. If she ever harbored any doubts about what she was doing, they ended the day she received that email.

I can't wait to take your name, she'd told him at the hotel. And so she had. Taken his latest fake name, and returned his real one to him.

PART 3

Thank heaven for little girls.

—*Alan Jay Lerner*

ICE

Athena could run. Boy, could she run.

She ran down the hill at full speed. Because she could, because the hill was there and when you are ten years old, running down a hill at full speed makes as much sense as anything else you might do. You can roll down a hill, too, but that is a game for lazier, gentler grassy slopes, with plenty of land to catch you at the bottom. This hill was studded with trees, which snapped and slapped unless you were fleet and nimble, short and skinny. Athena was all those things. Her brother lumbered along, slowed down by his size, crying out when he felt the stinging, winter-bare branches on his face. Those branches never touched Athena.

Athena flew down the hill, her lungs bursting with happiness. It was such a beautiful day, more beautiful than any January day had a right to be, more like March. They were off from school for Martin Luther King Jr.'s birthday, a holiday just for schools, nobody else. Her mama didn't have off, but she and her brother did.

It was funny, though, how boring a day off from school could become before it was over, how easy it was to use up all the fun. The day had started fine—Mama's kiss on the top of her head as Athena burrowed under her covers, enjoying an extra hour of sleep. Cartoons and Nesquik and Pop-Tarts, *Dialing for Dollars*. Then outside, a walk to the corner store with the dollar Mama had left for her. One for her and one for her brother. Then they had sort of run out of things to do until Bobby thought to go exploring in the woods behind Hillside Road.

And now here they were, running, running, running down the hill. There was a pond at the foot of the hill. It had never occurred to Athena, whose school bus crossed that pond on a bridge every day, that she could reach it on foot, yet here it was. The pond, still all ice after last week's hard freeze, looked like a shiny white diamond winking at her. If she ran fast enough, she could probably glide across it, like them skaters do. The Winter Olympics would be starting soon, and she liked to watch the skaters and the skiers, although her uncle Rodney always said those were sports for rich folks and white folks. Athena had puzzled over that because she was pretty sure that all rich folks were white folks, except for maybe Miss Diana Ross and the Jackson Five. Not even the people on Hillside Road were truly rich, big as their houses were compared to the one where she lived with Robert and Mama.

They were racing and she was winning. Robert was two years older, but she was faster and, oh, how it irked him, losing to his baby sister. *Can't catch me, I'm the gingerbread man!* Of course, when she got to the bottom, he could catch her. Wouldn't it be funny if she said exactly those words and didn't stop, just flew across the ice to the other side? Mrs. Burke had been reading them this story, about slavery and such, said it was important to know certain things if they were going to celebrate the birthday of Dr. Martin Luther King Jr. here in Baltimore, they needed to know how far they had come, how it used to be that the stories of Black people were listened to only when told by a white woman, and while this woman was a good white woman, Dr. King had showed the world that they had words, too, they didn't need white people to tell their stories.

Athena ran down that hill like Eliza running from Simon Legree, like Moses escaping Egypt. Go down, Moses. Go down, Athena. It would be hard to run on the ice. She had taken many a fall on ice in her time. Maybe she should try to walk across the spine of the rickety old dam, the one that created the little pond out of a stream that usually just tumbled and churned across rocks. But no, that dam was so full of splinters and stuff. She would just get up a lot of speed, then glide across the ice. It would be like surfing, not that she had ever done that, either. She ran straight at the frozen pond and launched herself across it, arms out, gliding, gliding, gliding. It was the closest a person could come to flying and have her feet on the ground, Athena thought.

She was almost to the opposite side when she felt the ice shudder. Could ice get cold? Or did ice shiver when it got warm? It shuddered once, twice, then gave way the third time, collapsed beneath her. If gliding had felt like flying, then this was like falling from the sky.

Athena couldn't swim. Neither could Robert. Her brother stood on the bank screaming for her, but Athena never surfaced. The water was barely over her head in the spot where she fell. But that was enough, that was all it took. The stream's murky waters, which looked so lazy and still on the surface, were strong enough to press her against the old dam and hold her there. She was cold, then surprisingly warm, so warm—

"AND THEY NEVER FOUND HER body, not even when they had to rebuild the dam after Hurricane Agnes," Gwen told Mickey, a flashlight beneath her chin.

They were sitting in Gwen's bedroom, under a makeshift tent made from Gwen's bedspread.

"That doesn't make any sense," Mickey said. "It's not more than six feet deep there, when the stream is at its highest. She was either there or she was washed over. And if she was washed over, they'd have found her right away, her head all busted and stuff on the rocks."

"It's a *mystery*," Gwen said. "That's the point of the story. She just ran down the hill and tried to cross the ice, fell through and was never seen again."

"The only mystery I can see," Mickey said, "is how it could have happened on Martin Luther King's birthday before Agnes. We didn't even have that holiday before 1972."

"I think we did," Gwen said. "I'm pretty sure we did."

"How would you know? You didn't live here then."

"My father told me. He heard about it down at the hospital.

They were talking about how we had a school holiday next week and someone said that it was so sad, how a little Black girl died on Martin Luther King Day the first or second time we had it. Just ran down a hill, right into the water. And her named for the goddess of wisdom, too. That's irony, my dad says. Do you know what irony is?"

"Of course," Mickey said.

She didn't. And even though Mickey understood Gwen was asking only because she liked to explain things, not because she thought less of Mickey for not knowing them, she wasn't going to admit her ignorance this time. Gwen knew lots of things and she liked to share them. If she had her way, they would play school in the afternoons, but the last thing Mickey wanted to do was play school after being there every day.

She was so tired of Gwen explaining things to her.

Gwen was her friend, her best friend. "Your only friend," Mickey's mom said, meanly. It wasn't her fault that there weren't any other eleven-year-old girls around here. And Gwen was a very satisfactory friend most of the time, with a cool house and a cool mom and amazing treats in a big drawer in the kitchen that you were allowed to have whenever you wanted up until thirty minutes before dinner. Gwen's mother went to the grocery store every Saturday morning and the rule was that all the kids in the house—Gwen; her older sister, Fee; her brother, Miller, before he left for college last fall—could pick anything they wanted, and as much as they wanted, then eat it as fast or slowly as they wanted. Gwen always picked out one or two treats for Mickey and when Mickey looked into the treat drawer and saw the package of circus peanuts—not real peanuts, but the orangey marshmallow ones—she felt like someone in a pirate movie, staring into a chest that made your face glow gold.

Lately, though, Mickey was getting tired of Gwen's stories. Gwen liked to talk. Mickey liked to *do* things. Not sports so much—she wasn't good at sports. But she yearned to spend the afternoons outside, roaming the wild, overgrown park that surrounded Gwen's house. Gwen could sit inside for hours, even on a beautiful day, moving her stuffed animals and dolls around in service of a story, playing tea party and school and hospital and drugstore. She really did tell wonderful stories, although Mickey was beginning to suspect she stole them from books. The only details Mickey contributed were usually taken from *Dark Shadows* and *One Life to Live*, the show you had to sit through in order to get to *Dark Shadows*.

But now it was January, a cold, snowless January. The promises of Christmas—promises that had failed to be kept in Mickey's case—had come and gone, and the year stretched ahead, with so little to look forward to. There would be Valentine's Day—cupcakes, cards. The teacher said everyone had to give a card to everyone, which was a torture for Mickey, as it meant getting money from her mom, or trying to go around her mom and wheedle it from her sort-of stepdad, Rick, who always gave her what she wanted—unless her mother decided to stop him. "On principle," she said, but the only principle Mickey could see was that her mother didn't want her to have things she wanted. That's how Christmas had gone down, her wish list ignored because her mother decided she should get "better" stuff, more expensive things. Stupid clothes and a little handheld hairdryer, which her mother used most mornings. Besides—the one-Valentine-for-everyone rule? It was so unfair. It was made for girls like Gwen, who was plump and too smart, so no boys liked her. Boys liked Mickey and she didn't even try to make them. She would have gotten a Valentine's Day card from every boy in the class *without* a rule. It seemed to Mickey sometimes that all the rules were made for people like Gwen by people like Gwen—teachers and such. Like, one day, a million years ago, some teacher didn't get a Valentine's Day card from a single boy, so she made a rule that everyone had to give a card to everyone. But that was unfair to people who couldn't buy the best cards. Mickey's mom would want her to get that awful pack of silly cards, the babyish ones without envelopes, with skunks and bears and puppies saying stupid stuff.

No, if Mickey couldn't get Rick to take her to G.C. Murphy's for the good cards, she'd rather not buy any cards at all. Maybe she should convince Gwen that it was a cool thing to do—

The overhead light snapped on, making them jump.

"Why are you inside, sitting in the dark?" Gwen's mother, Tally, the kind of mother who said, "Call me Tally," had sneaked up on them. She was generally cool, Gwen's mother, but she moved about the house like a cat, surprising them.

Gwen hid the flashlight beneath her skirt before pulling the bedspread from their heads. Mickey wasn't sure why it mattered if she had the flashlight. But Gwen's family was funny that way. There were things that Mickey would never touch in a million years—fragile things, valuable things—that Gwen was allowed to handle. But then Gwen's parents would get upset because she used a flashlight. They were nicer than Mickey's mom, no doubt, but at least Mickey knew where she stood with her mom. Tally was sweet most of the time, then she went on these tears. Mickey could see one forming now, as she moved around Gwen's room, pulling up the blinds so they snapped, grabbing and folding the quilt they had used for their game.

"Marimekko," she said to the quilt. "Do you know what this cost?"

"We were just playing."

"The sun's out. You should be outside."

"It's cold," Gwen said. It was really cold, and had been for a week, the kind of cold that made the inside of your nose freeze so it felt like the ceiling at Luray Caverns, all stalactites and things.

"The pond has frozen over. I saw everyone skating when I drove up to the store. You should go skating."

It sounded like a suggestion, but Mickey knew it wasn't.

"I don't have skates," Mickey said. She really didn't.

"There's probably an old pair around that would fit you. Maybe even mine, although we'd have to roll up a pair of socks and put them in the toes."

Now was the time to say that she didn't know how to skate. So why didn't she? It was hard for Mickey to say she didn't know how to do things. It was so much easier to pretend that things weren't worth doing. Like arithmetic, for example. Or making a diorama for Maryland Day. So much easier to take the zero than to try to explain that her mom didn't have an empty shoebox, much less the time to sit with her and help her make little arks and doves out of paper. Gwen had gotten an A on her diorama, but Tally had ended up doing most of it, even making a Father Andrew out of the kind of plastic doll you found on wedding cakes.

"That's okay. I'll just go home," Mickey said.

"Don't be silly," Tally said.

"Will you skate with us, Mom?" Gwen's voice was hopeful. Tally was pretty and, although not particularly young, she looked young, with her long hair and slender figure. She looked younger than Mickey's mom, in some ways, and Mickey's mom was one of the youngest in their class. But her mom was prettier, Mickey decided with a sudden, fierce loyalty. She never loved her own mom more than when she was around Tally Robison in one of her moods.

"No, I'm busy," Tally said. *Doing what?* Mickey wondered. Her mom worked, but Gwen's mom just sort of . . . floated. Gwen said she was writing a book, but that was the kind of lie that Gwen would tell. Oh, Tally did peck away at a typewriter some afternoons, but real people, people you knew, didn't write books, and it was silly to pretend they did. Mickey wasn't sure who, exactly, wrote books, but it wasn't normal people. People on television shows, maybe, or the president.

Tally's old skates actually fit Mickey without a pair of socks in them, although there was a little extra room in the toe. "It's the fit at the ankle that matters," Tally said, tying the skates tight while Mickey and Gwen sat on a broken concrete ledge that everyone apparently used for this purpose. "I worked at a rink when I was growing up in Boston and no one could lace a skate as tight as I could. I was also the only girl who ever drove the Zamboni."

"What's a Zamboni?"

"A machine that cleans the ice."

"Is it hard to drive?"

"Not particularly."

"Then why didn't they let girls drive it?"

"Sexism," Tally said. "Mickey—don't you want to skate?"

"Oh sure."

"Then why don't you?"

"Oh, I'm just—just warming up," she said. Gwen had already launched herself across the ice. Gwen wasn't athletic, but she had learned to skate somewhere and she made her way into the middle of the pond without falling. And it was okay to fall, apparently. People were falling all over the place, not just little kids. Up toward the far end of the pond, near the bridge that led to Mickey's house, boys were playing hockey.

Tally gave Mickey a hard look. "It's okay if you're not good at it. Falling is part of learning."

And everyone should get a Valentine from everyone.

But Mickey said only: "It's just been a long time."

Mickey knew that Tally would help her—but only if Mickey admitted she didn't know how to skate. And then Tally might summon Gwen back, order her to teach Mickey, which would be worse somehow. She would rather sit here a thousand years than admit that there was something else Gwen could do that she couldn't. Wasn't it enough that Gwen made A's and won the school poster contest and wrote poems that got put up on the bulletin board even though they didn't rhyme? She wasn't supposed to be good at outdoor things, too.

"I had a treat a little bit ago," she said.

"So?"

"My mom says ice-skating is like swimming. You can get cramps."

"Oh, Mickey—"

Fiercely: "My mom *says*."

So Tally left Mickey sitting on the concrete ledge, saying only: "Don't bang the blades against the concrete. It will dull them. Walk back when the sun goes down. It's not safe to skate here after dark."

It was cold, sitting still, especially if she couldn't swing her legs. Mickey could change back into her shoes and boots, walk home. Tally Robison wasn't the boss of her. But Tally would have called Mickey's mother by now, told her about dinner, and her mom would be mad at Mickey for leaving the pond without a grown-up's permission. At least, she would say she was mad about that. Mickey knew she would really be mad about having to make dinner when she thought she was off the hook.

Could it be that hard, skating? Mickey managed to stand, only to have her ankles collapse until her feet felt like two Ls standing back-to-back. Stupid Tally, who had laced her skates, announcing all along how good she was at lacing skates. Mickey edged back to the concrete ledge, retied them. Better. But she still couldn't figure out how to move in them. Gwen seemed to skate without picking her feet up at all. How did that work? Mickey tried to walk toward her, picking her feet up and down—and fell immediately.

"Damn it," she said, and a nearby mom looked at her with horror. Mickey knew worse curses.

She retreated again, removed the skates. Why couldn't she just wear her shoes and boots on the ice? Yes, she knew it would be slippery, but it wasn't like she had never walked down an icy sidewalk. She removed the skates and put on her boots. It was amazing how loose and free her ankles felt after being inside the skates. She stood, walked onto the ice, caught herself before she fell. Okay, this was going to be hard. But she soon found that if she rose on her tiptoes and ran, she could then slide for great distances. A few adults called after her, said things like "You're going to hurt yourself," or "You really should have on skates," but Mickey never had a problem ignoring adults. Besides, she wasn't falling, not that much, no more than Gwen, with her fancy white skates. People began watching her, Mickey, the girl in boots. She even joined in a game of Crack the Whip, taking the last position and letting the skaters pull her along, then laughing hysterically when they released her, flying so far up the pond that she almost ended up in the hockey game, where the Halloran boys, who were sometimes called the Hooligan boys, yelled at her and shook their sticks. Who cared? It was like flying. She had invented a new sport, shoe-skating. It was Gwen who had to remind Mickey that it was time to go when darkness fell.

The cold snap hung on for the rest of the week and Mickey went back every afternoon, refining her new sport. Gwen came, too, but she seemed to be mad at Mickey. She was jealous, Mickey decided. Anyone could ice-skate, but only Mickey could shoe-skate. By the third or fourth day, she almost never fell at all. "She must have a lower center of gravity than other people," she heard one mother say to another. "Or she's graceful, like a dancer," the other said. "It's almost as if her feet aren't touching at all." That's how it felt to Mickey—as if her feet barely touched at all.

The pond was still frozen the next Monday, when they had off for Martin Luther King Jr.'s birthday. Mickey had permission to spend the entire day at Gwen's house, and she wanted to go straight back to the pond. The weather was beginning to warm, the pond wouldn't be frozen much longer. But Gwen dawdled, allowing the hours to slip by, and suddenly it was lunchtime and Tally was in one of her moods, which meant they had to sit down and have tomato soup and grilled cheese sandwiches, neither of them normal. The soup was spicy, the cheese smelled funny, and even the bread was weird. But, finally, Gwen and Mickey were at the pond. Gwen sat on the concrete ledge while

Mickey practiced her "figures," tracing numbers and letters, not that anyone could see them. But she could. On a weekday, in the early afternoon, the pond was almost empty, only the Halloran boys there, no grown-ups. Only the kids got off for King's birthday.

Gwen continued to sit, refusing to put on her skates.

"I'm tired of doing this," she said. "It's boring."

"Try doing it like I do," Mickey said, knowing Gwen couldn't, enjoying her chance to be superior. She put her arms out, rose up on tiptoe, took her tiny little steps, then lowered her heels so she was flat-footed. She could cross almost the entire breadth of the frozen pond. She looked back to see if Gwen was admiring her, but saw that she had turned her back on the pond. In fact, she had her face pressed into her hands. Stupid Gwen. She was probably crying, baby that she was. If the Halloran boys noticed, they would tease her, then start in on Mickey. Plus, why was Gwen crying? She had her ice skates, she could come out if she wanted. She just hated for Mickey to be good at anything. And when Mickey was good at something—shoe-skating, getting Valentine's Day cards, knowing the names of plants and bugs—Gwen said it didn't count. Gwen was so unfair. Gwen was a bad friend. Mickey was going to go over there and tell her so. She rose up on her toes, got her usual running start, and—

She had not noticed how thin the ice was getting here, near the shore, the dam. It seemed to wobble beneath her, sort of like hard Jell-O. Then, just like that, it broke beneath her and she plunged into the water.

She was drowning.

That was her conscious thought, her only thought: *I am drowning.*

She looked up: There was sky above her, or at least a patch of promising brightness. She had gone straight down, so the hole was above her head. The danger, she knew, was that she would be sucked toward the dam and under the ice and she would not be able to break through. She had to fight her way back to that brightness. Mickey could swim, she was a decent swimmer, but her clothes were heavy now as they took on water, so when her toe found the mushy bottom and pushed off, she felt heavier than she had on the surface, quite the opposite of what she usually felt in the water, where she flipped and turned like an astronaut in zero gravity. She rose slowly, slowly, slowly, but her head finally broke the surface and she was able to heave her body out of the water, back onto the ice, where she stayed low, afraid to move. Gwen was screaming, but doing nothing. The hockey-playing boys didn't even seem to know what was going on. At any rate, they did not stop their game.

Mickey flattened herself on the ice as much as possible. Maybe if she moved upstream, toward the bridge, the ice wouldn't be as weak. She probably should retreat toward the middle of the pond, where the ice would be thicker, less affected by the thaw. But the shore was so tantalizingly close. Mickey edged toward it on a diagonal like, hugging the ice. That should work. She crawled like an inchworm, humping her butt up and down in the air. Flattening, humping, flattening, humping. Oh, she hoped the Halloran boys didn't look now. They would never let her live it down.

She was three feet from shore when the ice gave way again. The second fall was worse, in part because she belly-flopped in, so her face and body took the shock, but also because she knew now how hard it would be to get out. She heard Gwen screaming, screaming, screaming and then it was quiet, the way it always was in movies when things happened underwater. Her feet found the bottom again. She was in over her head, only barely. She should be able to push to the surface, but the water was stronger than she was and it was taking her now, moving her, bullying her, forcing her up against the dam, away from the light.

She heard her own voice: *I'm going to die.*

No, you're not, a voice in another part of her head insisted. *Push.*

I can't. I tried. I'll just hit the ice.

Then break it.

What?

Push. With your hand. It will give way. But you gotta hit it hard.

This was not her voice. How was a voice in her head not her voice?

Show me.

Can't. But you can do it.

She raised her arms above her head. How could this lazy stream of water have so much strength below the surface? She pushed off, tapped the ice, but nothing happened.

Harder.

I can't. I can't.

Yes, you can. You have to. It's the only way out. You can't swim back now. You gotta break the ice.

I can't.

You wanna live, you better. I can tell you this much—you don't want to stay here.

Mickey looked straight ahead and saw a pair of green eyes almost glowing in the murky water. They could be—what? The eyes of a catfish or whatever else might live here in the long-polluted stream. But she knew these were not a catfish's eyes, and they scared her so much that she found the strength to push toward the surface again, the voice calling after her, insistently in her ear, almost as if someone was riding piggy-back.

Make fists. Hit that ice like it's somebody you want to hurt. You ever want to hurt anyone?

Yes. Yes, I've wanted to hurt people.

Me, too, the voice said. *Me, too.*

And with that, Mickey cracked the ice above her head, broke the surface, then let the water pin her into the corner formed by the dam and the concrete ledge. There, clinging to the rough side, she caught her breath and let Gwen help her out. She probably could have gotten out on her own, but it felt good to see Gwen's arms reaching for her.

"Don't tell my mom," Gwen said.

"Of course." Again, this was one of the things that Gwen's

parents would get upset about, while Mickey's mother wouldn't mind, given that she was alive.

"We'll go in through the basement, wash your clothes and put them through the dryer. You can sit down there in a towel until they're ready."

"Sure," Mickey said. "Gwen, when I was under the ice—"

"You had a tetanus last year, right?"

"Yeah, and I didn't get cut, I just swallowed a lot of water. I'll be okay. Gwen—that story, about that girl. The one who ran into the water. Did it really happen?"

"I told you it did. My father told me about it. You're lucky you're not her."

"Why was she running like that? Across the ice?"

"Just playing some stupid game with her brother. Tag or something. I don't know. She tried to run across the ice and she fell in. You really shouldn't wear shoes on the ice."

Not shoes, Mickey thought. It wasn't about the shoes. Something else happened to that girl. Athena. How did she know her name? She just did. There was a girl, named Athena, who had tried to run across the pond and fallen in. Why had Athena been running? Athena, who had ridden Mickey's back up and out of that filthy water, she hadn't waited around to tell her all she wanted to know. There wasn't time to tell the white girl about how Athena's brother had brought a boy to the house, a boy he was specifically forbidden to bring around. Marvin. Ugly, thuggish Marvin. Bobby wasn't supposed to bring anybody to the house when Mama wasn't there, and Marvin wasn't welcome even when Mama was there. Athena didn't want to be in the house with them, so she went outside, sat on the back steps, hands thrust into her pockets because she had forgotten her gloves. It was only one P.M. Mama wouldn't be home until five o'clock.

The boys came banging out the back door. There was a small, sad tree in the yard, naked and cold. Marvin broke a branch from it. Mama would be mad. She loved that tree, a dogwood, bloomed pink every spring. "Let's play a game," Marvin said. "Like hockey. And your sister will be the puck."

Athena turned to go back in the house, but Bobby blocked the way. There was nothing to do but run past Marvin and through the back gate, then into the woods beyond Hillside Road. The boys were slower, in part because Bobby had to grab his own branch, and carrying the sticks slowed them down, but she could hear them behind her.

She ran down the hill, almost blind in her panic, while they shouted at her, saying terrible things about what they would do. She was smaller than they were and able to duck the branches that snapped and whipped around them, but what good was being faster when she ended up at the pond, trapped? She could run along the shore, but she wasn't so fast that she could get back to the road before they caught up with her. She would have to go across the ice. That was the only way. There were houses on the other side, and houses meant people. They couldn't do whatever they meant to do to her if people were around. It seemed safer to walk along the dam line, where Athena would have something to grab if she slipped. She inched her way across, her brother and Marvin standing on the shore, shouting horrible things at her but scared to follow. She was almost to the other side when the ice seemed to hesitate beneath her, just like the girl in her class who never knew the answer to anything. "And what is the name of Dr. King's most famous speech, Quintana?" *Ummmmmmmm.* "We are working on our seven times today. What is seven times seven, Quintana?" *Ummmmmmmmm.* And then Mrs. Burke's pointer would slap across her desk. "Pay attention, Quintana, or I am going to have to send a note to your mother."

So the ice said *Ummmmmmmm* and then cracked beneath Athena's feet, the sound as sharp as Mrs. Burke's pointer slapping across a desk. Athena plunged into water colder than anything she had ever known. An igloo could not be this cold. The cold seemed to make the water thick, too, even where it was not ice. And although the surface was only six inches from her head, it might as well have been a hundred miles. She didn't know how to swim, didn't have the first idea what to do. Her legs, so fleet on the ground, pedaled as if on an imaginary bike, her arms waved as if she were trying to signal a school bus that was pulling away from the curb, leaving her behind. The water pushed her, lazy but determined. No matter how she battled it, the water came back, nudging and pushing, telling her where to go until she could go no farther. The dam's rickety boards caught on her clothes and hair, held her there.

And there she stayed, the little girl who ran into the pond.

Because she was silly, because she didn't know better, because she couldn't swim. She could hear it all, the stories told over and over again. Did you hear about the girl who just ran into the pond? That was Robert's story, not hers. She heard her brother's lying words, heard her mother's tears. She watched the light change above her, signaling the seasons, calculated when the dogwood bloomed—and when its flowers dropped. One year, two years. She saw the light grow dim when the ice closed over her again, saw children's feet, agonizingly close, moving above her. Winter, spring, summer, fall. Her mother's tears were not as loud or frequent, people spoke of her less. Three years, four years. The story stopped being told.

Did the girl know, the one who had fallen, that Athena had grabbed on to her back and ridden her to the surface, then just kept rising? Had she felt Athena's fingers digging into her sweater and hair, her breath in her ear? They had broken the surface together, but where the other girl reached for her friend, Athena kept rising. The last thing she saw, as she looked down at the pond that had held her so long, was that soggy white girl clinging to her friend—chest heaving, hair streaming water. Did that girl even know how lucky she was to be alive? Probably not. But she would say she did and that was all that mattered. Would she remember Athena? Probably forever. There would be a new story now, about a different girl, a new warning. There would always be cautions and stories, stories told to scare other children. Athena understood that now. The girl who played with matches. The boy who didn't look both ways. The girls who talked to strangers. The boys who walked home in the storm. Athena had been held in place not by the water or the splintery boards, but by her own story. Now that there was another story to replace hers, Athena was free. Athena was gone.

Athena could run.

THE LAST OF
SHEILA LOCKE-HOLMES

Years later, when relatives tried to tease her about the summer she turned eleven and opened her own detective agency, she always changed the subject. People thought she was embarrassed because she wore a deerstalker cap with a sweatshirt and utility belt and advertised her services under the name Sheila Locke-Holmes, which was almost her real name anyway. She was actually Sheila Locke-Weiner, but it was bad enough to be that in real life. The only case she ever solved was the one about her father's missing *Wall Street Journal* and she disbanded her agency by the summer's end.

Besides, it didn't begin with the deerstalker cap, despite what her parents think they remember. She was already open for business when she found the cap, in her mother's side of the walk-in closet, in a box full of odd things. Because her mother was Firmly Against Clutter—a pronouncement she made often, to Sheila's father, who was apparently on the side of clutter— this unmarked box was particularly interesting to Sheila. It contained a deerstalker cap, although she did not know to call it that; a very faded orange T-shirt that said GO CLIMB A ROCK;

a sky-blue wool cape with a red plaid lining; and a silver charm bracelet.

She took the box to her mother, who told Sheila that she really must learn to respect other people's privacy and property. "We talked about this. Remember, Sheila? You promised to do better."

"But I have to practice searching for things," Sheila said. "It's my job. May I have the T-shirt? It's cool, like the shorts people buy at Abercrombie, only even better because it's really old, not fake-old."

"Don't you want the cape, too? And the charm bracelet? I think those things are back in style as well."

Sheila maintained a polite silence. Her mother was not the kind of mother who was actually up to date on what was cool. She just thought she was. "I like the cap. It's like the one on that book that Daddy is always reading, the one he says he wants to work on if it ever becomes a film."

Her mother looked puzzled. "Sherlock Holmes?"

"No, the one about the stupid people who fought for the South in the Civil War."

"Stupid people?"

"The dunces."

"The dunces—oh, no, Sheila, that's not what the book is about. But, yes, the man in *A Confederacy of Dunces* wears a cap like this. And writes things down on Big Chief tablets, sort of like you've been doing."

Sheila could not let this pass. "I use black-and-white composition books like Harriet M. Welsch in *Harriet the Spy*."

She took the cap, though, to be nice. Grown-ups thought they were always watching out for children's feelings, but Sheila believed it was the other way around just as often. Sheila was tender with her mother, who was sensitive in her own way, and indulgent of her father, who was dreamy and absentminded, usually lost inside whatever film he was editing. He had worked on some famous films, but he worked in an office, no closer to the movie stars than Sheila was when she watched a movie on her computer, so no one at school thought what her father did was cool. Her mother was a lawyer, which definitely wasn't cool. It wasn't uncool, either. It just was.

Sheila sometimes went to her father's workplace, all the way downtown, on Canal Street. This usually happened on school holidays because her mother's law office never recognized holidays or during the summer because of what her parents called child-care chaos. They had a lot of child-care chaos the summer that Sheila was eleven. On these days, she learned her father took the 1 train, which irritated her father because it was a local, but she liked all the extra stops. There were more people coming and going. She tried to make up a story about each person in the car. They tended to be sad stories.

Her father worked at a big Mac computer and it started off exciting—for the first half hour or so, she would even start to think that maybe she would be a film editor. She enjoyed her father's lectures about the choices he made, how he sometimes had to find the film that the filmmaker failed to make, that it was like trying to cook a meal with only what was already in the pantry. But it was slow, tedious work. She eventually got bored, wandered into the lunchroom where bagels were set out, or asked if there was a computer she could use, played games on her father's phone. Most often, though, she pulled out a book, usually a mystery or something with magic.

"You're on a crime spree," her father joked. But she was not an indiscriminate reader of mystery books. She started with Encyclopedia Brown and tried very hard not to cheat by looking at the solutions in the back, but some of the clues were awfully small. (How was she supposed to know that Southerners called the Battle of Bull Run the Battle of Manassas?) She read books by Zilpha Keatley Snyder, which were sort of like mysteries, and *Harriet the Spy* and *The Long Secret*, the sequel, which she liked even better. Despite her deerstalker cap, she did not read Sherlock Holmes. Nor did she read Nancy Drew. Sheila *hated* Nancy Drew, who reminded her of a girl in her class and not just because she had red hair. Like Nancy Drew, Trista had two friends, Caitlin and Harmony, whose job seemed to be to advertise her wonderfulness. *Oh, Trista*, they would moan, *you are so smart, you are so pretty, your clothes are the best.* They said this over and over again and somehow it all became true. When it wasn't, not in Sheila's opinion.

Sheila would talk to her father about Trista and her friends because her father was interested in why people did the things they did, whereas her mother said such conversations were merely gossip, which she forbade, along with *Gossip Girl*. Her father said it was psychoanalysis and that gossip was fine, anyway, as long as it didn't become like the gossip game in *The Last of Sheila*, a film he particularly liked. Sheila pretended to like it, too, because it seemed important to her father. He needed her to like *The Last of Sheila*, *Paths of Glory*, *McCabe & Mrs. Miller*, *The Magnificent Ambersons*, *Miller's Crossing*, and *Funny Bones*. So she did, and she never told him that *Funny Bones* was very scary for what was supposed to be a funny movie and that she didn't understand what anyone in *Miller's Crossing* was talking about, no matter how many times she watched it.

"It's like this Trista has her own PR firm," Sheila's father said.

"Puerto Rican?"

"What?"

"That's what they call the Sharks in *West Side Story*. PRs."

Her father had shown her the film on television, telling her to look at the color of the sky as Tony walked through the alleys, singing of Maria. He was critical of the editing, although it had won an Oscar, according to the white-haired man, the one who talked after the movies on that channel. "Awards don't mean anything," her father told Sheila, yet his awards—none of them Oscars—were framed and hanging in his office.

"Oh, I meant public relations. You know, people who are hired to tell other people how great people are."

"Can I have someone like that? Instead of a babysitter? Could you hire someone to tell people I'm great?"

Her father laughed. But she was serious. She had not had a good year in the fifth grade and she was dreading sixth grade. She was not sure a vintage GO CLIMB A ROCK T-shirt could solve all her problems, although she hoped it would be a start. But how much easier it would be if someone would go to her school and tell everyone she was great. *Sheila the Great*. There was a book by that name, a Judy Blume, but it made her sad, because the Sheila in that book was so obviously not great.

However, Sheila did not realize how bad fifth grade had been until her parents received a call from the school, suggesting that they come in for a conference before the new school year began. "Just to make sure we're all on the same page as far as Sheila's behavior is concerned." She knew this because she picked up the extension in her parents' bedroom and her father caught her.

"Eavesdroppers hear no good of themselves," he said.

"It's part of my job. I have to know things. That's how I found out what was happening to your newspaper. I heard the super claiming to the doorman that people were subscribing to newspapers and leaving them downstairs for days at a time, so he was just going to start throwing them away if people didn't come down to get them by nine."

"I'm down by nine."

She gave her father a look. "Almost never. You leave for work at ten or eleven and, most nights, don't come home until after my bedtime."

He gave her a story by Saki. How weird for someone to be named the same thing as what her mother drank from the little carafe at the sushi place. The story was about a cat, Tobermory, that learned to talk and told everyone's secrets and the people then plotted to poison him. They didn't get a chance—he was killed in a fight by another cat—but that didn't worry Sheila.

She knew how to get around being poisoned. You just made sure that someone else tasted your food first. She also decided that if she was ever allowed to have a cat, she would name him Tobermory and call him Toby for short. She thought about changing the name of her stuffed white-and-gray tabby, which had been passed down to her by her mother, but it didn't seem right, changing someone's name when he was so old. Her mother was fifty, so her stuffed animals must be . . . almost fifty. Sheila had wanted to change her own name. Last year she had asked if she could be Sheila Locke instead of Locke-Weiner. She argued that a girl should have her mother's surname, that it was good for women's rights. Her mother said a change would hurt her father's feelings, that he had managed to grow up with the same name and all Sheila had to do was remind people, politely, that it was pronounced *whiner*.

Like that was so much better.

After solving the case of her father's missing newspaper, Sheila felt she needed more work. She put up a small note advertising her services, but the super scolded her and said such postings were not allowed in the hallways. Her family's building had a lot of rules like that, almost more than school. For example, no delivery people were ever allowed past the lobby, which was part of the reason that all those newspapers ended up on a table and then got thrown away by the angry super.

People in the building were always stressing that this rule was very good for the kids because they could come and go throughout the building and their parents would know that they would never meet an outsider. But there weren't that many kids and Sheila wasn't friends with them anyway, so she would have gladly traded that rule for having Chinese food brought right to the door with everybody already in pajamas. There was nothing cozier than eating Chinese food with her parents with everyone already in pajamas. But because someone had to go downstairs to fetch it they never ended up doing it that way. Besides, they seldom ate dinner as a family because of her father's hours. He said he couldn't help being a night owl. Sometimes her mother ate with Sheila; sometimes she drank a glass of wine while Sheila ate dinner by herself. They had a formal dining room, but it was rare for them to eat in there because it was so formal. They were not formal people, her father said. They all preferred the little breakfast bar in the kitchen, which was bright and cheerful.

But everyone else, guests and strangers, loved the dining room with its scary crimson walls and the chandelier that looked like something that might become a monster at night. *It's a beautiful apartment.* That's what everyone said, upon entering. *What a beautiful apartment.* They praised her parents' taste. They expressed envy for the bookshelves, for the tiny study that her parents shared, for the floors, which were parquet, which Sheila eventually figured out was not a type of margarine. But whenever her mother led someone down the hall with the bedrooms, she would say apologetically, "The bedrooms are kind of mean." Sheila felt this made their bedrooms sound much more exciting than they were. They were small and square with such limited closet space that the smallest one, in the middle, had been transformed into a walk-in closet/dressing room. Her father got one side, her mother got the other. Sheila remained stuck with the little stinky one in her room.

The summer she turned eleven, she began to spend a lot of time in the walk-in closet and that was how she found her mother's deerstalker cap.

"Were you popular?" she asked her mother, twirling the cap on her index finger. "When you were my age?"

"I was kind of in the middle. Not popular, but I had lots of friends."

"Were you pretty?" Her mother was one of the old mothers at her school and although there were quite a few old mothers, she was one of the *old*-old mothers.

"I didn't think so, but I was, actually. I had shiny hair and such a nice smile. When I see photographs of myself from that time, I kick myself for not really realizing how pretty I was. Don't make the same mistake, Sheila. Whatever age you are, you'll look back ten years and kill to look like that again."

"I don't want to look like I'm one year old. I was fat and I had no hair."

Her mother laughed. "Later, I mean. At thirty, a woman wants to look as she did at twenty, so on and so forth."

Sheila had shiny hair and she supposed her smile was nice, but that was not enough, not at her school. Things must have been much simpler in her mother's times. Then again, she grew up in Ohio.

Sheila spent entire days in the closet and her babysitter didn't care. The summer babysitter was old, a woman who didn't want to go anywhere and had to visit the doctor a lot, which was why there was so much child-care chaos. Sheila found she could hear whatever her parents said in their bedroom, if she crept into the closet late at night after a bathroom run. They talked about her at times. It was neither good nor bad, so her father wasn't exactly right about eavesdroppers. Her parents were worried about school. They talked about bullies and cliques. Trista's name came up. Trista was a bully, for sure. She was the worst kind of bully, the kind who had other people do her bullying for her. Her hair was shiny, too. So shiny hair was part of being popular, but it wasn't the only thing that would make a person popular. In her composition book, Sheila began working on a list of things required for popularity and came up with:

1. Shiny hair
2. Nice smile (no braces, lip gloss?)
3. Good clothes
4. Being nice to most people but maybe mean to one person
5. To be continued

She continued to search the walk-in closet. Her father saved everything. Everything! Single cuff links, keys to forgotten places and key rings with no keys, coasters, old business cards. He had a box of Sheila's baby clothes, nothing special, yet he kept them. It was embarrassing to see those stupid clothes, especially the Yankees onesie. Girls shouldn't wear baseball onesies.

But it was in her mother's jewelry box, the one that Sheila was never, ever supposed to touch, where she looked and found the heavy engraved card with her father's name and a woman's name and an address downtown, on Chambers Street. She did not know her father had been in business with a woman named Chloe Beezer. Sheila had never met Chloe Beezer, or heard her father speak of her. The card was pretty, cream-colored and on heavy paper, with a thin green line around their names. Beezer—what an ugly name. A person would have to be very pretty to survive such a name.

There was a photograph clipped to the back. Her father, with a mustache and longer hair, tilted his head toward a woman with blond hair. They were somewhere with palm trees, bright orange drinks in front of them, and orange sky behind them.

"Dad, who was Chloe Beezer?" she asked him on the 1 train, coming back from his office. It was the final week of her summer vacation and the train was very hot and smelly.

"How do you know that name?" he asked her.

"I found a card, with her name on it and yours."

"Where?"

Why did she lie? It was instinctive. Instinctive lying was part of the reason that she was in trouble at school. She took things. She lied about it. But how could one tell the truth about taking things? How could she explain to anyone that Trista's billfold, which had a pattern of gold swirls and caramel whorls that reminded Sheila of a blond brownie, had seemed magical to her? A *talisman*, a word she had found in the books by E. Nesbit and Edward Eager, writers her father insisted were superior to

J. K. Rowling. If she had a billfold like that, she would be powerful. And she was very considerate, which was probably why she got caught: she removed the money and the credit card and the other personal items and put them back in Trista's purse, taking only the billfold. Trista's family was rich-rich. A billfold meant nothing to her. She would have a new one in a month or two. Whereas Sheila's family was comfortable, according to her parents. Except in their dining room, which made them all uncomfortable.

She was not supposed to snoop. But she also was not supposed to go into her mother's jewelry box, which sat on the vanity that separated her father's cluttered side of the closet from her mother's neat, orderly side.

She decided to admit to a smaller crime.

"I found it in a box you had with cuff links and other old stuff."

"You shouldn't be poking around in other people's things, Sheila."

"Why? Do you have secrets?"

"I have a reasonable expectation of privacy. Do you want me to go in your room and search through your things?"

"I wouldn't mind. I've hidden my composition book. You'll never find it." If there was a lesson to be learned from Harriet the Spy, it was to maintain control over one's diary, not that Sheila had anything juicy in it. "Who was Chloe Beezer?"

Her father sighed. "You know, I think, that I was married once before. Before your mother."

She did know that, in some vague way. It had just never been real to her.

"The card was something she made when we got married and moved in together. We sent it to our friends. We didn't have a wedding, so we wanted our friends to know where we had set up house."

"Was she Beezer-Weiner?"

He laughed, as if this were a ridiculous question. "Chloe? No. No. She wanted no part of Weiner." He laughed again, but it was a different kind of laugh.

"Did she die?"

"No! What made you think that?"

"I don't know. Did you get divorced?"

"Yes."

"Why?"

"It's an odd thing, Sheila, but I don't really remember. We married quickly. Perhaps we didn't think it through. Are you ready for school next week? Don't we need to make a trip for school supplies?"

She knew her father was changing the subject. She let him.

But once at home, she had to know if her mother was aware of this extraordinary thing about her father. "Did you know Daddy was married before?" she asked her mother when she came home. "To someone named Chloe Beezer?"

"Yes," her mother said. "I did know that. You did, too. We told you, years ago."

"I might have known, but I guess I forgot."

Her mother looked at her father, who was reading his *Wall Street Journal* at the breakfast bar. Because he had to come home early with Sheila, they were going to have takeout from City Diner. "Why is this coming up now?"

Before Sheila could answer, her father said: "She found an old piece of paper in a box of my stuff. I told her she should respect our privacy more and she said she would. Right, Sheila?"

"Right," she said, although she didn't remember agreeing. "And a photograph. There was a photograph paper-clipped to it."

"Do you want sweet potato fries, Sheila?" her mother asked.

"Yes, with cinnamon sugar."

That night, as her mother put her to bed, Sheila was thinking about lying. She wasn't supposed to do it even when it made sense. But what about when someone else repeated one of her lies? Her father was the one who said she found the card in his boxes, but it had been in the jewelry box, which she was specifically forbidden to touch. Didn't her mother remember it was there? It was right on top, in clear view. She would see it tomorrow morning. Her mother went to that box every workday, pulling out golden chains and silver bangles. Her mother was very particular about her jewelry. She spent more time selecting jewelry than she did on making up her face. "An old face needs an ornate frame," she said, laughing. It was an old face, even as mother's faces went. Sheila wished this weren't so, but it was. She could see that her mother had been at least medium-pretty once, in the same way that she had been medium-popular. But she wasn't pretty now. It might help if she were. Trista's mother was pretty.

"Mom, I went into your jewelry box."

"I figured that out, Sheila. That's okay. It's good you're being honest about it with me. That's the first step. Telling the truth."

"Why did you have that card?"

"What?"

"The card, with the photograph."

"Oh, you know how hard it is to keep things in order sometimes."

Yes, on her father's side of the closet. But her mother's side was always neat, with shoeboxes with Polaroid pictures of the shoes inside and clothing hanging according to type and color. Everything was labeled and accounted for on her mother's side.

"Daddy thought it was in his boxes."

"It probably was."

"Do you snoop, too, Mom?"

She didn't answer right away. "I did. But it's wrong, Sheila. I don't do it anymore." She kissed her good night.

Two days later, Sheila disbanded Sheila Locke-Holmes. She left the deerstalker cap on a hook in her closet, put her almost-blank notebook down the trash chute, and took apart the utility belt that she had created in homage to Harriet the Spy. She told her mother that she would like to wear the charm bracelet, after all, that charm bracelets were popular again. She wore it to school the first day, along with her mother's T-shirt. Sixth grade was way better than she thought it would be and she began to hope she might, one day, at least be medium-popular. Like her mother, she had shiny hair and a nice smile. Like her father, she was dreamy and absentminded, lost in her own world. There were worse ways to be.

Sheila's mother was not dreamy. She did not indulge conversations about why people did what they did. She did not stop movies and show Sheila the color of the sky or explain how Dr. Horrible could go down wearing one thing and rise up and wearing another a second later. But she was sometimes right about things, as Sheila learned with each passing year. At thirty, Sheila would sigh with envy over her twenty-year-old face. At forty, she would longingly look back at thirty.

She would never yearn for that summer when she was eleven. Whenever someone brought up the time she wore the deerstalker cap and started her own detective agency, she changed the subject but not because she was embarrassed. She could not bear to remember how sad her mother looked that night, when she confessed to snooping. She wanted to say to her mother: *He saves everything! It doesn't matter!* She wanted to ask her mother: *Why did you take the card? Did you want him to know you took it? Why did you put it somewhere you would have to see it every day?* She wanted to ask her father: *Why did you keep it? Do you miss Chloe Beezer? Aren't you happy that you married Mommy and had me? What was in those orange drinks?*

But all these things went unsaid. Which, to Sheila's way of thinking, was also a kind of lying, but the kind of lying that grown-ups approved of.

FIVE FIRES

"There was another fire last night." That's the first woman. Tennis skirt, Lacoste polo, gold chain with a diamond on it, like a drop of water.

The other woman—I don't know either of them, you can't, even in a town as small as ours, know everybody—says: "That makes three this month, doesn't it?"

"Two. The one at the vacant—you know that place. And now behind Langley's."

And the playhouse, I want to say. *The first one was that playhouse*. But I don't say it, because, again, I don't know them. But three is right. There have been three since August 1, and it's only August 10.

"Do they know the cause?"

"Lightning."

"There wasn't a storm last night. There's barely been a drop of rain since Memorial Day. Good for the beach towns, but nobody else."

"I know, but there was heat lightning. You could see it in the sky."

"Heat lightning doesn't cause fires."

"Why not? It's still lightning."

"But it doesn't strike the ground, does it?"

"It must strike somewhere. There's no other explanation. No evidence of arson. I suppose, at Langley's, someone could have thrown a cigarette in the dumpster, but there's nothing that can make a vacant lot catch fire, 'cept lightning."

But the playhouse had electricity. Or did it? I'd never been in it, of course, but I'd heard about it. The two-story house that Horace Stone had built for his only daughter, Becca. It had a kitchen and a bedroom and real furniture and, I think, running water. But not electricity. Or maybe it had electricity but not running water? It definitely had a bed. But everyone in town knew that. About the bed.

Now that I think about it, I'm pretty sure it had running water. And maybe a little minifridge with ice. There had to be ice. Not that I ever knew Becca Stone to play with. She's a lot older than I am, four years ahead of me in school, going into her senior year at Princeton. She may want to be my friend, all things considered. But right now, I'm going into my senior year at Belleville High School, and it's hard to imagine a day when I'll be friends with people so much older. Even people who are inclined to like me, like Becca Stone. At least I *think* she likes me. Or would, if we got to know each other.

The women take their sandwiches and go. They never said a thing to me the entire time they were in the store, except: "Wheat bread." "No mayonnaise." And: "Do you have any other chips?" It was like I wasn't there. So I don't say goodbye. I don't know them, although I might know their kids, if they have any. Kids don't come to the deli. It's not cool. Most of the kids go to Subway or McDonald's, maybe the Sonic, although only to get food to go, not to stay and eat in their cars, despite the fact that it's a drive-in. That would be uncool, too. I've made a study of what's cool and what's not, but it's harder than it looks. Why is it cool to get Sonic food to go, but not eat there in your car? I don't know. I just know that's how it is.

IT'S ALMOST FOUR, WHEN I get to leave, if Wendi, who works the next shift, is on time. Big *if*. Wendi's boyfriend is working as a lifeguard at the community pool this summer, but she's not sure of him, so she goes to the pool and stays until the last possible minute, then comes here, smelling of lotion and chlorine and french fries. I think she's silly. He's not going to do anything while she's around, and watching him until the last minute isn't going to make Jordan behave. I don't know, if some girl were watching me that way, I think I might feel obligated to do something.

And when Wendi finally gets to work, she wants me to stay and listen to her complaints and suspicions about Jordan, even though I've punched out. Wendi is one of those people who doesn't seem to exist when she's alone. But she never talks to me anywhere else, so I don't see why I have to linger past the time I'm on the clock to listen to her talk about Jordan. True, I used to like it. Back when she was more positive about him, when I could be a good influence. Back last fall, when people said some nasty stuff about Jordan, I told Wendi she should trust him. She seemed to appreciate it.

"And then Patsy—she's such a slut—"

"I've got to go, Wendi."

"Why?" she asks. Meaning: *You don't have anywhere to go.* Wendi knows how to do that, put a lot of meanness into words that aren't necessarily mean.

"Actually," I say, "someone's waiting for me."

"Who?" She thinks I'm lying. Won't she be surprised when she finds out who's back. But that's a secret, for now. I've promised not to tell. So I just smile. Enigmatically. That's one of my vocabulary words. En-ig-mat-i-cal-ly. I'm not going to take the SAT, but if I did, I bet I would get a pretty good score.

There are exactly seven ways for me to walk home from the deli. I worked it out. It's sort of like an algebra problem. I've always tried to vary it, even before this summer, because I like some variety.

"More like geometry," Tara says, falling into place beside me at the corner of Tulip and Elm. The north–south streets are named for trees, the cross streets for flowers.

"No," I say, conscious that she's smart, that she got into a good college, even if she decided not to go there in the end. Her decision, no one else's. But that doesn't mean she's always right. "It's not about the shapes. It's about the variables. If I go straight on Elm, then there are three possible places to turn right—so those would be x, y, or z. But if I choose to go right here, on Tulip, there are still two more possibilities. So that makes Tulip x, or—"

"BOR-ing," she says, the way she used to in class some-times, in a light, high voice, almost like singing, that all the boys seemed to think was funny. "Is there anything more bor-ing than figuring out how many ways you can walk between your job and your house? Except this town."

"Well," I say, "you didn't have to come back to Belleville if you think it's so boring. And you don't have to stay."

"Of course I have to stay," she says. "At least for a little while."

"Why? Your family moved away last spring. Why did you come back?"

"You know why," she says. I don't know why she thinks that. I mean, I know she's here, staying with a friend, I guess. But she hasn't explained, and it's not like we were close in school.

NO ONE'S HOME AT MY house, 333 Rose. My mom's working four to eleven this week. "I can't have people in when my mom's not home," I tell Tara. "You know that."

"Like you've never broken that rule."

"I haven't."

"Only because no one's ever wanted to come over to your house."

That's not true. Okay, it's true, but it's not nice. But Tara was never that nice, despite what some people think. She wasn't mean—it wasn't like the movies, where the girls are so nasty you can't quite believe it. She just made it really clear that she thought she was up there and other people weren't. True, she was pretty and a cheerleader, but her family didn't even move to Belleville until she was a junior. And, sure, she made varsity cheerleader without ever being on JV, but so what? It's not like she was the only girl who ever did that. Becca Stone made varsity as a freshman and also graduated at the top of her class, went to Princeton. There's a world of difference between some-one like Tara Greene and Becca Stone, and Tara never seemed to get that. My mama always said that the Greenes didn't un-derstand Belleville, that you don't move into a place and try to make it be like you. *You* have to learn to be like *it*.

I guess Tara came back because she's a few credits shy of her diploma. But if she's not in college, she has no one to blame but herself.

I shut the door, leaving her on the walk. "See you tomor-row, Beth!" she says, but I'm already thinking if maybe there's a new way to walk home from the deli, a way that will keep Tara from waiting for me. It was interesting at first, having her seek me out, trying to be my friend. Now I'm not so sure. She's sneaky. I don't know what she wants from me, but I don't owe her anything.

I don't mind coming home to an empty house, although I feel bad for my mom, who hates the night shift. But if she's here when I get home, she's on me. Even when school is out and there's no homework to do. She tells me to take a shower because I smell like salami and sweat. She tells me to put my clothes in the hamper, then says, "Can't you see that hamper's full, Bethie? Start a wash." She stands nearby when I count my tips—at the end of your shift, if you've worked alone, you get everything in the tip jar, although there's a tradition that you leave a dollar for the next girl. I don't know why, but I do it. Wendi doesn't, though. She's not . . . honorable. It's silly not to do it. It's not as if you lose out. Because, of course, if everyone does it, no one loses a dollar.

I still hide my tip money from my mom, although she's okay now. I can't imagine her going through my room again, looking for my savings. Well, I can, but if it happened, I would know what to do. I'd tell her to call Bill, the guy responsible for getting her through the rough patches, and if she wouldn't, then I would. That's happened only once, and if you ask me, it was kind of Tara's fault. I mean, things got so crazy there for a while and it was hard on my mom. People said mean things. I was okay with it, but she was fragile, taking it one day at a time, like they say, and she had a bad day. One. Only one. I'm really proud of her.

Thinking about my mom, and how she loves me and wants the best for me, makes me want to be good to her. So I do all the things she would tell me to do. I take a shower. I start a wash, gathering all the dark clothes, except that one bright red T-shirt at the bottom of the hamper. It's not that I'm ashamed of it, not at all, it's just that I won't know what to do with it once it's clean. Plus, once it's clean, then, I don't know, it's as if everything will be over, and I really don't want things to be over. I keep thinking that maybe it's just summer, that life will be exciting when school starts again, but I'm not sure. Daniel Stone graduated, and he's going to Johns Hopkins on a lacrosse scholarship. Some people say it's wrong, Daniel Stone getting money he doesn't need, but I don't see why he shouldn't get a scholarship. I mean, it's for being a good athlete, and if having a poor family shouldn't keep you out of college, then having a rich one shouldn't keep you from being recognized for your genuine talents.

I wanted to go away to college, but my mom says it's community college for me unless the sky rains money sometime between now and next spring. I'm a good student, but I don't have any kind of special talent that gets you scholarships. It's not that I wouldn't get *some* aid, but my mom is dead set against loans and says it has to be a free ride or nothing if I want to go away.

Last fall, I talked to a recruiter from Delaware State University, but my mom got this look on her face and said, "Over my dead body." I told her that it wasn't an all-Black school anymore, hadn't been for a long time, that it's ranked very high on some lists and a U.S. congressman went there. I kept in touch with that recruiter, telling her of my situation, and she seemed really encouraging until this winter, when she suddenly said she didn't think the school would be a good fit for me. I figure my mom went behind my back and said something. What can I say? My mom is prejudiced. Lots of older people are.

Also, my dad left her for someone from Dover, and I think she has a grudge against Dover. She's lived in Belleville all her life. Me, too. My dad didn't move here until he was in first grade, and he stayed here until he met that schoolteacher from Dover. She got a flat tire on the way to the beach. This would have been the summer I was three years old, but I remember it.

Well, I remember him packing up, moving out. My mother told me about the schoolteacher, her red Miata, how she rode in the truck with the tow truck driver, wearing a shift that was barely a shirt over her bikini. *Slut*, my mother said. *Nice example for a third-grade teacher to set.*

The teacher had a summer share over at Dewey Beach with a bunch of other schoolteachers. My father started taking weekend shifts at the garage, coming home on Saturday nights with a two-tone tan—dark brown on his forearms and face, a paler brown on his torso and legs. And he smelled of beer and the sea, without a speck of grease on him. He would try to get into the shower fast, he'd be a blur moving toward that bathroom, but my mother knew and she threw him out, expecting him to come crawling back. (She's told me this story more than once.) So he packed up and went to Dover, and next thing we know he's sending Christmas cards, addressed only to me, with one baby boy, then two, then three. His new wife encouraged him to push himself, and he switched to selling cars. He pays child support, and he used to visit, but it wasn't fun for either of us, so we let it go when I was twelve or so. "You have your own life now," my father said. "You'll be too busy on the weekends to see your old man. You'll go out for cheerleading, start dating." I thought he had information that I didn't, that those things happened when you were a teenager, almost by law. I was a little puzzled at first when life turned out differently, but I didn't mind.

"Your father never knew what the hell he was talking about," my mother said. "Besides, he's got those other kids now. He's too busy driving them to soccer and baseball and whatever else they do. Well, he always wanted a son, and now he has three. I hope he's happy."

I don't think she does.

My dad kept up his support payments, though. And he says he'll help, if I get into a school, but he can't pay the full freight or even put up enough to bridge the difference between what I've saved and the full cost.

Del Tech, here I come.

Luckily, the Georgetown campus offers an associate degree in criminal justice, and it's only twenty miles away. I just have to make sure that I don't take Friday afternoon classes during the summer term, because the beach traffic will make even that short drive hellish. People who don't live here can't understand what it's like, in the summer, to live in the kind of town that people are forever driving through, how you have to put everything on hold for much of Friday through Sunday, and it's annoying. Today is Thursday and everyone is running around like a storm is coming—going to the grocery store, getting gas, whatever—because by noon tomorrow you won't be able to cross the highway. My mom and I are lucky that we live in town, but even that gets crazy, as there are a bunch of people who think they're so slick, skipping the bypass and going through town. Why do you think they built the bypass? They come roaring through in their big SUVs, bicycles strapped on the back, kayaks and canoes on the roof, the cargo space filled with beach toys. Belleville comes at the point in the journey when most of them have been on the road long enough to be impatient, but there's still more than an hour of driving ahead of them. You can almost feel how cranky the kids are, even from behind the deli counter.

"They don't use half that stuff they pack," my mother says. "The boats and the bikes. You just know they don't even get it off the car. It's only a week, two at the most, and they pack like they're going to Siberia."

I've lived thirty miles from the beach my entire life, and I go only once a year, at most. Not even that anymore. It's a hassle, and my mom always says, "For what? To get a sunburn and a pound of sand in your underwear." Besides, you can break your neck bodysurfing. She read about a guy in the newspaper who did just that.

I don't even know how to swim. That's one reason I don't go to the community pool, where Wendi keeps watch over her boyfriend.

I hang the laundry. We have a dryer, but we try not to use it in the summer unless there's rain, because it heats up the house so and you have to run the A/C even higher and my mother says she doesn't work all the hours she works to keep the wives of Delmarva Power executives in fur coats.

I make a bowl of microwave popcorn for my dinner—it's a diet I've been trying: normal breakfast and lunch, but microwave popcorn for dinner, and I'm down six pounds—and fall asleep in front of the TV. The next thing I know, I'm dreaming and there's the bonfire, but it's the weird kind of dream where I stand outside myself, I see myself in my red T-shirt and I don't care what anyone says, I think I look pretty, but then there is a pounding, pounding, pounding sound and these women in fur coats start looking around and Daniel Stone puts his arm around me and says, "Thank you, Beth," and it's not clear if he's protecting me or I'm protecting him, and the pounding keeps coming and I think it's Tara, at the front door, ignoring my mother's rules, but—

Shit. It's raining, a hard, intense rain pounding the roof. I grab the laundry from the line and put it in the dryer, hoping the cycle runs before my mom gets home. I don't know why I'm so tired. But it was busy at the deli, it being Thursday and all, and I was on my feet for five hours. ("Now you know how I feel," Mama says when I talk about my feet hurting. "I do it for eight, and I'm twenty-five years older than you.") And wouldn't you know, the rain stops almost as fast as it started and the sky looks clear, although there are flashes of heat lightning to the east.

Sure enough, before my mother comes home, I hear the sirens of the Belleville Volunteer Fire Department heading out into the night.

Fire number four.

This one's at the snack bar of the community pool, and they decide to close the place for the rest of the summer, seeing that summer's almost over anyway.

"ARSON," WENDI SAYS. "THERE'S YELLOW tape up and everything."

It's been a slow day—a Friday in August, so the main highway is clogged and people are in their hives, as I think of it, just staying put. Like in the high school cafeteria. Did you know that queen bees are determined before they're born? The potential queen eggs are laid in queen cups, and the queen develops differently because she gets more royal jelly, the name for a protein that's secreted by the worker bees' glands. There can be only one queen bee. Tara was one of the wannabes. Wannabees? Anyway, I guess she learned her lesson. She wanted royal jelly and she got it.

"Why are they so sure it was arson?" I ask.

"They found something. Unlike the others. It looked like the person tried to set it in the trash can, but everything was wet after the rain. So someone broke the lock on the gate they pull over the snack bar at night, turned on the gas. It blew up like a fireball."

"That could be an accident," I said. "I mean, the guy who works there—he's from that place for grown-ups that need help. He might have left it on. Plus someone would have to climb the fence."

"Boys climb that fence all the time," Wendi says. "The lock on the gate had been broken, and gas doesn't just *ignite*." She's excited. Jordan won't be at the pool anymore, so she won't have to hang around there, watching him from behind her sunglasses. Wendi is a redhead. Having to keep tabs on her lifeguard boyfriend hasn't been good for her looks. She has fair skin, set off by her bright red hair and green eyes. Did you know that only 2 percent of the population has green eyes? I didn't, until

Wendi told me. I checked it out: turns out she's right, although 20 percent of Hungarians have green eyes. I asked Wendi if she was Hungarian and she said no, they were Lutheran.

I leave, taking my tips, putting a dollar in the jar for Wendi, knowing she won't do the same at the end of her shift because she's closing. Wendi doesn't understand that there's a psychology to the tip jar, that you want at least a dollar in there all the time, because it gives people the *idea* to tip. It sets the tone. My mom hates tip jars. "If anyone's going to have a tip jar, it should be me, on my feet at the cash register at Happy Harry's for eight hours." She's not wrong, but there's nothing I can do about it except rub her feet, bring her coffee in bed the weeks she works the night shift. I did that this morning. She was awake, staring at the ceiling.

"Did you hear the sirens last night?" she asked me while she sipped her coffee in a mug I made for her when I was ten. Well, I didn't make it, but I decorated it. She was the one who told me the fire was at the community pool. She saw the trucks on her way home. I decide to go by there, too, after work. I plan to take law enforcement classes at Del Tech, although I doubt I'll be an arson investigator. Arson is scary. You have to be crazy to set fire to something. I mean, something that's not supposed to be set fire to. Every fall, just before Halloween, there's a big bonfire in Belleville, a pep rally for the game against our big rivals from Christiana. Everyone goes. It's my favorite night of fall. It makes up for not having trick-or-treat anymore, now that I'm too old for it, for the cold, gray days that come rushing in once it's November. Winter usually isn't a big deal here. Schools close more often for fog than they do for sleet or snow. But last year, we missed eight days for snow and had to make up five of those days. Except for the seniors, which didn't seem fair. They graduated, and we still had another week.

There's yellow crime scene tape at the pool, just as Wendi said, and a state trooper's car. Not the first time I've seen that in Belleville, but it's real rare. Tara's standing off to the side, watching them. I'd thought I'd avoid her, coming by here, and I make a point not to catch her eye. But when I start walking home, she falls in step beside me.

"What do you think?" she says.

I look down at her feet. "About your new sandals? It's a shame how muddy they are."

"They're not new. They're the same sandals I wear every day. No, I meant what do you think about this fire?"

"None of my business, I guess."

"That didn't stop you. Before."

My mom taught me that when you don't like what someone's saying, just don't say anything.

"I was a Brownie," Tara says. "And a Girl Scout, before I moved here. I bet you think that's corny. But I was disappointed that they didn't have a troop here. I had so many badges and insignias, the most of anyone in my troop back home in Philadelphia."

Back home in Philadelphia. *Exactly*, I think. *That's your home. Go back there.*

"I was really good at camping. I can start a fire by rubbing two sticks together. Honest," she adds, as if I won't believe her. But I believe her. About that, at least.

"Big deal," I say. "I suppose anyone who watches *Survivor* knows how to do that. Or who has YouTube."

"Yeah, but can you do it?"

"I don't want to do it. And I don't want to talk about it."

"I had so many badges. So many insignias. You could barely see my uniform for all of them. And that was in—"

"Philadelphia, I know. You were forever talking about Philadelphia." I'm tired of Tara, tired enough to be rude. "Nobody liked it. How much you talked about Philadelphia, how everything was better there. You kept saying all you wanted to do was go back there, and you did. So why are you here?"

"Believe me," she says, "it wasn't my idea. But I've got to finish up."

"You mean you have to get your credits before you can go to college?"

"Something like that."

We walk a few blocks or so and she doesn't talk for a while. We're almost to my house when she says: "Did everyone really hate it?"

"What?"

"When I talked about Philadelphia? I did it only because I was homesick. And new."

"Well, 'hate' is strong. But you did talk about it. A lot."

"Daniel seemed interested," she says. "He asked me lots of questions. He said he was considering Penn."

"Oh, I know you thought Daniel was interested."

"You're mean, Beth."

"No. No, I'm not. I was never mean. You were. You never talked to anyone. You never talked to me, and you only talk to me now because I'm one of the few people in town who wouldn't run away from you. You were stuck up."

"I wasn't." She looks close to crying, and I admit I feel something I haven't felt in a while. It's powerful yet scary, making someone like Tara cry.

Today she doesn't even ask to come in, just stands on the front walk for a while, staring at my house. It frightens me, the way she looks at our house. I don't sleep at all that night, not even after Mama comes home, because I can't tell her what I'm scared of, what I suspect.

The sirens sound at one A.M.

This time it's only a few blocks away, but on the other side of Alamo, which makes a world of difference. I bet you're thinking: *But you said the streets are named for trees and flowers.* Well, *alamo* means "cottonwood." Belleville was settled by a group of priests, including one who was Spanish. The houses on the other side of Alamo are the grandest ones in town. The Stone family lived at the dead end of Iris; their land backs up to the river. The sirens keep going and going and I can't help myself. I sneak out my bedroom window. It's not something I've ever had to do, but I've practiced a couple of times, in case my life takes a turn and I become the kind of girl who sneaks out of windows at night and goes to meet other kids. Wendi does that. Tara did, too, as everybody found out. I bet even Becca Stone did it.

I follow the sounds and the smells and the lights and find myself standing across the street from Tara's old house at the corner of Iris and Oak. She's out front, alone, hugging her arms as if it were cold. But the night is warm, and the fire makes it warmer still. *Step back, step back*, the firemen say. I've never seen someone fight a fire before. It's amazing how fire moves, how quick it is. I watch a flame race up a tree. "It's going to jump, it's going to jump," someone shouts, and the firefighters aim their hoses at the house next door, trying to wet it down. The paint is bubbling on the place next door, and the windows give way from the pressure. I feel bad for the people there, but the fire is strangely beautiful. There are people in town who say they want to end the bonfire, in part because it's dangerous, especially after this summer of drought. They say it's irresponsible, bad for the environment. But it's a tradition; it's what we do in Belleville. Traditions are important.

"I'm sorry," I say to Tara.

"No, you're not," she says. "I'm not, either. It's not as if my family were ever coming back here, you know. And they can't sell it. Whoever did this did them a kindness."

"But where will you stay now?"

"With you?"

"Our house is pretty small, only two bedrooms, and my mom—"

She laughs in my face. "As if I would ever live with you, Beth. You know the house was empty, that I've been staying somewhere else. Is it true your real name is Bethesda, that your mom saw it somewhere and thought it was pretty?"

"It is pretty."

"Then why don't you use it? Why didn't you use it when reporters took your photograph and asked your name? Were you ashamed?"

"There's no talking to you," I say. "I said I was sorry, and you just turn it on me. You're the mean one. And you're named for a plantation, so who are you to talk?"

I walk home. Belleville is a safe place. A girl can walk home at three A.M. in Belleville, knowing nothing would ever happen here. And if it happened, it would be because of a stranger, someone passing through, one of those long-haul truckers. A long time ago, when I was eight or so, a magazine put us on the list of the ten best small towns in America. I never read the article, but I heard about it. Last fall, everyone kept saying that. "One of the best small towns in America in which to live . . ." Although they never mentioned that was ten years ago and Belleville never made the list again. But I guess we still are, despite what happened. Despite these fires. I bet it is heat lightning. That's the only explanation. Even at the pool. Lightning could have sparked the fire if the gas had been left on, right? And heat lightning must travel to the ground, and I don't believe Tara was a Girl Scout, much less that she knows how to rub two sticks together. She was the kind of girl who acted as if she needed protection from the silliest things—insects and dogs and puddles. Everyone remembers the story of how Daniel Stone lay down in a puddle—didn't just put his jacket on it, the way Sir Walter Raleigh supposedly did, but lay down in the puddle, and let Tara walk across him. Sir Walter Raleigh never did that, but Daniel Stone did, and half the school saw it. She traipsed across his back, giggling, acting as if it were her due.

The trees seemed to be whispering as I climbed back through the window. A breeze is kicking up. It never fails, no matter how the weather changes: Every August, before school, before Labor Day, a front moves through. It drops temperatures for just a few hours. The next day it's hot again. But it's not the same kind of hot. It's like someone has knocked summer down in a fight and it gets back up, but it's staggering, weaker. It's going to get knocked down again. Again and again and again, until it no longer gets up.

Then fall will come, my favorite season. In the fall, anything is possible. I'm going to buy some new clothes at Kohl's up in Dover. I might go all the way to Wilmington, or even Baltimore, to get my hair cut. I'm going to be a senior. It probably won't be as exciting as last year, but it might be. Last fall was the best fall of my life.

EVERYTHING BEGAN AT THE BONFIRE, the first one. The cool kids had a plan to go drinking afterward. I don't drink, so I couldn't have gone even if they asked me. But I love the bonfire. I stood at the far edge of the circle, listened to the speeches, watched the cheerleaders flip so close to the flames. Their shadows were huge. *We've got spirit, yes we do.* Tara, the lightest, was hurled to the top of the pyramid. She had entered school the winter before, but we still thought of her as the new girl because no one newer had come along. New people are rare in our high school. I guess most families wouldn't move when their kids were halfway through their junior year. Why did Tara's family move here? They said it was because they wanted a simpler life, as if Belleville was simpler than Philadelphia. Smaller, sure. But not simpler. Still, Tara would not shut up about how amazing Philadelphia was. God, how tired everyone got hearing Tara hold forth on Philly cheesesteaks, as if that skinny twig ever ate anything. You know how some people yell, "Eat a cheeseburger" at skinny girls? I always wanted to yell, "Eat a cheesesteak." I didn't, but it would have been funny if I had. I bet Daniel Stone would have laughed.

The crowd dispersed, the boys leading the way. Daniel didn't play football. He didn't have the build for it. He played lacrosse, which in some ways was a bigger deal, because our lacrosse players went on to good college teams and our football players almost never did. Tara and her friend Chelsey scampered after him. Scampered like puppies trying to keep up with a big dog.

"Where are we going?" I heard Tara ask.

"Stone Manor," Daniel said.

"Stoner Manor," put in his best friend, Charley Boyd.

They giggled. I heard them. They giggled.

Stone Manor was what Daniel called his sister's playhouse. It wasn't like any playhouse you've ever seen. For one thing, it was two stories, a replica of the Stone house, painted the same soft green color, the paint freshened every few years. The front door even had a lock, but it was never used. Most people in

Belleville don't lock the front doors to their houses—another detail that the reporters seized on. Did the Stones know what went on in the little house? They said they didn't, but I guess they did. Look, kids drink and get high. I mean, I don't, because of my mom, but it's not a big deal. Kids drink, and it's up to girls to police themselves. Sorry, but that's just how it is, even in a place like Belleville, where you can walk home at night without a worry. Tara was from Philadelphia, as she reminded us every day. She was smart. As she reminded us every day. She went to Becca Stone's playhouse with Chelsey and four boys. Do the math. What did you think was going to happen?

She knew. She knew.

And the video: What did it prove? For one thing, it proved it was only Daniel and Charley, not the other two boys, Wendi's Jordan and a guy named Bobby Wright. Nothing happened to Chelsey. No one forced Tara to drink all that punch. Sure, she looks groggy and out of it, but she doesn't say no. She never says no. It's weird that Charley filmed it, but—I know this sounds odd—it looks kind of romantic. The bed even had a canopy, and Daniel whispered in Tara's ear as he moved on top of her, slow and careful. "Are you okay?" he says over and over. "Are you okay?" He cared about her. I mean, he wasn't in love with her, and that's probably why she got mad, but in that moment it looked like he was being real sweet.

And it was only after everyone started sharing the video that Tara filed charges. Said she didn't remember. How could she not remember? Her eyes were open; she was with Daniel

Stone. I'd remember every minute. She said Charley raped her, too, but there's no video of that. Conveniently. She's just a slut. And that's why I wore the T-shirt to the second bonfire, the one where we stood up for Daniel and Charley and our town, Belleville. My T-shirt said:

SKANKVILLE
population: 1

The letters were white. Red and white are the school colors. Go Cardinals! There was a photo of Tara under the letters. And for once, I didn't stand at the edge of the circle around the bonfire. I went straight up to it. I led the cheer. *Slut, slut, slut, slut . . .* And everyone yelled with me. I can't imagine it feels any better, flying to the top of a pyramid.

The Wilmington paper ran my photo. It went everywhere. People around the world saw me. Some people said I was angry in the photo, but I wasn't angry. I was righteous. Our town, our boys. That's what the signs said. We love our town. We love our boys.

On the internet, people wrote some nasty things about me under that photo. I learned to stop reading those comments, though. And while I'm on Facebook, I keep it tight, just my real friends or Candy Crush, so I didn't see the things people said there. Daniel Stone told me personally that he was grateful for my support. He said it just that way: "I'm so grateful for your support. That girl tried to ruin my life."

And Charley's, too, I guess, but he complicated every-thing by agreeing he had done it. But, again, it wasn't what you think. The police told him he could be put in jail because he was eighteen—he has a late-summer birthday, his parents held him back a year so he'd be more competitive at football—and Tara was only sixteen, but that wasn't even true. They put him in a room by himself and said all sorts of things that weren't true, that Daniel was blaming him, said it was his idea, that he was having consensual sex with Tara but Charley sneaked up on them, taking that video with his phone, then said he deserved a turn. Later, Daniel told Charley that not a word of it was true. Who knows what really happened? Tara had no bruises, no marks. They couldn't do a rape kit, because she didn't even tell anyone for almost a week. She looks fine in the video. If she threw up and they carried her home, left her in her yard, well—they did ring the bell. They thought her parents were there. She had sneaked out before, several times. How could they know her parents had gone away for the weekend, that she wouldn't be found until the morning? She just made up that story to keep from getting in more trouble with her parents.

"Don't drink around boys," my mom told me. "You'll get what you deserve." This whole thing upset her. My mom is third-generation Belleville, used to lord it over my dad. We didn't like seeing our town in the news, seeing a good boy from its best family accused of a horrible crime. It's not that we don't understand date rape. We're not stupid or unsophisticated. We watch the same TV shows you do, go to the same movies. We have Facebook and smartphones and DVRs and computers and internet. Just because there's cornfields and Kiwanis barbecues and produce stands along the highway, just because you drive through at sixty-five miles an hour—the speed limit is fifty, by the way—with your windows up and your kayaks and your bicycles, you don't know us. You don't know anything about us. The Stones are good people. Their name is on the old theater and the scoreboard and the snack bar at the community pool, which hires mentally slow people and contributes its proceeds to the booster club. They own a grocery store and a seafood restaurant, and they're not the least bit stuck up. My mom would love to work for them instead of Happy Harry's, but chains are buying up everything now.

When my photo appeared in the Wilmington paper, it wasn't a big deal. I mean, it was on page one, and a lot of kids said, "Go, you," and not at all sarcastic. A week later it was online, in a newspaper all the way in London, England, and it said: THE FACE OF BELLEVILLE. Well, I'm not, but I would be proud to be that. And the part underneath, "A Town Unites in Hate Against Rape Victim," wasn't true. Because Tara wasn't raped. No charges were filed; her lawsuit was dropped because her parents got cold feet, and they went back to Philadelphia. What about Daniel? What about Charley? I imagine them this fall, off at school, saying their names, saying where they're from. She ruined their lives, or tried. And Charley's not much, but Daniel Stone is the nicest boy you'll ever meet. He lay down at her feet and let her walk across his back, and she says these things against him? *Slut* is kind, if you ask me. Girl gets caught having sex, says it wasn't her idea, puts it on the boy.

Sure, Tara, sure.

And now she's back. If she wanted to apologize, things would be different. But she's never going to admit she was wrong. Never.

The playhouse. The vacant lot where we held bonfires. The dumpster behind Langley's. The snack bar at the pool. And now the Greene house, which no one wanted to buy. I bet it's insured. I bet it's insured for a lot of money. "Jewish lightning," my mother says the next day. I had forgotten the Greene family was Jewish. Outsiders made a big deal out of that, but that didn't matter to us. And Tara got lots of extra holidays. I think she made half of them up. She was a liar, and that's what liars do: make things up.

I KNOW WHAT I HAVE to do, but I don't want to do it. I don't want to go to the cops, tell them about Tara. The mud on her sandals the night after the rain, the fire at the pool. How I saw her standing outside her own house when it went up in flames. If I go to them, I'm a snitch. Like her, only I'll be telling the truth.

Tara must know what's going through my mind, because she doesn't follow me home on Monday or Tuesday. Or maybe I start leaving just a few minutes earlier, now that Wendi's on time, since the pool closed down. But Wednesday, after I stop by the high school to make sure I'm not missing any major requirements, she's waiting for me at the edge of the lacrosse field, under the John and Adelaide Stone scoreboard, the one with the ad for Langley Seafood along the bottom.

Then she sees the state trooper's car, parked across the street, and she runs.

Two men get out. "Beth Ennis? Can we talk to you? Just a few questions. Can we talk to you?"

I look around. No one's there, no one will know if I talk to them. Tara might, but that's her problem, right? She was tagging after me, they saw her, she ran. They think I know something. But I don't. I can't know anything. I make up my mind that I'll talk to them but I won't volunteer anything. They teach you in kindergarten not to be a tattletale.

They take me to the state police barracks. In the car, on the way over, they ask me my age and I say eighteen. I guess they don't believe me, because I see them exchange a look and they ask for my actual birth date, like I can't do math. I turned eighteen two weeks ago. My mom had the option to hold me back, so she did, so I wouldn't be the smallest in the class. The thing is, I'm kinda the biggest. I hit six feet at age fourteen.

"My mom held me back," I tell them. "So I wouldn't be the smallest. I mean, the youngest. I was never the smallest. But it wasn't like it was with Charley Boyd's parents. They wanted him to have an advantage when he tried out for football. They call that redshirting—which is different from Redshirts, which is a *Star Trek* thing."

I read a lot of science fiction and fantasy. *Speculative fiction* is the better term, I think. Because fantasies are that *Shades of Grey* stuff, about love and sex. And science fiction sounds as if it's about science. When it's still about the people, you know? It's all what if. *What if?*

They ask me again for the year I was born and I tell them.

AT THE BARRACKS IN GEORGETOWN, they offer me anything I want from the vending machines—anything. I don't want to appear greedy, so I ask for a Diet 7Up and a bag of Utz crab chips. They're both really nice. Good cop, good cop. After all, I'm not a suspect. I'm just someone who knows things I wish I didn't know. The mud on Tara's sandals. Seeing her watching her own house burn. The thing she said about knowing how to make a fire from sticks. When I feel like I'm about to tell them something I shouldn't, I eat a big handful of chips, sip my soda. *The policeman is your friend. The policeman is your friend.* That old song comes back to me from kindergarten, back when I was normal size, right in the middle of the class when we lined up by height.

"You know the house that burned, right?" one asks me.

"Know of it, sir. I was never inside."

"And the playhouse? The snack bar?"

"Again, I know about those places, but they're not places I ever went."

"The vacant lot, the dumpster at Langley's."

They're not from Belleville. They need my help.

"Well, the vacant lot is where we have the bonfires in the

fall. For pep rallies. And, and, for other things. Langley's is a seafood restaurant. It's owned by the Stone family. Daniel worked as a waiter there, modest as you please. He didn't need to work. But his family has what my mom calls good values. They believe in work. Daniel waited tables there in the summer. They have a really good fried oyster sandwich. My mom and I went there for her birthday once. But it was March, so Daniel wasn't there."

"So," says one of them. They look so much alike, they might be twins. Tan suits, short dark hair. "If you think about it, every one of these fires is tied to the Stone family or the Greene family."

"Well, not the vacant lot, sir. Everyone in the high school went there."

"Still, it's interesting, don't you think?"

I don't. I really don't. But I'm out of chips and soda, and I don't know what to do with my hands. I tent my fingers, then put my palms flat on the table. They're really sweaty, and now my fingers have that crab dust on them from the chips.

"Sirs? There's something I probably should tell you. I don't want to, and I would appreciate if you didn't let it get out. That I told you. Because, while I plan to major in law enforcement at Del Tech, kids can be very cruel. They'll say I'm a snitch. I'm not. I'm the opposite. But Tara Greene is back in town. I've seen her. I don't know where she's staying, but I see her every day, almost. She was at the school just now. Did you see her? She ran away when she saw you. She walks home with me from the deli. And the day after the fire at the pool, there was mud on her sandals, and I saw her at the fire at her house. I don't know why she would burn down the snack bar, although I think she and Daniel first started flirting there"—Wendi told me that—"and I don't know why she would burn down her house, although her parents can't sell it; maybe she thought they would get insurance money—"

They interrupt and say: "You know, we probably should call your parents."

MY MOM IS GETTING READY to go to work, and she's pissed. But when she comes in, she says, "Let's make this quick."

I say, "Mom, I had to tell them. Tara did it. Tara started all those fires. And she's been following me around for weeks now. I didn't let her in the house, although she kept asking to come in. I don't owe her anything."

The cops do that thing where they exchange a look, then leave. My mom, so old, so used up, so not the pretty schoolteacher with the convertible that needs a new tire, does something that she hasn't done since I was eight years old. She takes me in her arms, although she's so tiny it feels odd. It's like one of those birds who rides on the head of a hippo decided to give it a hug. Not that I'm that big, just that my mom is that small. By the time I was fourteen, when she had bad nights, I could pick her up and carry her, put her in the tub, put her to bed. I hated doing that, yet I miss it sometimes. She doesn't need me as much as she used to.

"Oh, Beth, oh Bethie, what have you done?"

"Nothing, Mom. I wasn't even sure until now that it was Tara. I—"

"Oh, baby," my mom says. "You know that Tara Greene's been dead since last May. Killed herself a week before graduation. She drove down here from Philadelphia and slit her wrists in that playhouse. You know that. Everyone in town knows that."

The cops come back in. I bet they were listening to us all along. It's one-way glass, usually, so they can see in, listen to what you say. Everyone knows that trick.

"But she set those fires," I say. "Sorry, but she did. I don't want to tattle, but I saw her, I saw her—"

"Beth," the one cop says, "we need to go through where you were. Every night there was a fire, okay? Can you prove where you were?"

"She was home with me," Mom says.

"Are you sure, ma'am? Are you sure?"

I say, wanting to be truthful, wanting to keep Mom from looking like she's covering up for me: "I did go out the night of the fire at the Greenes' house. But only after I heard the sirens. That's how I know Tara was there. I went out my bedroom window. But I wouldn't go out to do anything bad. You know that, Mom. I would never do anything bad."

The two men in the tan suits look to my mom, who is crying now and rocking in her seat.

"Been working four to eleven since August 1," Mom says.

"The night shift. The fucking night shift. I don't even look in on her when I get home. She's always in her room with the door shut. At least—I thought she was in her room."

Poor Mom. I probably should call her sponsor tonight. It makes her so nervous when I'm at the center of things. She doesn't think I can handle it. That's why she had that bad night last fall. But I'm a hero, Mom. I'm proud. I'm righteous. I don't mind telling these police officers what Tara's been up to, if that's what I have to do. I'll help them catch her, too. That will be exciting, almost as exciting as last fall, when I was the face of Belleville.

PART 4

The chains of marriage are so heavy that it
takes two to bear them, and sometimes three.

—*Alexandre Dumas*

WACO 1982

They called them black beans, although no one in the *Waco Times* newsroom could explain the origin of the term. They were just "Lou's Black Beans," dreaded equally by one and all. They appeared in the form of memos typed on scanner paper, the coded sheets that were threaded through IBM Selectrics when there were not enough computers to go around—and there were never enough computers, not in the crunch of afternoon deadline, not when one was the low woman on the totem pole. Forced to use a typewriter to file her copy, Marissa belonged to one of the last generation of journalists to type *-30-* to denote the end, but of course she could not know this in the summer of 1982. She also couldn't know that she would give up on newspapers by year's end, although the briefness of her tenure would not keep her from bragging, many years in the future, that she had once typed her copy and put *-30-* at the end.

Black beans arrived in one's mailbox cubby, innocuous slips of paper until unfolded. Then they became the black plague. Death to advancement, death to career, death to ambition.

*Marissa, Go down to the park and write up a little
something on the groundbreaking ceremony for the new
public restrooms (no big deal). Best, Lou*

*Marissa, There's a program over at Baylor for young
entrepreneurs, in which kiddos learn the ins and outs of
business. But please—don't give us a lot of cute stories
about kids. Focus on the business basics. Best, Lou*

*Marissa, Where does navel lint come from? And why do I
have so much of it? Best, Lou*

The last one never happened. But it could, it might. Marissa came to believe that she would spend an eternity chasing down every idle thought that rolled through the mind of Lou Baker lonely as a tumbleweed, something Marissa had believed she would find in Waco, Texas, knowing very little about the state's topography before she arrived there for a job interview on a sweltering April day. She feared that she would spend the rest of her life in Waco, Texas, because she had graduated in the middle of a recession and all the good newspapers insisted that applicants have at least five years experience and she was never, ever going to have five years experience.

Marissa was twenty-one years old.

The day she turned twenty-two, in late August, she found another black bean in her mailbox:

Marissa, Wouldn't it be interesting, as summer comes to an end, to find out what is in the various lost-and-found boxes at motels, restaurants, the Texas Rangers Hall of Fame, et cetera? Best, Lou

No, she thought reflexively, as if the question were not rhetorical.

She made a dutiful effort to shoot it down. First rule of a Lou Baker Black Bean: Shoot it down. She called the motels. Mostly clothing. She called the restaurants. Clothing, a pair of binoculars. She called the Texas Rangers Hall of Fame and they seemed strangely proud of having nothing—nothing!—in the lost and found, as if part of being a Texas Ranger was making sure that a person was never, ever separated from a beloved hat, fanny pack, or billfold.

But when she dutifully reported back to Lou that there really didn't seem to be much in the various lost and founds, the city editor asked for a list of the places she had called and scanned it with a puckered frown.

"I don't see the Waco Inn on here," Lou said.

That place. "I thought you wanted me to focus on the tourist destinations, along the interstate. The Waco Inn is pretty far off the beaten track."

"But Tatum Buford, who owns the Waco Inn, was the person who gave me this idea. At the Rotary Club luncheon. He said, 'Wouldn't it be interesting if someone looked to see what was in the local lost and founds at summer's end? I think it would be.'"

"Oh, it was a great idea in concept. But sometimes even good ideas don't pan out."

"Sure, if you just sit at your desk, making phone calls. You should go and ask to see the contents. Feet on the street, Marissa, feet on the street." It was one of Lou's favorite expressions, as mysterious in origin as the black beans.

"At every motel?"

"At every motel."

"What if they won't show me?"

"They have to, by law. Freedom of speech. Look, don't forget the five *W*'s—they work, Marissa. You know what they say—no stupid questions!"

Marissa was pretty sure that the First Amendment did not apply in this situation and that there were plenty of stupid questions. But she resigned herself to spending a day or two visiting every motel in Waco and asking to see the lost-and-found boxes.

Lou tottered off, smoothing her too-tight skirt down over her hips. Lou was Louisa Busbee Baker, the first female city editor at the Waco paper. She had worked there her entire career, as she frequently reminded Marissa, starting in 1967 as a clerk in the features section—it was called Brazos Living, after the river that ran through town. She had moved up from taking paid wedding announcements to reporter, then to editor of Brazos Living and, for five years now, city editor. She was the only woman in management on the news side, a fact she frequently referenced. "As the only woman . . ." She favored tight skirts and high heels, although she always seemed uncertain in the latter. The general impression was of someone who used to be a knockout and didn't realize that her knockout days were behind her. Lou was, by Marissa's calculations, at least thirty-eight.

Marissa started on the interstate frontage road, where the motels were close together and she could cover a lot of ground. She had already interviewed clerks at almost every one, but no one seemed to remember her or the conversation, so she had to go through her spiel all over again. Perhaps they were as bored as she was on this despairingly hot August day. At any rate, they either brought out the box of left-behind clothing immediately or asked the manager for permission to do so, in which case the manager, also bored, did the honors.

The boxes themselves were remarkably the same from motel to motel, almost as if they had a single supplier or there were state regulations stipulating what could be used as a lost-and-found box at a motel. Plain cardboard, beginning to sag and soften in that way that cardboard does over time.

The contents, too, were similar. Clothes and more clothes, an occasional paperback, usually a romance.

The young clerk at the Motel 6 said: "Off the record?"

Marissa thought that hilarious. *Off the record.* As if this were Watergate, which was part of the reason she was a journalist. It was the reason that almost everyone in her generation had become a journalist. *Follow the money, bring down a president.* That's what she should be doing, not staring into a cardboard box of dirty clothes.

"Sure."

"You're not going to find anything good."

Tell me something I don't know. "That's what I've been trying to explain to my boss. She seems to think I'm going to find, like, bowling balls or a live alligator if I ask the right questions."

"No, I mean—the valuable stuff, jewelry and the like, it's not going to be in the lost and found, not for long. It may never even get to the box. The maids get first crack and you can't blame them for taking what they find. People are pigs. The nicest-looking people will do things you can't believe to a motel room." Actually, Marissa could believe it. "But even if someone does do the right thing and brings an item in, the boss lets them keep it if no one calls within a week. That's why it's all crap clothes and pantyhose. No one wants this stuff, not even the people who once owned it."

Marissa wondered if there was a story in this. *Rampant thievery at Waco motels.* But given that Lou had gotten this hot tip from a motel guy at the Rotary Club, that idea probably wouldn't be met with much favor.

Lou got most of her ideas from lunches and associates and neighbors. She didn't seem to have a life outside the paper. She didn't seem to read the paper, either, and often assigned stories that had already been published. On the rare occasions she had ideas of her own, it was because she had been jostled by a pothole or seen a billboard on the way to work. Many of Lou's Black Beans began: *Saw a sign on the way to work today, which got me to thinking . . .*

The most frequent supplier of Lou's ideas, if one could call them ideas, was the man who owned the Mexican restaurant on the traffic circle, where Lou went every Friday and had the taco salad with exactly one frozen margarita. She was very proud of that frozen margarita, which is why her staff knew about it. She seemed to think it signaled a wild streak, a *Front Page / His Girl Friday* type of devil-may-care shenanigans. Drinking! At lunch! But the frozen margarita at that restaurant was about as potent as a Slurpee.

The young reporters liked to drink beer and shots at a bar near the newspaper, a dive-y place called Pat's Idle Hour. Even as they sat there, drinking cheap beer and complaining about their bosses, they knew that one day they would enjoy telling people about Pat's Idle Hour, where the clientele ran to VA patients and the jukebox played Glenn Miller's "A String of Pearls." The young reporters were hyperconscious of the camp factor in their lives, the dives and the aptly named diners, the hilarious items at the flea market on the traffic circle, the bowling shirts and vintage dresses discovered at yard sales, although the elderly widows of Waco were surprisingly savvy about the value of their Depression-era china.

"She hates me," Marissa said that afternoon, as the young staffers closed out the week at Pat's Idle Hour, drinking the cheapest and best beers of their lives. To her horror, no one contradicted her.

"She doesn't have any reason to hate me," she tried again.

"Well," Beth said, "you *are* cute."

"So are you," Marissa said with automatic courtesy. Beth was cute. Cute was exactly what Beth was. She was the kind of girl who never lacked for a boyfriend. In fact, her boyfriends usually overlapped by a little. Marissa was attractive in a different way, sultry and exotic. Most of the men she met here thought she was Mexican, but she was a quarter Lebanese, from her mother's side.

"You're totally cute," she repeated to Beth for emphasis. "And so is Veronica. So how can that be the problem?"

"Hey—thanks," Veronica said, caught off guard by the compliment. She was a pretty girl, if slightly overweight and in need of better clothes.

The two guys in their group, John and Jonathan, wisely kept their own counsel.

"Lou doesn't have the intellectual discipline to hate more than one person. She has a favorite"—Beth indicated Jonathan, who, not being a girl, simply nodded, acknowledging the truth. "And she has an unfavorite. That's you, for now. But it will change. I think it's just her personality. Which is to say, her lack of personality. She doesn't know who she is, so she fixates on the person she envies. You're cute, you went to a really good college back east, you drive that amazing car that your parents gave you for graduation."

"That amazing car," Marissa reminded Beth, "doesn't have air-conditioning. Because my parents never thought I'd end up in Texas and neither did I. Especially not Waco, Texas, for god's sake. My parents thought I was going to Yale Law School, which I turned down to go into journalism."

John nodded. "Yes, we know. You went to Williams, you got into Yale, you have parents who will pay the full freight if you decide to abandon journalism and go to law school. We all know. And Lou knows. Lou knows that you have complete and utter disdain for the place that she has spent her entire adult life, since arriving at Baylor when she was eighteen. Lou grew up in Rosebud, Texas. Waco is the big city to her."

"We all want out," Marissa said. "Not a single person sitting here wants to work for this paper one more goddamn day than necessary."

"True," Jonathan said. "But the rest of us are a little more diplomatic about that fact."

Easy for Jonathan to be so lofty. The cop reporter, he had the best story of the summer so far, a suspected homicide, juicy by local standards. A Baylor coed had been found in a ditch off Robinson Road about a month ago. Although there were strange markings on her—the sheriff's office was being deliberately vague about just what they were—the cause of death had not yet been determined and was awaiting a more thorough autopsy down in Austin. But the death of a Baylor student was a big deal, under any circumstance, even a drunk-driving accident.

"That's so *unfair*," Marissa said, even as she hoped Jonathan was right about the source of her disfavor. Because she could change her attitude, if that was all Lou held against her. She could be kinder, sweeter. She could pretend wild enthusiasm for Lou's Black Beans. She could stop mentioning that she had given up Yale Law School for "all of this," waving her hand at the small newsroom, the town beyond. She had, come to think of it, said that more than once.

On Monday, newly energized, she attacked her list of remaining motels, the drives longer now that the motels were farther apart. By eleven A.M., her seat belt had left a wet stripe across her dress and her hair looked a wreck from driving with the windows open. It was the penultimate day of August and Lou wanted the story for next weekend, which would be Labor Day. Back at school, the days would already be pleasant, the nights verging on cool. Marissa had arrived in Waco with fifteen Fair Isle sweaters, sweaters that remained in boxes of mothballs. With only one motel to go by lunchtime, she decided to reward herself for her thoroughness with a coconut milkshake at the ironically named Health Camp, a burger place on the traffic circle. It wasn't far from Lou's beloved Mexican restaurant, but it was a Monday. Lou would never drink a frozen margarita on a Monday.

Marissa preferred her margaritas on the rocks, at a bar on the river that thought it was cool. She was having what her friends back home called a *Looking for Mr. Goodbar* phase, which made her something of a throwback, but then—Waco was something of a throwback. Her friends in Waco didn't know what she did on weekday nights after work. Beth, who had never been without a boyfriend, would have been shocked, Veronica worried, John and Jonathan tantalized. Besides, what could be safer than picking up men in Waco? The men that Marissa allowed to take her home for a night were, for the most part, wildly grateful. Almost every one said he wanted another "date," but she gave them fake names and numbers, cut them dead if she encountered them again. Her pickups were Baylor boys and cowboys and Rotarians. They made her feel sophisticated, in her vintage black sundress and high-heeled sandals, her sunglasses up on her head. It was a heady sensation for someone like Marissa, who until arriving in Waco had had sex with exactly two men, both long-term college boyfriends, the second of whom had broken her heart when he made it clear, rather late in the game, that he didn't want her to follow him to Columbia's j-school, or even to New York.

But it was surprisingly hard work, getting these men to take her home. Most of them had to get drunk first, really drunk. After the first encounter, Marissa decided never to get in a man's car again, that the drive was the real risk. She followed them to shitty off-campus apartments and depressing duplexes and apartments that looked like cheap motel rooms and sometimes actual motel rooms. "Are you on the Pill?" every single one asked, usually just seconds before, hovering above her. "Are you on the Pill?"

She was.

One man had not asked, had not said much of anything. He also needed the least persuasion, instructing her after one drink to follow him to a motel room. Once there, he posed her, he told her what to do, still using as few words as possible. She found herself doing whatever he wanted, and he wanted some unusual things. Of all the men she had been with, he was the one she would have liked to keep seeing. But no matter how many times she went to the bar along the river, he never showed up again.

He said his name was Charlie, but that wasn't how he signed the register when they pretended, for the benefit of the night clerk, to be newlyweds who had driven up I-35 from Nuevo Laredo.

Fortified by a coconut milkshake and an order of onion rings, Marissa headed to the last motel on her list, the Waco Inn. A dull panic began to set in as she drove, because she had now spent two days on this assignment and established only that she was right and Lou was wrong, which Lou would find particularly unforgivable.

At the Waco Inn, the manager showed her the usual collection of abandoned clothes, stained and torn and smelly items so awful that it was possible to imagine someone checking into a motel just to get rid of them.

"There's one more item, but the owner keeps it in his office safe."

"It must be valuable," Marissa said.

"Oh, it is. I'll ask Tatum if he wants to show it to you."

Ah, yes, Tatum, the Rotarian who had suggested the story to Lou, probably inspired by this very item, thinking it would bring publicity to his not-very-nice motel, whose customers were seldom tourists.

"I can't imagine someone leaving a beauty like this behind," Tatum said, lifting a black leather belt with a heavy silver-and-turquoise buckle from his safe. It was the first item of value that Marissa had seen in all her travels. Not to her taste, not at all, but clearly expensive.

"How long have you had it?"

"About four weeks."

"I'm surprised you haven't let someone on staff take it."

Marissa expected the owner to deny the practice of divvying up the lost-and-found spoils. Instead, he said: "No one on the staff has the initials CB."

She took the belt in her hands. It was the first time she had touched it, but not the first time it had touched her. She remembered it around her wrists, her throat, and, later, its brisk strokes on her back and ass, stinging but not hurting. "You are a very bad girl," the man she knew as Charlie told her in a low, strangely dispassionate voice. He didn't really hurt her. That was his gift. That was why she wanted to see him again. He knew how to take a girl right up to the edge, how to make sex scary, but not too scary. He had very dark hair and lots of it—on his head, on his forearms, on his muscled legs, on his chest, but not on his back. He had tightened that belt around her neck and she had let him, never the least bit tempted to tell him to stop, trusting him to anticipate the perfect moment. No, she couldn't be wrong. It was the same belt. But then—it was the same motel. Four weeks. It had been five weeks since Marissa had been here with him. Five weeks and five days. Five weeks and five days of going back to the bar by the river, but he was never there. She traced the initials on the buckle. CB.

"They call us the buckle on the Bible Belt." That's what one editor after the other said to Marissa the day she interviewed for the job at the *Waco Times*. The executive editor, the managing editor, the assistant managing editor, and, finally, Lou. They seemed to be warning her, or at least challenging her commitment. But Marissa needed a job and she had started the hunt late, given that she thought she would be at Columbia in the fall, getting a master's in journalism alongside her boyfriend, with whom she had worked on the college paper. But he didn't want her there. And Columbia didn't want her there, which was almost as hurtful. Marissa decided to get a real newspaper job, show her ex that she was ready to do what he was only *studying*.

"They call us the buckle on the Bible Belt, Marissa. A little sleepy for young people, but it's a great place to raise a family."

The male editors all had families. Only Lou, married to her high school sweetheart, did not. The gossip was that Lou had the steady job in her family, that her husband called himself a developer, but he was just a man with a lot of raw land south of town.

The Waco Inn's owner, Tatum Buford, father of this bastard black bean, reached for the buckle, but Marissa did not surrender it. "I'm surprised you didn't try to find the guest who left this behind."

"We did," Tatum said. "But he paid cash and the name in the register, it wasn't with these initials."

"And when did you say this was?" Marissa asked.

"Four weeks ago. Maybe three. But no more than a month."

Five weeks and five days. When he was done, he stood up and she watched from the bed as he dressed, fastening the buckle, tucking in his shirt. "See you around," he said, and she had taken those words to heart. She didn't care that he had ripped her dress under the armhole; the seams in old dresses gave way sometimes. She didn't care that he spoke so little. She didn't care if he was married, raising a family in this town that was so good for families. She assumed he was married. But she couldn't imagine why he didn't want her again. Had she been too compliant, too eager? Should she have fought more, pretended fear? If she could find him again, she'd do it however he wanted.

"You should let me photograph this for my story," Marissa told Tatum Buford.

"Shouldn't I pose with it? A photo of a belt is awful plain."

"Oh, yes. But we'll need a studio shot, too, and that has to be done at the office, with proper lighting."

"You'll bring it back? After it's photographed?"

"Of course," Marissa said.

She often made such blithe promises, only three months into what she thought would be her career. She promised to give back photographs, scrapbooks, any and all artifacts that were beloved by their owners, of no consequence to her. She promised to inquire how someone might buy a photograph once it was in the paper. Sometimes she did, and sometimes she didn't, but it never worried her. It was something she said in order to get what she wanted. That was what reporters did. They said whatever it took, to get what they wanted.

In this case, she knew she wouldn't bring the belt back. Because in this case, the man who owned the belt would call her and she would give it to him, face-to-face. *Face-to-face*.

"The silver has tarnished. You ought to shine it up for the photograph," the owner said.

"I will," Marissa said. "I will."

She took it back to the newspaper, excited to have found a way into the story she had been trying to kill. When Lou came out of the afternoon meeting, Marissa was waiting at her office door, a puppy dog who had finally learned to play fetch. *Here's the stick! Love me! Pet me! Say I'm your favorite!*

Lou looked at the belt and said, "Come on in."

Her office was small, windowless, without much in the way of personal touches, quite unlike the offices of her male colleagues, which were filled with evidence of the families that thrived in Waco. The young women who worked for Lou surmised that she believed she was not entitled to a private life, or even photographs of one. Lou had to prove, every day, that her head was in the game.

Lou turned the buckle over and over in her hand, while Marissa talked about how it was the only interesting thing she had uncovered, that it would be better to focus on the discovery of this one beautiful object, that the owner might come forward and then they would have another story.

"From the Waco Inn?" Lou asked. "And the belt's owner never called and the motel didn't call him?"

"No, he never called and there's been—some screwup. They're not sure who left it there. The maid forgot to write down the room number. Or she didn't turn it in right away. I'll have to check my notes on that one detail."

"And they couldn't match it to the initials in the register?"

"No, but it could be an heirloom. The man might not even have those initials."

"It's tarnished," Lou said, tapping it with a manicured finger.

It was. "I need to shine it, I guess."

"Yes, you do that."

Marissa did. She polished the belt, she polished her story and turned it in, structuring it like a mystery, a safe one, the kind of breathless tale that the Happy Hollisters might take on. The assistant city editor thought it was good, for what it was. But the story didn't run and it didn't run and it didn't run. September continued hot; it felt like summer to her. Suddenly it was October, which was hot, too. When she finally asked Lou when they were going to run her story, Lou said: "Oh, it doesn't feel timely anymore."

"What?"

"Summer's over. We don't have a hook."

"It's really not so much about the lost-and-found boxes, the end of summer, not anymore. It's about this beautiful belt left at a seedy motel, whether it will be reunited with the owner."

"The Waco Inn isn't seedy. It's just—fighting a tough location. Tatum's doing what he can to bring it along. He's even going to add a continental breakfast."

"Still, if we could reunite this buckle with its owner—"

"That's another thing. How are we going to evaluate the claims that come in? Any man with the initials CB could say he owned this and how would we prove he didn't? I don't know, Marissa, you did a good job, but I was wrong. It's not a story."

"What should I do with the belt?"

"Tell photo to send it back." But photo had lost the belt, as it turned out.

Unexpectedly, Marissa stopped being Lou's unfavorite about this time. The steady diet of black beans went to Veronica now, poor thing. Marissa even got to share a byline on Jonathan's story when the state police lab determined that the girl in the ditch had a blood alcohol level of .02, but death had been caused by strangulation. The rape kit had been ambiguous—evidence of sex, but not force.

One day, an almost autumnal Friday, Marissa had a hankering for taco salad and talked Beth into going to the Mexican place, despite knowing that Lou would be there with her one frozen margarita. Veronica, firmly entrenched as the unfavorite, wanted no part of the escapade, but Beth agreed. The taco salad was a good one, the bottom of the shell-bowl giving way at just the right moment, the perfect combination of crunch and moisture.

Lou was alone with her margarita and they waved at her warily, fearful she would summon them, but she didn't seem at all interested in their company. A few minutes later, a man joined her. A dark-haired man, very thick hair combed straight back from a widow's peak.

"Damn," Beth said, "I'd be the breadwinner, too, if I could go home to that. Even with that werewolf hair."

Marissa watched as Lou drank *three* margaritas that day, then led her husband out of the restaurant, giggling girlishly. She stopped by their table on the way out. Bumped it, actually with her hip, miscalculating how much space she took up.

"Girls, I don't think I've ever met my husband. I mean"—

another fit of giggles—"I don't think *y'all* have ever met my husband. Charlie, this is Beth and Ma— Ma—"

"Marissa," she supplied, staring at the man's midsection. At his belt.

"Weekenders due by two, girls, to make the bulldog," Lou said. "Hank is editing, though. I'm going to take the afternoon off. I don't feel so good."

She winked at them. Beth would regale the others for weeks about that wink, but Marissa never joined in the laughter.

Charlie Baker nodded at Marissa and Beth, courtly and regal. "You be good to my wife, girls. Treat her right. She's very precious to me."

Lou wobbled out of the restaurant, Charlie steady in her wake.

A few weeks later, a black bean appeared in Marissa's mailbox. *Marissa, Tatum Buford has done such a good job fixing up the Waco Inn. How about a little profile on him for the Sunday paper? Don't forget to mention the continental breakfast. Best, Lou.*

On her way to the Waco Inn, Marissa took a detour down Robinson Road, finding the spot where the Baylor girl's body had been dumped. The road, also known as US-Texas 77, eventually led to Rosebud, home of Lou Busbee Baker. And, by inference, her husband Charlie Baker, her high school sweetheart, a man who took girls to the Waco Inn and wrapped a belt around their necks until they told him to stop.

Maybe he didn't always stop.

Marissa turned around, but instead of driving to the Waco

Inn, she went to her apartment, a dowdy duplex full of second-hand furniture. She put everything she owned into her car, piled it in willy-nilly, and began driving north, then east. Five hours later, she called her notice in to the night assistant editor, Hank, from Texarkana, making sure she was on the Arkansas side of the line. She then called her parents in Philadelphia and said she wanted to start law school that January, if possible. And if she had to defer until next fall, then she wanted to work at her father's office, doing whatever she could to be useful.

She sat in her motel room, hugging her knees, shivering despite the chugging space heater beneath the window. *Follow the money.* Follow the belt buckle. A motel owner finds a belt with a distinctive buckle, one that he recognizes, evidence of nothing more than an indiscretion. He makes sure that an editor at the newspaper knows that he has it. But he couldn't know what had happened, why a man might leave a room in such haste that he would forget his belt. *And Lou can't know, either. Can she? The husband, reunited with his belt, forgiven by his wife, will be more careful in the future. Won't he? It was an accident. Wasn't it?* There are no stupid questions, Lou had told her.

But there are terrifying ones.

When Marissa checked out the next morning, she left some of her clothes behind. Not the ones she had been wearing the day before, but a vintage black sundress with a ripped seam and a pair of high-heeled sandals pulled from the trunk of her car at the last minute. She had no doubt that the items would end up in the lost and found. They belonged there, in a sagging cardboard box full of things that were torn and stained and shameful.

SLOW BURNER

Hi, it's Phil. New phone (who dis). I
got a second phone.

Pourquoi

Regular # for business, this # for
trying to bring you up to speed on
seminal films of the 1980s and '90s.
Welcome to the friend zone, matey.

Funny

No parking in the friend zone—
remember when I showed you
the movie Airplane! that time in
Santa Monica?

Yeah

Thrilled to be working with you
again. You are absolutely aces,
the best in the biz. Would have
been devastated if you didn't want
to work with me again but not

surprised. I'm really sorry I
crossed the line. Crossed the
streams, if you will.

?

Ghostbusters reference.

Loved the new one. Never saw
the old one

Opposite for me.

Misogynist

Hey!

JK

I'm in SF next month,
maybe dinner?

Lemme check calendar.

LIZ IS GATHERING THE LAUNDRY when the phone slides out
of Phil's khakis' pocket. It's a cheap basic model. It looks like
a toy, but why would Phil have a toy? Liz and Phil don't have
kids; they don't even have friends with kids.

She looks at the phone on the bathroom floor. What to do
with it? It seems natural, innocent even, definitely innocent, to
pick it up and manipulate its buttons until this single, solitary

text thread comes into view. Liz has found several lost phones on the sidewalks of Chicago, and she has always done her best to reunite them with their rightful owners. Liz is a goody-goody. She assumes Phil came upon someone's phone while walking their dog, then didn't follow through on returning it.

Only—Phil is the not-so-rightful owner, hiding behind a Utah area code. His correspondent—San Francisco area code—is a contractor, HW, who almost wrecked the Kelseys' marriage eighteen months ago. That was the code Phil used for her in his contacts, HW. A private joke, one Liz never sussed out.

And now Liz has a problem. She cannot put the phone back in Phil's pocket and then put his pants in the wash, because the phone will be destroyed and he will replace it with another phone, one he will safeguard more carefully.

Yet she also cannot ask Phil about the phone, much less the text. Because also eighteen months ago, she promised she would never spy on him again. It was an easy promise to make and keep because she believed they were happy and there would be no reason, going forward, to look at his phone, go through his computer.

She believed they were happy until the phone clattered to the bathroom floor.

It is early April in Chicago; jackets are still being worn. Coats, even. Phil left his denim jacket slung over the sofa when he came home last night, a habit of long standing, and headed out the door this morning in a heavier coat. He had to walk ten steps past the hall tree in the foyer to avoid hanging up his jacket, but he does that almost every day. He doesn't think that hanging up jackets is important. Liz does. She has tried every-thing to encourage Phil to hang up his jacket. Finally, at great expense—Phil's expense, to be fair, but he's in VC and she's a private-school teacher—she hired a carpenter to come to the house and restore the foyer that a previous owner had disman-tled.

Sometimes regression is a good thing. Their Bucktown house was built in the early twentieth century, it wasn't meant to have an open floor plan; Liz has spent much of their ten years here having the walls put *back*. One now enters a toasty ves-tibule with a mission bench, hooks for coats, cubbies for wet shoes, and an antique umbrella stand before passing through to the house. Phil sits on the mission bench and takes off his shoes, he puts his umbrella in the stand—then pushes open the heavy oak door with the stained glass window and throws his jacket on the sofa.

Liz puts the phone in the denim jacket's right breast pocket. Phil is a man who is forever losing keys, wallets, phones. (In approving profiles, this absentmindedness is deemed proof of his genius.) Clearly, he is not in the habit, not yet, of taking this second phone everywhere he goes. He won't remember that he left it in his khakis. All he will feel is relief at finding it.

Later that night, she notices him roaming, fidgeting, pick-ing up piles of magazines and newspapers, poking under the mission bench.

"Are you looking for something?" she asks.

"I thought I had left—my keys in my pocket."

"I hung your keys by the front door." There is a charming metal bracket by the front door with multiple hooks for keys. Phil never uses it.

"Oh." He continues to pace, poke, search. At some point, he must slide his hand into the pocket of his denim jacket, where his new friend waits for him. At any rate, he comes into the den, where Liz is reading, suddenly jovial and relaxed.

"Do you want to watch a movie?"

"Sure," she says, although she doesn't. She curls into his side on the sofa. He chooses *Ghostbusters*, the all-female reboot.

"How old were we when the original came out?"

"I was ten, you were nine." She has never minded being older than he is. It's only a year and Liz knows she looks good for her age.

She also knows the old saying that cautions men to remember, whenever they meet a beautiful woman, that somewhere, someone is tired of her.

Throughout the movie, Phil's fingers twitch, yearning for purchase, the feel of the new phone. *Who you gonna call? Who you gonna text?* He will write about this later. The movie, his memories of the original.

But she will not be part of the story.

You were right about Ghostbusters.
I love the original, but I think the
all-female reboot is better.

Yeah

I can't believe all the misogynist
crap it had to withstand. Not
to mention the racist stuff. You
were right. Sometimes, I'm so
embarrassed to be a man.

Love Kate McKinnon!

"NO BREAD FOR ME," PHIL says at dinner. "And no potatoes."

Dinner is roast chicken, with carrots and potatoes roasted in its pan juices, homemade cheddar biscuits, and a salad. It's a perfect meal for a blustery night. Phil eats only white meat chicken and preempts the salad course.

"Are you doing . . . keto?"

"Nothing that formal. Just cutting out bread, starches. They make me logy. And you know I'm never really off the clock because I'm working with people across time zones. London's six hours ahead, San Francisco is two hours behind. I have to keep a clear head. Been reading this book, *Grain Brain*. It's interesting."

"You used to say that all diets were frauds, that every eating plan was, at bottom, a gimmicky way to reduce caloric intake."

"And I still think that. But I also find my head is so much clearer now. Giving up alcohol helps, too." He takes a sip of La Croix.

Liz pours herself another glass of wine. It's a pinot noir, which pairs better with chicken than most white wines. There's no way she's going to give up alcohol right now.

> I ran five miles today.

Good 4 u

> Started again a few weeks ago. Gotta get fit. I'm an old man in a young man's game. Gotta keep up.

You're not old

> Says the 29-year-old who looks like she's 22. You can't imagine being old. But you know what? I can't imagine you being old, either. You will never be old.

;)

> Hey I had a meeting with Willoughby.

That creep

> Did I ever tell you how I came to know him? It's a funny story. Three years ago, I was in Seattle . . .

HE HAS LEFT THE PHONE in his jacket pocket, but the April day is mild, a classic Chicago tease, and his jacket is hanging in the vestibule. Liz hears a muffled ding when she comes in with their dog, Pugsley. She can't help herself. She slides the burner out of the pocket. It makes her sad, embarrassed for him, to see the inequity of the exchange—Phil's long, logorrheic style, the girl's terse replies that she only fitfully punctuates.

This is how it happened before, eighteen months ago. He became conscientious about food, exercise. He bought new clothes. Liz started snooping, found his love letters to HW, who clearly was keeping him at arm's length.

They went to counseling. Liz admitted all her flaws and then some. She had been cold, she had been resentful of the chasm between their worlds, the high-flying venture capital-ist and the high school English teacher. She saved her mar-riage.

Or so she thought.

It's me, HW, on a burner.

Why are you using a burner?

It's . . . fun. Like a secret club,
walkie talkies. Like that TV show
you're always talking about

The Wire

That's it

I can't believe you still
haven't watched it.
Everything OK at home?

J saw that you were texting me
again. It's easier if you don't pop up
on my screen.

We're just friends. It's no big deal.
But I get it. Liz's life—I feel like she
needs to stir up drama because
she doesn't really have that much
going on. She blows everything out
of proportion. Or she renovates.
And now that she's renovated
every room in our house, she's
buying art. She's bored.

Bummer

"MISS KELSEY?"

"Ms.," she corrects absentmindedly, her thoughts far from this classroom, her thoughts locked into the 2.8-inch display of a flip phone. "Mssssssss. Or Mrs. Kelsey. But not Miss."

"*Msssssss.* Kelsey—why was Zeus so awful?"

"Awful?"

"He's, like, you know, a rapist."

Liz has been teaching a Greek mythology unit every spring

for ten years now. She begins with Demeter and Persephone; Chicago Aprils make it easy to imagine a world where spring might never come again. It's a progressive school, verging on what her mother called hippie-dippy, and her students have always been quick to seize on the vagaries of the gods.

Since #MeToo, however, they are increasingly disturbed by how the gods behave. Hades is a kidnapper, plain and simple. Why should Persephone be punished for eating a few seeds? Why is Medusa punished for being raped? Why does Zeus force himself on unwilling women? (Liz has always encouraged that inquiry, teaching the Yeats poem, leaning hard on the word *terrified*.) To teenagers, the gods are like adults, taking themselves much too seriously, demanding respect they have not earned, changing the rules as it suits them while torturing the puny mortals in their care. The gods are hypocrites.

The students are not wrong.

"As a god," Liz says, "he believed himself entitled to what he wanted."

"Why does Hera put up with him?"

"There aren't a lot of choices for gods when it comes to marriage."

"She's his SISTER."

"Gods can't be married to mortals. Mortals can't even look at the gods in their authentic state. Remember what happened to the mother of Dionysius when she asked to see Zeus in his true raiment."

"Hera tricked her into asking that. Why does Hera go after the women? Why doesn't she kill Zeus?"

"Because he's immortal."

Phil is not a god, but he gathers money for ideas that might change the world. He does not force himself on young women, he does not take on disguises to seduce them, nor does he turn them into creatures to hide his dalliances from his wife of almost twenty years.

Phil's weakness—his Achilles' heel, Liz thinks—is that he cannot resist the delight of being new to someone, anyone. To tell the stories that Liz already knows, having lived through many of them.

> Did I ever tell you about the time
> that I realized I was sitting in front of
> David Foster Wallace at the theater?

Don't think so.

> It was in New York. A production
> of Lysistrata that had been a big
> hit at the Edinburgh Fringe Festival
> had been brought over. It was a
> hot ticket. They set it in the 1970s—
> the design, the look was borrowed
> from a satire of Marin County life
> called The Serial.

The podcast?

> No, not Serial. _The Serial_. It ran
> in a newspaper in San Francisco,

just like Tales of the City by
Armistead Maupin.

Gesundheit.

Funny. Anyway, they took the
humor really low. Scatological,
even. There was this running joke
about a woman with bulimia. It was
gross. Maybe it worked in Scotland,
but it was dying in New York. The
third or fourth time the character
fake vomited, the theater was dead
silent—and then this big, booming
laugh came from behind me. Turns
out David Foster Wallace loved a
good vomit joke.

IT WASN'T DAVID FOSTER WALLACE, Liz thinks, staring at the phone. *It was William Styron.* How could he confuse the two? Then she realizes—HW wouldn't be impressed by Styron, assuming she even knows who he was. But DFW is a writer her generation is more likely to revere. Phil is not only changing the story, he's tailoring it to make it more appealing to HW.

And, of course, no mention of Liz, who recognized William Styron, who chose the production. It was her thirtieth birthday weekend. She felt so old. She was so young.

She's surprised Phil even remembers *The Serial*, a book that was quite dear to her. As for *Tales of the City*—he never read the books, but he watched the television adaptation with her. He liked Laura Linney.

She closes the phone. They say eavesdroppers hear no good of themselves, but that's the point of eavesdropping. It's a form of espionage, a device, used by the Greeks and Shakespeare and daytime soap operas. The difference is that nowadays the device is done via device. A phone this time, his laptop last time. What will it be next time?

And there will be a next time, Liz realizes. She's not the only one in need of drama.

What's up?

Not much. Work. Life.

Same here. Work. Wife. Life.
Damn autocorrect.

Yes, last I checked, you don't have a wife, but you young people are so— what's the word—fluid. Or maybe J told you he's going to transition?

That's a weird thing to say.

If J didn't exist—would that change things?

For me? Of course

> And me? What would
> it mean for me?

We're friends remember

> We are. But things can change. I'm
> sorry if this lands on you unwanted.
> But things could change, if we both
> wanted them to change.

Don't cross the streams

LIZ FLICKS THROUGH HER PHONE, looking for a selfie taken on their trip to Barcelona last year. It's blurry, unflattering. A shadow mars half her face. (Bad foreshadowing, shadow! Too obvious. Too on the nose. THE SHADOW IS LITERALLY ON HER NOSE.) But she loves this photo of herself because she looks insanely happy.

Loved, she *loved* the photo, past tense. Now the photo is simply evidence of how dumb she was to believe herself happy. The trip to Barcelona had been a business trip for Phil, but also a celebration. They had survived the darkest days of their marriage. It hadn't been easy. Phil did not see how his emails to HW could count as a betrayal when there had been no sex. A kiss, yes, just one kiss, and they had agreed the next day it was a mistake and it would never happen again.

"Agreed?" Liz had said in counseling. "She basically stopped answering your emails after that time you kissed her."

But that had been a mistake, because it wounded his ego. It also reminded Phil that Liz had spied on him and he insisted that was as egregious as what he had done. He rejected the term *emotional affair*. His needs weren't being met at home; he should be praised for *not* cheating.

THAT WAS THE SUMMER OF 2017. The fall of 2017 brought #MeToo, but Phil had a clear conscience. He hadn't masturbated in front of anyone. He hadn't lured vulnerable young women into his hotel room and taken off his clothes, or dangled quid pro quo deals in front of them. He had fallen in love. He was Lancelot. Liz guesses that makes HW Guinevere and she's— Arthur? Funny, she doesn't feel like a king.

Then Phil's company began working with a start-up that desperately needed the exact service HW provides, an HR consultancy that helps tech man-boys behave like humans. She wanted the contract. If she didn't get it—well, who knows what might happen? Phil hadn't understood at the time that he had done anything wrong, given that she was no longer under contract when he started mooning after her. In fact, the kiss had occurred after a simple wrap-up dinner to commemorate the project's end. As a cheater, Phil was very ethical.

Now he gets it. *Now.* He understands that the patriarchy never sleeps, that he might have ceased to be HW's supervisor, but he still had power over her, which forced her to be polite about the kiss, which was awkward for her, as she, too, had a spouse. What could he do? He had to give her the contract or she could go public with his blunder.

By the time he told all this to Liz, he had, in fact, already given HW the contract.

"Well, here's another fine mess you've gotten us into," Liz said when Phil came clean. He didn't even recognize the reference, much less its significance. Their first real date had been to a Laurel and Hardy film festival.

Well, it was a very long time ago.

Good morning, what city are you
waking up in?

W-ville.

?????

I don't visit cities. I occupy a series
of interchangeable W hotel rooms.

If there was a city outside
your room, what would it be
called on a map.

Checking. All our instruments
agree: I am in London.

London! Oh, I have a great
restaurant suggestion. Wait—you
don't eat meat.

Nothing with a face.

But you can do Indian, right?
There's this amazing place in
Mayfair that I stumbled on a few
years ago. Hard to get a res, but
there's a communal table and a bar.

KNIGHTSBRIDGE, LIZ THINKS WHEN SHE reads this exchange. *It was in Knightsbridge, Phil. And I was the one who found it.*

Their therapist had a word for the stuck-in-second-gear nature of the emotional affair, but Liz has forgotten it. Besides, #MeToo has changed the emotional affair. Why is no one talking about this? People thrown together in work environments, so very very aware of the new rules, are probably more likely to have emotional affairs. Perpetual anticipation, as the Sondheim song warns us, is not good for the heart.

Liz used to love musicals. Lately not so much. They are too linear about love. People fall in, people fall out. Also rom-coms. Has anyone noticed how easily people jettison their partners in rom-coms? Liz has.

At any rate, she recognizes Burner Phil, as she thinks of him. It is a Phil she knew a very long time ago, when they first started dating—solicitous, eager to share, impress. Solicitous Phil wanted to recommend restaurants and books and obscure films. Solicitous Phil wanted to take you on adventures! "Let's get in the car," Solicitous Phil would say, "I've got a surprise."

They had been together ten years when Liz realized that

the whole point of Solicitous Phil's surprise quests was that he determined the agenda. They went where he wanted to go, ate what he wanted to eat. By casting his plans as surprises, he always got what he wanted. Heck, she made him go to that awful production of *Lysistrata* only because she yearned, on principle, to be the one who made the plan for once.

Still, she loves him. That's what rom-coms get right. Love isn't logical. Only in rom-coms, the two people seem mismatched, then find their antipathy is really their way of fighting their mad attraction to one another.

Whereas in real life, the mad attraction feels logical and then these rifts are exposed, yet you go on loving the other person anyway.

She loves Phil. That's the problem.

What's up? Who's up?

Me. My body's in California, but it
thinks it's still in London.

You do get around.

So ashamed of my
carbon footprint. :{

Oh, I'm sure you have the daintiest
of carbon footprints. In fact, I bet
there is a prince out there with a
glass slipper, trying to find whose

sooty sole it fits. Did I ever tell you
the story about when I was 7 and
I tried to bluff my way through a
paper on Cinderella by watching
Cinderfella? I just so hated to read
when I was kid . . .

NOW THIS IS PHIL'S STORY and Liz knows it well. It's a first-date story. Maybe second or third. Again, this is what happens when a relationship is stuck in the second gear of "friendship." Chug, chug, chug. Charm, charm, charm. Has he not noticed that HW never responds in kind? Her texts are short and to the point. Of course, she's younger, a millennial. Her generation grew up with texts. (Part of her TED Talk centered on an excruciating experience with AOL Instant Messenger, in which she claimed to have a terminal disease and traumatized her entire eighth-grade class.)

Phil is a Gen Xer. Like Liz. Not old enough to be HW's father. Just old enough to be her creepy uncle.

She almost feels sorry for him. Almost.

I'm going to be in SF next month.
Lunch? Dinner?

OK

Where do you want to go? Your
town, your pick—but I pay

No

It's a write-off for me. You're
my contractor.

I'll wear a tool belt

IT'S NOT SPYING TO READ something in plain sight, Liz tells
herself. It's normal, it's human nature, like walking down an
alley and stealing looks into lighted windows. Liz had been
strangely disappointed to find out that other people did this.
She thought she was the only one.

As a teen, Liz was a lonely, gawky girl, convinced of her
own unattractiveness despite the insistence of those around her
that she was lovely. Her mother was a great beauty, a fate Liz
wouldn't wish on anyone. Except, possibly, HW.

She met Phil junior year of college. She worked at the information desk in the student center. He bought a Friday *New York
Times*, sat down in a nearby easy chair and worked the crossword puzzle in forty-five minutes, then put it in front of her.

"What do you think of that?"

There's a line in a novel that haunts her. She can't remember the novel, she can't remember the exact line, and she wor-
ries that it's a bad novel, that she would be embarrassed to
have one of its lines stuck in her head for eternity. But the line
is about how everything that would come to characterize a
relationship, for better or worse, was there from the beginning. Liz wishes she had said to Phil: "I think I'm not your

mother." Or: "I think you must be very good at crossword puzzles." Maybe: "Have you mistaken me for your second-grade teacher?"

What she said was: "Wow—I can't even do Wednesdays by myself."

And because it was 1998, they went out for a beer and the next day they did the Saturday puzzle, in bed. He told her all his stories. She told hers. But they were young when they met and they ran out of stories quickly. So they made stories together. The hilarious mix-up in Merida. The Indian restaurant in Knightsbridge. The handsy tailor in Turkey who cupped Phil's balls when measuring him for a suit and said, when Phil objected: "But this is the most important part."

What they didn't make was a child. By the time they got serious about it, Liz was in her late thirties. Her body wouldn't make a baby and Phil started the new company and adoption was hard and he met HW and who needs a baby when a twenty-seven-year-old wunderkind is batting her baby blues at you, explaining to you that your "tech type" wasn't just a random collection of tics and social inadequacies but the very heart and soul of your success.

Really, what kind of man-boy brandishes his crossword puzzle at a stranger and demands her attention? The one that Liz married, the one that Liz loves, the one that is stuck in this permanent not-quite-a-betrayal-but-definitely-a-humiliation loop. How will they ever get out? How does this end?

But Liz knows the answer to that question. It's never going

to end. He needs to be new and that's the one thing he can never be with Liz.

> What happened? I was so worried
> about you when you didn't show and
> then I got the message at my hotel.

Sorry! I lost the phone! And then
J surprised me with a reservation
at our favorite place and what
could I do? I totally spaced that it
was our anniversary.

> Freudian slip?

No one wears slips anymore.
Freudian camisole, maybe.

> But you have it now?

OBVIOUSLY. ;)

> Glad you're safe. I was just
> disappointed. Was looking forward
> to seeing your face.

It's aging rapidly.

> Don't be silly.

I spend $175 on face cream.

Again, don't be silly. Anyway, I'll
be back in San Francisco next
month, staying at my usual place.
We can try again.

Can't wait.

OH, PHIL. YOU'RE BEING PLAYED. *Can't you see?* But Liz knows he cannot, that men have no understanding of the subtle ways in which women keep them on hold forever.

When Phil is home in Chicago, he's careful with the burner phone, keeping it in his desk. Sometimes she notices him absentmindedly stroking the desk while he's talking to her. It's really the phone he's in love with, not HW. He's in love with the idea of love, he's in love with this eternally puerile game. His texts might as well read: *Do you like me? Yes. No. As a friend.*

There should be a fourth alternative: *You're just another horndog man I tolerate for my job but if you want to think this is mutual, go for it.*

So the project is coming to an end.

There will be more.

Yes, but—I don't think there
should be.

Why not? I love working with you.

Maybe too much.

What?

The minute I got this burner—we
both know this isn't right.

We're FRIENDS.

Right. Friends who hide our
friendship from our spouses.

I don't. Liz knows everything
now. EVERYTHING

Srsly?

Srsly

But that doesn't make it right. This
is not right.

LIZ BREATHES IN SO SHARPLY it feels like a little knife in her
diaphragm. *This is not true, this is not true.* Phil has said nothing
of the sort to her.

But even after this exchange, she is not prepared when Phil
announces he wants a divorce.

He doesn't ask right away. There are several days of stormy
moods, blowups over nothing. He's still texting, but no replies
are coming back, Liz is sure of it. You wouldn't need access to a
phone to know that. All communication has ended. He has been
cut off. He has been used. Liz has been waiting for this day to

come. She assumed he would be happy to run back to the safe haven of their marriage, to the woman who has always stood by him, no matter how much he humiliates her.

Only Phil doesn't know that, does he? He really believes Liz knows nothing, believes she has given up spying. And she can't tell him what she knows unless she's willing to tell him *how* she knows, and that's unthinkable. She has to keep the moral high ground. Especially now that he's saying he wants to end their marriage.

Of all the scenarios she imagined, she never thought that he would see this as a sign that he needed to leave her. Had HW really made him that happy?

"I know—" she begins that night at bedtime, then stops. What does she know?

> This isn't about you, but—I'm definitely leaving Liz.

[A day later]

> Did you really give up the burner?
> Or are you just ignoring me?

[Eight hours later]

> Do you talk to other people
> on this burner? Do you have
> other burners?

[A day later]

Dammit, HW, I'm going to call you
on your other phone.

Please don't.

Are you seeing these messages?

Yes.

Ok.

I don't know what to say.

My marriage has been over for a
long time. Again, this has nothing
to do with you.

I'm married.

I know.

I'm happy.

If you say so. Clearly some need
was going unfulfilled.

Still be open to working with you.

Of course. We're friends.

Yes, we're friends.

> I wouldn't want to make
> you uncomfortable.

You never do.

> So many shitty men out there.

You're telling me.

THEY GO BACK TO THERAPY. Liz literally doesn't know what to say. She has been spying on Phil for so long, it's hard to remember what she might know and what she can't know. She isn't temperamentally suited to this level of deception. By nature, she is an honest person. Whereas Phil has always been in favor of the judicious lie, the lies people tell while rationalizing that they are sparing someone else's feelings. Living with Phil is like the old riddle about the island with the one—oh dear, that riddle has aged badly. Say, the island with a Native American who always tells the truth and one who always lies and you have only one question to figure out which is which.

(What is the question? Are they brothers? Do you ask, "Does your brother tell the truth?" No, that's not it because both of them would say no.)

So she says to the therapist, "He seems very distracted to me. Since last spring." It's summer now. She has too much free time. She exercises more, she gets a new haircut.

Phil says: "She's so cold. All I want is love and affection. When I walk through the door, I feel as if I'm just a giant inconvenience."

"He travels a lot."

"For my job."

"You don't have to travel that much."

"You could travel with me."

"I have a job."

"You don't have to have a job."

Without a job, who would she be, what would she do? There's nothing left to renovate, not in the house, not on herself.

Hi

Hi

How are you?

Fine. How's therapy going

Ok. I guess I owe it to her.

To yourself, too.

Thanks. You're a good friend.

We're better as friends,
don't you think?

Shrug

I'm happy with J

What changed?

I was taking him for granted. If you
really love someone, embers are
always there

           I feel that I'm taken for granted.
           She doesn't even have a real job!
           Our lifestyle, our house—she just
                    takes that as her due.

Maybe she feels taken for granted?

           Maybe. Hey did I ever tell you the
           story about the time my father
           tried to teach me how to score a
                  baseball game?

IT'S A FUNNY STORY, YET a sad one, too. Liz knows it well.

They had been together for three months. She and Phil were
in bed in her room in the apartment she shared with three other
girls. Her room was the largest, but it wasn't well-insulated. That
was the trade-off. Huddled beneath two blankets and a quilt for
warmth, they began telling new kinds of stories, the tragic stories that people think define them when they are young. She
talked about her father, a serial cheater who was forever sneak-
ing out to meet up with other women. "The Dark End of the
Street," Phil warbled mournfully. She had never heard the song
before.

Then Phil told her about *his* father, who did the fatherly

things, but never in quite the right way. The day he tried to teach Phil how to score a baseball game he ended up screaming at him, calling him a moron.

She did the thing women were never supposed to do: she said "I love you" first. And he did the thing that nineteen-year-old men were not supposed to do three months into a college romance: he asked her to marry him. They were engaged for eighteen months, married a week after their graduation.

And now here is Phil's familiar story, text box after text box, with barely a comment back. Her husband is preening for this other woman, strutting with his feathers in full view.

According to the Greeks, the peacock owes its appearance to adultery. Hera asked the watchman, Argus with his one hundred eyes, to keep guard over a white cow, one of Zeus's loves that he had tried to disguise from Hera's wrath. It was Zeus's solution to send a disguised Hermes to Argus. He talked and talked and talked until finally all one hundred of Argus's eyes closed.

And Hermes killed him.

Argus's eyes were added to the peacock's tail. And what became of Zeus's love? Hera sent stinging flies to torture her, until she ran all the way to Egypt and regained human form, one of the happier endings for a lover of Zeus.

Liz loves Phil. She loves him so much that it hurts, watching him make a fool of himself over this young woman, who clearly has no interest in him. How can someone not love you when you love him this much?

She and Phil have the exact same problem, but she can never tell him that.

I'm going to be in SF again
at month's end.

Oh

Dinner?

I don't know

We're friends. Friends
have dinner, right?

No one has dinner anymore except
Insta influencers.

Funny

[curtsy]

No, seriously, can we have dinner?

Where are you staying?

Fairmont

Nice. Old school, but nice.

I'm old school. But nice.

<g>

So dinner?

Date?

NOT a date! DINNER.

Haha You know what I mean.

Oct 30.

That works. J will be in Shanghai.

If he were here, would you tell him
you were meeting me?

Does Liz know you're still
talking to me?

We're separated as of last week.

Oh

Not that it's relevant to you.

I don't know what to say.

I'm going to be happy. This has
nothing to do with you. I deserve
to be happy.

You do. Everyone does.

THEY ARE NOT SEPARATED. HE floated the idea of a trial separation at their last counseling session. Liz refused to discuss it. The only way to save a marriage, she believes, is to stay and fight. Once Phil is out the door, he will never be back.

But he also will never stop straying. She knows that now. And she is no Hera. She cannot send stinging flies after the poor girl trapped inside the white cow. It's not this girl's fault and it won't be the next girl's fault.

HE WHISTLES AS HE PACKS for San Francisco. Liz realized long ago, the first time, that he is kindest to her when he believes his relationship with HW is going well. He must think that she is going to leave her husband for him, despite the denials. Phil has always gotten what he wanted. A short man, boyish and charming, he has a big personality. He's irresistible. It's only a matter of time before he gets what he wants.

He whistles and packs, packs and whistles. The blue Thomas Pink shirt Liz gave him for his last birthday, the handmade Italian shoes. Of course, his money really paid for those gifts. He owns everything.

It seems to Liz that he's packing a lot for a two-day trip to San Francisco.

Let's have dinner in your room.

Really?

For discretion's sake. It's a small
town in its way. People know me.

Whereas I'm nothing but a face in
the crowd.

Text me your room #

I promise I'll behave.

What if I don't want you to?

Can you be here by 7:30?

Leave the door unlocked so I can
slip in. I don't want anyone to see
me knocking on someone's hotel
room door.

Dark End of the Street.

What

An old song. I'll play it for you.

WINTER COMES EARLY TO CHICAGO that year, with measurable snowfall the second week of November. Still, Liz likes to walk after dark, no matter how cold it is, and Pugsley is happy for the extra exercise. She walks and walks and walks and the neighbors who recognize her give her space, respect her need for solitude.

Besides, no one knows what to say to a widow, especially such a young widow in these circumstances.

Once upon a time, the story of Phil Kelsey's death might have been kept to the circumspect old-school media coverage. PROMINENT CHICAGO INVESTOR KILLED IN HOTEL ROBBERY. And those were the facts. He was a prominent man, a rich man. Someone had entered a hotel room—no sign of forced entry—and shot him as he showered, leaving with his wallet and his watch.

The internet, however, was not so polite, was happy to gossip. The flirtation between PK and HW was well-known in the incestuous world of tech; she had confided in her friends, after #MeToo made the news, how confused she was by his attentions. Yet she had chosen to go back to work for him. Friends said he had promised her he would be professional and, for the most part, he was.

Phil's phone, the second phone, told a different story. Although he had been diligent about deleting all the texts from HW within a day or two, nothing ever really disappears. There it was, the story of their communication, the plan to meet. She denied it all, professed amazement, and her husband stood by her, in a fashion.

Still, despite what her texts claimed, her husband was not in Shanghai, had never been in Shanghai. He had returned the night before from Seattle; they had been at dinner together when Phil Kelsey was shot.

A door was left unlocked. A man with a gun walked through it. Or maybe a woman with a gun. A watch and a wallet were taken, two phones had been left behind with tantalizing clues, but it was just gossip.

As for Liz Kelsey, the sad cuckquean—the female term for cuckold, seldom used, perhaps because it's simply part of the female condition—had been at a school event two thousand miles away, a showcase for students' artwork. One of her students from last year had, at Liz's suggestion, done a series of pastel profiles of the collateral damage of Zeus's infidelity. Io and Argus and Echo and Callisto and Leto—it was quite a gallery.

Deep in her down coat's right-hand pocket, a phone vibrates.

"It is time to discuss your invoice."

"Of course. And you will invoice me for—"

"Item #2728. It's an oil painting from the midcentury. Unsigned, but in the style of a mid-Atlantic artist whose bigger canvases have gone for as much as $250,000. He's back in vogue because he was featured on some movie star's Instagram account. All you have to do is hit the 'Buy Now' button. You won't be able to use a charge card, but we're set up to take bank transfers. In a few weeks, you will receive the painting. It's a very pleasant landscape. We do recommend hanging the work. And don't try to resell it or insure it."

"May I ask—where did you get the painting?"

"We scout flea markets and garage sales for items that could credibly be of value. The young woman who finds them for us assumes it's a simple art scam."

He is assuring her, Liz realizes, how few people know just what, exactly, Vintage Works LLC sells to its customers, those canny art lovers who are enterprising enough to enter the underworld of the dark web to find what they really need.

She has reached the Chicago River. "It runs backward, you know," Phil had told her on one of their early dates, and she hadn't known and she had been so impressed. As students at Northwestern, she and Phil had loved coming downtown. They felt so grown-up, with their fake IDs and true love. And when they actually could afford to buy their dream house, that had been more amazing still. It was their forever town, where the river ran backward but they were going forward, forever forward even as Liz took their new house backward, to what it used to be. *Chicago, Chicago. I saw a man, he danced with his wife.*

"Well, goodbye," she says.

"Pleasure doing business with you."

She has been speaking to her "art dealer" on a flip phone that is the exact same model as Phil's burner. There will be no record, no proof that she is anything but the grieving widow she appears to be. And she is grieving, that part is true. That will always be true. Next week, $125,000 will go out of her bank account, but an oil painting believed to be by a somewhat fashionable midcentury painter will arrive at her home. She will hang it in Phil's office.

She pulls a second flip phone from her left coat pocket. This was her first burner, the one she obtained a few weeks after she found Phil's. She had, after all, promised not to spy on him. So she bought a burner phone and texted her husband, pretending to be the woman with whom he was infatuated. Then she watched her husband woo the other woman.

Eavesdroppers hear no good of themselves, fair enough. But did she also have to discover the high regard in which her husband held this other woman?

Liz was everyone in this story. Liz was Hera. She was Zeus, disguised as a swan. She was the swan. She was Io, driven mad by flies. But Zeus always came back to Hera in the end. Phil was adamant—on his flip phone, speaking to what he believed was another woman—that he was going to leave Liz.

Zeus and Hera, Hera and Zeus. How much damage they caused to everyone around them. Why, her student asked, did Hera hurt the women and not Zeus? Because Zeus is immortal, Liz said. Why does Hera take him back? Because gods must marry gods.

Phil was not a god. Neither is she. But, for a few months, she had seized their prerogatives. To spy, to fool, to lull.

To kill.

Liz throws the second phone in the river and walks home into the stinging rain.

JUST ONE MORE

Columbo

Drama—10 Seasons—TV-PG

A Los Angeles detective solves murder cases

They were watching a lot of television. Who wasn't, in the spring of 2020? Kelley and Tom watched Netflix and chilled; they caught up on those HBO bummers they had long ago pretended to watch when their coworkers brought them up. They enjoyed some truly corny sitcoms on Hulu that were not unlike the meals they prepared—old-fashioned, comforting, throwbacks, the TV equivalent of meatloaf and tuna casserole with potato chips.

Then they discovered that Peacock, a new streaming service, had all sixty-nine episodes of *Columbo*. Kelley's mother had loved *Columbo*, or maybe the actor playing him. At any rate, Kelley had some dimly happy memories of watching the show with her mother in the early 1990s. Kelley and Tom decided to watch them all, one every night, which would get them almost to July 1, when Tom was sure that the curve would be flattened and life would be, if not back to normal, back to normal-ish.

They made other goals, too, to fill the hours bestowed on them. Kelley vowed she would finally do something about their garden, perhaps with the help of her friend Amy, a landscape architect. It was okay to be outdoors with people; she and Amy were already taking Saturday hikes. Tom took up running— well, he ordered some shoes from Amazon and planned to start running when it wasn't so cold. He had wanted to buy a bike, but the local stores were so besieged with back orders that he was told it would be late summer before the model he liked could be delivered.

Sure, Kelley was putting on a little weight, but so was Tom, and yes, she was living in sweatpants while seldom working up a sweat. Still, they were intensely aware that they had many reasons to be grateful as they hunkered down during that strange, cold spring. They could both do their jobs from home, and their home, while modest, had enough room that each could have an office of sorts. Their decision not to have kids, which others had implied was selfish, now looked prescient, even righteous. The world was a shitshow, but they had each other and they were delighted to be reminded that this was more than enough. Together fifteen years, since they met in their junior year of college, married for ten. "You're lucky," Kelley's single friends liked to say, and that was *before* the stay-at-home advisory. She couldn't imagine what it must feel like to be single now.

Perhaps it was in that spirit of gratitude and smugness that she said to Tom one cold April night:

"I think we should sign up for a dating app."

He laughed.

"No, seriously."

They were in the den, where they now spent every evening together, on a new, velvety sofa that was long enough for Tom to spread out. His head was in her lap and she was rubbing it. Per the rules of the household, this meant she had control of the remote. She was wandering in what Tom called the lady thicket of cable, killing time until *Columbo* o'clock, which they had decided would be at nine thirty every night. But even though the rules allowed the person with the remote to choose whatever program she (or he) desired, Kelley was considerate, avoiding reality shows, which Tom detested. She settled on the last forty-five minutes of a rom-com, one of those where two mismatched people somehow disentangled themselves from their old relationships with surprising ease. Inevitably, every commercial break was full of ads for dating apps, each one claiming superior scientific power.

"I'm quite serious."

"Why would we do something like that?"

"As an experiment. And a diversion. We would both join, then see if the service matches us. Just for grins."

"And what if it doesn't?"

"Of course it would," she said.

"Sounds like a waste of money. Time for *Columbo*."

Tonight's installment was "Lady in Waiting," in which a mousy millionairess murdered her domineering brother, who was trying to force her to break off her relationship with a man she loved. The act of homicide, which she staged so it looked like an accident, seemed to liberate her. She changed her clothes and her hair, became more assertive in the family business. Lieutenant Columbo and her boyfriend did not like this new version of the mousy millionairess. In some ways, it felt as if that was her true crime—not killing her brother, but becoming blunt and forceful in her opinions.

"I can't wait to get a haircut again," Kelley said, examining her split ends through her fingers.

"I like it long, actually."

Did she have long hair? But they had agreed to leave that discussion back in 2019. Sometimes the past was the past.

Blueprint for Murder: Columbo orders the excavation of a huge pylon, in search of a missing body, but finds nothing.

"My mom went to a summer camp where Forrest Tucker was sort of the patron. The main theater was named after him."

"And to think that I thought there was nothing new for us to learn about each other after fifteen years together. Where was this summer camp?"

Kelley realized she did not know. Her mother had been a nonstop talker, loud and charming, always "on." Kelley had assumed she would have a lifetime of asking her mother questions. "Somewhere in Wisconsin? She talked about it a lot. She even wanted me to go there."

"Why didn't you?"

"Musical theater camp? No thank you. I chose lacrosse camp, to her everlasting disappointment. That's how I ended up at Towson, remember? I had an athletic scholarship."

"Your mom was the best."

Also the worst, Kelley thought. She had adored her mother. But everything that made her fun and exciting—the spontaneity, her indifference to rules, her free-spirit persona—had also led to four husbands, bankruptcy, and her death, which was ruled an accidental overdose, but Kelley always wondered how accidental it was.

Forrest Tucker was the victim in this episode. But it was his ex-wife, not his current one, who was determined to prove he had been murdered when no body could be found. The ex-wife, who was named Goldie, made lots of references to "gold lamé" and was a remarkably good sport about the younger new wife.

"They seem so different," Kelley murmured. "And both should be able to do better than Forrest Tucker."

"Well," Tom said, "he's rich. That would have been a big draw back then."

"Women still go after men for their money, for your information. Or power."

"Is that why you chose me? Because I was willing to buy you whatever your heart desired at the Swallow at the Hollow?"

The Swallow was a dive bar with great mozzarella sticks. They still went there sometimes. It was like going on a double date with their younger selves. When would they go to a restaurant again? They could order delivery from the Swallow, but it wouldn't be the same. For one thing, mozzarella sticks never arrived hot. When would life be normal?

"That's why we're lucky," Kelley said, leaning into him. "We met when we were blank slates. Practically babies. Soon, we'll have spent more of our lives together than we have apart. But what if we met *now*? Do you think we would still choose each other?"

"Are we back to that stupid compatibility test?"

"I think it could be fun. And funny. It will match us, or it won't. It's something to *do*."

He nuzzled her neck. "Of course it would match us. The bigger question is, would we choose each other, once this highly scientific system paired us?"

"You're telling me that if you're matched with 'Kelley' from North Baltimore, you're not going to click or swipe or do whatever people do on dating apps?"

"I'm saying this would only be worth doing if you take the idea a little further. Use fake names, fake photos. Nothing that automatically identifies us. We have to be us, but with slightly different histories."

It was an alluring idea. It was an alarming idea. How did her husband know so much about dating apps?

"So I have to create a new bio for myself? Am I the me I am now, or the one you met in our college economics class?"

"Ground rules," Tom said, taking the remote and pausing the episode. "We are who we are now, but we can alter our ages slightly. Or not. Let's say we can go three years in either direction. We use generic photos from the internet, people we judge to be of equal attractiveness to us, but not identical to us. We fudge facts, but we are truthful about who we are, what we want, our values. Like, not wanting to have kids, for example. Or our politics."

"You warmed to this idea quickly," Kelley said.

"We would need safe words, too—once we're sure we're talking to one another, we'll invoke them. And we'll live happily ever after. Again."

He kissed her neck again, reached under her hoodie and found the place at the center of her back where she loved to be lightly scratched. The bra-strap place, they called it, although a bra rarely made it under Kelley's clothes these days. That was one of the good things about being with someone for fifteen years: He knew her spots, just as Kelley knew what he liked, wanted, needed. And if there had been some challenges along the way, those moments were safely in the past now, averted disasters.

At bedtime—they made a point now of always going to bed together, which they hadn't been doing before—she found a slinky slip in the back of her underwear drawer and made sure not to wear her socks to bed, although it was freezing. In fact, Tom jumped back when her feet grazed his.

But she wrapped her legs around him and let him stay on top. She thought she would have to fake her orgasm—she had never been able to climax in this position—but she was intensely excited, feeling as if she were with someone new, or about to be.

Should I be a widow or divorcée? she wondered, Tom's movements quickening, his breath getting ragged. He was clearly excited. A widow felt almost too tragic, and Tom might be a bit miffed when they finally found each other. But she hated the idea of identifying as a divorcée, something she never wanted to be. She couldn't help it; when her female friends got divorced, she pitied them. Old-fashioned and sexist of her, but she never doubted it was on women to hold on to their men.

It never occurred to her to be single at thirty-five. That would truly be the worst.

She squeezed her legs harder around Tom's hips, thrusting against him, kissing him the way people kiss in the beginning. She felt so sorry for her single friends, who couldn't kiss anyone right now if they wanted to.

Étude in Black: The mistress of a symphony conductor plans to go public with his extramarital activities.

She found her new face by typing "generic 35 year old woman" into a Google Images search. She was tempted by the possibility of a dramatic makeover. In particular, there was a woman with a heart-shaped face and cascading curls piled in a messy topknot. But if Tom chose that woman—no, Kelley had to keep her new image in her wheelhouse, so to speak. She varied the hair color, going from light brown to blond, kept her blue eyes, went rounder with her face shape. Her girlfriends had always complimented Kelley's cheekbones, but it was her sense that men didn't even notice them.

She selected the name "Catie"—like hers, a common name with an uncommon spelling—and used her real age, thirty-five, which Tom had said was fair play. They had agreed that they could use any Baltimore neighborhood but their own, Anneslie. She chose Federal Hill, on the city's south side. They had lived in Riverside, which was adjacent to Federal Hill, right after graduation. Kelley had loved it, but Tom insisted they move to the north side so he would have a shorter commute.

Work? *Magazine writer.* Not strictly true; she was a technical writer. She had wanted to be a journalist, but Tom had lucked into a marketing job at Stanley Black & Decker right out of college and Baltimore didn't have much on offer for a twenty-two-year-old with no real reporting experience. Still, it was her choice to stay here and live with Tom. She owned that. She had wanted Tom more than any job, and look at the state of journalism now, anyway.

The much-touted questionnaire didn't seem magical to her or particularly intuitive. It reminded her a little bit of the Minnesota Multiphasic Personality Inventory, which she had been required to take in a college psych class. Kelley's results had been disappointingly normal. She didn't have a devious bone in her body, apparently.

And like most questionnaires, this one had one glaring flaw: it relied on the veracity of the person filling it out. The questions struck Kelley as so banal that she was almost tempted to write off-the-wall things. But then she began to think about the questionnaire as a version of that old TV show, *The Newly-wed Game*, in which the aim was to guess what your spouse would say. Whom would Tom choose? What was Tom's vision of Kelley? That was the real challenge.

Her favorite book? Only one? Should she pick one that made her sound smart, or an obscure title that established she was a little quirky? What about one that could double as a sly joke, like *The Wife Between Us*? Of course, she hadn't actually read it yet, but it was in her TBR pile, along with a lot of other books whose titles featured wives and girls and daughters; Kelley thought she might write a suspense novel during the pandemic. Did Tom ever look at her TBR pile? Did he know what she was reading? Did he care?

Oh, this was so much more complicated than she had realized. She was committed to telling the truth about herself, but that truth was predicated on the idea that Tom knew the true Kelley. Did he? Did she know the true Tom?

She would come back to books. She moved on to music. That was easier. She wrote down Taylor Swift, without apology.

Requiem for a Falling Star: A secretary is mistakenly ensnared in an aging actress's plot to murder a gossip columnist.

Slowly but surely, Catie, thirty-five, came to life. She was a journalist who considered Taylor Swift a guilty pleasure, whose ideal first date involved a long walk, who was not open to having children, was looking for long-term relationships but not necessarily marriage. Kelley felt a little bit like Dr. Frankenstein, although her creation was seamless and scar-less, practically pore-less. Her online self was her real self, only a tiny bit better. That's probably what everyone did, right? It was no different from applying a filter to a selfie.

Now what? She put her profile in play, declining push notifications. She always declined push notifications. She knew herself, how easily distracted she would be. Besides, it would ruin the game if she and Tom heard their phones chirping to each other.

It was Tuesday morning, which was set aside for grocery shopping. After much discussion, she and Tom had worked out what they called their Covid style. They fired their cleaning ladies—a corporate entity, so Kelley felt no guilt about that. They used delivery services as much as possible and quarantined packages in the garage. But they had decided it was okay for Kelley to go to the grocery store once a week, as long as she went to a small one and did her shopping in under thirty minutes.

She worked out their five-day meal plan: turkey meatloaf, chili, Alison Roman's shallot pasta, Italian sausages with greens and white beans, sweet potato hash. (They had carryout on Fridays and leftovers on Mondays.) She shopped at Eddie's, the only Baltimore City grocery store that sold liquor, making the errand an efficient twofer.

As she selected wines for that week's meals, Kelley allowed

herself a covert thought: *I'm so much happier than I was a year ago at this time.* It seemed a terrible way to feel, but it was true. No, she didn't want people to die and she was worried about the economic effects if the pandemic kept going. But sheltering in place with Tom, which would have been challenging six months ago, was cozy, almost blissful. If they had to be under a stay-at-home order, thank goodness it was now, when their troubles were behind them. Oh, they still saw Dr. Blau every other week, using a telehealth portal, but that was just *maintenance.* They had done the hard work. They were in a good place, watching *The Good Place*, relatively certain that soul mates really existed.

Sure, sometimes she felt a surge of anger—how could he, how dare he? *It wasn't about you.* That was the worst part of all. How could it not have been about her? If it wasn't about her, then what in their marriage was about her? Was anything ever about her?

You don't have to forgive him, the therapist had told her at one point. But if you can't forgive him, then it's hard to see how the marriage could continue.

That only made her angrier. She was the victim, she was the wronged party. "Why do I have to do anything?" she had asked.

Dr. Blau repeated himself. You don't. But that's a choice. And that choice has consequences.

"Didn't Tom's choices have consequences?"

Tom had looked at her with stricken eyes. "We're here," he said. "I've done everything I can to convince you that I want to be with you. But you're so angry with me. I'm living with my consequences every day. I've hurt you and I've—"

"Please don't finish that sentence," Kelley said.

Dr. Blau: "Kelley, you have to let Tom talk."

"Why?"

The Most Dangerous Match: An American chess champion plays a private match with his challenger and kills him.

You have a beautiful smile.

Hi.

You're sexy.

Hi.

Love those blue eyes.

Hi.

Kelley had known, expected, hoped, that more than one man would contact her via the dating app, that Tom would be a needle in a small haystack. But the sheer volume of responses caught her off guard. She preened a little over the interest in "Catie," despite the fact that the photograph was literally "generic 35 year old woman." The soul was hers, even if the photo was not. These were *her* matches.

But why were the responses so, well, stupid? Was that what worked? Was this what the world had come to? Her friend Amy had complained about her experience with dating apps, but Kelley had assumed Amy was extraordinarily picky.

Of course, Kelley's first meeting with Tom wasn't exactly Shakespeare-grade dialogue. He had missed a class, then asked if he could borrow her notes. She hadn't even realized he was making a move, not in the moment. It was only later, in his apartment—under the covers, clothes off, her notebook tossed to the floor long ago—that he confessed it had been a ruse.

"I would never ask to see your notes if I really cared about making up the work," Tom said. "Your handwriting's terrible, for one thing."

"How do you know what my handwriting looks like?"

"I've been sitting behind you for most of the semester, looking over your shoulder."

"Why?"

"You have the prettiest neck. And I like the way you fiddle with the locket that you wear." He touched the silver disc softly with his index finger. "Tell me about this."

There wasn't much of a story to tell. Her mother's third husband, stepfather number three, had gone on a business trip when Kelley was sixteen and brought her this locket for her birthday. She was pretty sure it was from the duty-free shop at Heathrow. She had never even bothered to put a photo inside it. Still, how she thrilled to those words: *You have the prettiest neck. Tell me about this.* That's how beginnings were supposed to work.

Online, it was all so generic, as if the men were casting wide nets with the most basic chum. *Hi. You're sexy. Hey beautiful. Love your photo.* And although she would feel a frisson at those compliments—sexy, beautiful, cute—she would quickly remember they were not for her, but her computer alter ego. Who, Kelley had decided, was not quite as pretty as she was. She wished the men who liked Catie could know that Kelley was even better-looking.

Also, quite a few of the men in her mailbox were way too old. She fiddled with her preferences, made it clear that she would not consider anyone over forty.

The one thing she was sure of was that not a single one was Tom. She wondered if he had even taken the test yet.

Lovely but Lethal: A manufacturer is suspected of
killing a chemist who stole a cosmetics formula.

"Let me get this straight," her friend Amy said. "You signed up for a dating service to meet your own husband?"

They were hiking a trail in Leakin Park, a bit of a drive from their North Baltimore homes, but blissfully isolated and sparingly used. The two friends had been hiking weekly for almost two months now and were desperate for novelty. The Gwynns Falls Trail went on for miles; it was possible to walk or bike to downtown. Once upon a time, Leakin Park was famous as a dumping ground for dead bodies, but with most of its roads blocked to cars, it was now a sylvan glade. Or so Amy, given her professional interest in plants, kept insisting. Kelley couldn't tell one tree from another and the Gwynns Falls, splashing across rocks in the ravine below them, was clearly polluted.

They were walking six feet apart, talking on their phones, masks at chin level. Masks were not required in outdoor spaces. Kelley had bought several cute ones, but she quickly tired of wearing one while hiking. So she and Amy took their phones on their hikes and talked that way, which prevented them from having to yell across the six-foot gap.

She explained her idea, glancing at her friend's face from time to time as she spoke. Amy looked a little like the woman Kelley had wanted to claim as her dating app avatar. Tendrils of curls worn in a messy topknot, heart-shaped face, large and alluring gray eyes. They had been friends for about ten years. If they had met when Kelley was single, Kelley often admitted to herself, a friendship might have been impossible. She would have felt competitive with Amy, the kind of bright spark who drew men. There was a line in a movie in which a woman said men were always crossing rooms to talk to her best friend. That's what life would have been like if she and Amy were both single.

"You should let me see your profile," Amy said. "In fact, you should let me manage it."

"Why?"

"Because I have so much more experience at this."

This was true. Amy's dating apps were almost like a second job to her. She even kept a spreadsheet.

"I've already taken the questionnaire."

"What about photos?"

"I had to use a fake one that I found on Google and now I can't add any because they won't match."

"Start over. Take that one down. I'll find someone on Facebook or Instagram and copy their photographs."

"Is that ethical?"

"Do you think what you and Tom are doing is ethical? There are real people looking at your profile, you know. People who are going to be disappointed when they engage with you, only to find out it's all some game."

Kelley hadn't thought about it that way. She wasn't trying to deceive anyone. She just wanted to test the test. She wouldn't be entirely disappointed if she and Tom didn't find each other. In some ways, that would only solidify in her mind that they were fated, that soul mates can't be found through a written test. Lord knows, they had been tested in other ways. This was a diversion, a way to entertain themselves during this strange, cold, dull spring.

Only so far, it wasn't very entertaining. Maybe she should let Amy manage her profile.

Candidate for a Crime: A senatorial candidate
exploits death threats, fabricated for publicity, to kill
his manager.

"They always overthink it," Tom said. "So much fucking around with clocks and watches and airtight alibis."

"And creating alternative suspects."

The episodes about infidelity were hardest to watch. Luckily, infidelity was rare in Columbo's world and the wives were not the victims. Well, they weren't the ones that the cheating husbands chose to kill. In a *Columbo* episode, *discovery* of infidelity was a thing to be avoided at all costs. People killed to avoid shame, to protect their careers, to get or keep money. But they seldom killed for love.

"Funny to think," Kelley said, "that a divorce was once political suicide and we now have a sitting president who cheated with a porn star."

"I'm beat," Tom said. "I'm going to turn in."

Kelley went with him, then stared at the ceiling as Tom slept. It was almost a year ago to the day that she had seen a text on Tom's phone, a series of hearts and kisses from a contact listed as "Arnold Murphy." A joke, she tried to tell herself. Surely it was a joke. A homophobic joke, but a joke. Nothing was going on.

Then why was she looking at Tom's phone in the first place?

She asked Amy to meet her for a walk in Lake Roland Park. She worried that if they met in a bar, or at Amy's apartment, she would break down completely. On a walk, it would be possible to avoid eye contact and thereby maintain her composure.

They had barely gone ten feet down the path when she blurted out, "He's having an affair." She described the text she had seen.

Amy gasped. "How can you be sure? Have you seen other texts, or emails, or—"

"I just *know*. He claims to be working late or working out. He runs odd errands at odd times, things that could easily wait— and shouldn't take as long as they end up taking."

"Who do you think it is?"

"Someone from work, most likely."

"Have you confronted him directly?"

"No. Because I'm scared he'll confirm it."

"What are you really scared of, Kelley?"

"That he loves someone else. That he's going to leave me."

She sank to her haunches and began to cry. Amy knew Kelley well enough not to try to hug her when she was this vulnerable. She crouched, keeping her gaze fixed somewhere over Kelley's left shoulder.

"Would that really be the worst thing, Kel? Do you want to be with someone who loves someone else?"

"I don't know, I don't know, I don't know." She hugged her knees, rocking back and forth. She couldn't imagine life without Tom. He was the love of her life, her destiny, proof that she had broken her mother's sad, chaotic patterns. Sure, she'd had other boyfriends before Tom, had even believed herself in love with one of them. But being married to her college sweetheart—*that* was the story that defined her, her essence. It was, in some ways, the most interesting thing about her. Kelley Atkinson, raised by that silly, dippy hippie, finding stability and certainty. Of course she and Tom had their ups and downs. Everybody did. But this was too far down. If she was right. She might not be right.

"I think you should confront him," Amy said. "He owes you

the truth. I gotta be honest—you've always seemed unhappy in your marriage to me. I'm not sure you and Tom are right for each other. And, in my opinion, marriage itself is wildly over-rated."

This was new information. No one had ever said such a thing, not to Kelley's face. Other friends, family, agreed with her view of them as the perfect couple. They *matched*. In looks, in goals, in temperament. Even Kelley's mother, who was a bit soured on matrimony after the fourth husband came and went, never had a bad word to say about Tom.

Kelley left the park that day determined to cool her relationship with Amy until she could sort out what was going on with Tom. She needed supportive people around her while in a crisis, not someone with an anti-marriage agenda. The crisis lasted longer than expected. But when she asked Amy out for drinks at year's end, she showed off the watch Tom had bought her for Christmas. It wasn't flashy, one of the name brands that a Real Housewife might flaunt. But it was vintage and he had added an inscription on the back: *Always Time for You.*

"Did he have an affair, though?" asked Amy.

"He called it a dalliance, said it was meaningless. Sort of a midlife thing."

"He's only thirty-four, Kel."

"Well, Tom was always precocious. And now he's gotten it out of the way and we can get on with our lives."

"Once a cheater—"

"Please don't, Amy."

A Friend in Deed: A man murders his wife and has a
friend cover up the act with a burglary.

Amy had worked wonders on Catie's profile. The men who
started filling her virtual mailbox were more plausible matches.
Almost too plausible. Was this Tom, this floppy-haired doctor
in Fell's Point? Or could the superfit hiker in Hampden be Tom?
Kelley was overwhelmed by the possibilities.

Of course, it wouldn't be *fatal* to be wrong. This was not
"The Lady, or the Tiger?" with only two possibilities. If she
got the wrong fish on her line—and she was still sure she would
recognize Tom within one or two exchanges—she would do a
quick catch-and-release. What was the harm?

The new Catie was pretty, almost too pretty. Should Kelley
be flattered that Amy saw her that way, or insulted that Amy assumed she needed an upgrade to catch her own husband's eye?
The gallery of photos showed Catie playing tennis, something
Kelley had never done; sitting with a glass of white wine, something Kelley had done frequently; attending a formal event, her
high-heeled shoes in hand.

However, the photo that drew the most responses was a
simple portrait of "Catie" holding an armful of roses. The shot
(almost certainly filtered, by Amy if not by the real Catie) high-
lighted her eyes, a startling blue in this photo and staring directly into the camera. "Catie's" gaze was bold and direct, with
a hint of a sexual challenge in it. Yet her dress was modest, her
hair pulled back in an unfussy ponytail. Still, this was the photo

that seemed to excite the most men. It excited most of them to utter the usual banalities.

Pretty!

Sexy!

Cute!

Hot!

And then from a man named Matt: Funny, you don't look like a woman who would like roses.

Kelley was not a woman who liked roses. Oh my God, she was not—and yet Tom didn't know that. Did he? When they were young, he gave her supermarket bouquets. It was only in the past few years that he started giving her roses, clearly expensive ones, and she didn't know how to explain to him that she preferred peonies. Maybe he was paying closer attention these days? Maybe he noticed that the bouquets she picked up at the grocery store tended toward hydrangeas and tulips?

Tell me about this. A finger on a locket, at her throat. She felt something she had assumed she would never feel again: the thrill of a beginning. Maybe this was how a settled couple made themselves new again to each other.

She wrote back: Truth be told, I prefer peonies.

He replied almost immediately: I hope we'll always tell each other the truth.

This was tricky. If Matt was Tom, and he suspected Catie

was Kelley, he knew they were both lying. If it wasn't Tom—oh dear, Kelley's head hurt. But it could be Tom. It must be Tom.

Then the worst possibility occurred to her: What if it was Tom, but he didn't believe Catie to be Kelley?

Cross my heart, she wrote back.

Then she put her phone in the laundry hamper and joined Tom on the sofa for another night of *Columbo*. She was not disappointed when "Matt" failed to reply by morning. After all, she had been by Tom's side all night.

Forgotten Lady: An aging actress plans to return to a Broadway musical against her husband's wishes.

"Do you remember the piña colada song?" Amy asked on their next hike.

"My mom had it on an *album*. She loved it. She actually met my dad through the classifieds, those old 'in search of' posts that ran in the alt weekly. He saw her at a bus stop and couldn't get her out of his head."

Despite the warm day, Kelley felt a chill. Kelley hadn't heard from her father in at least three years. He hadn't even bothered to attend her mother's funeral. Go figure, a man who met women by placing classified ads turned out to be less than reliable.

"I never understood how they could both laugh it off," Amy said. "In the song. She places an ad, clearly determined to cheat. He answers an ad, hoping to cheat. So then they're going to live happily ever after, knowing they have one important thing in common: they're both cheaters. The only thing that would make sense is for that song to end in murder."

A good case for Columbo, Kelley thought. "What's your point, Amy?"

"I think you're playing with fire."

"That's the *opposite* of what Tom and I are doing. Besides—I think I've already found him. Tom, I mean."

"Really?" Amy stopped on the path. "Toss me your phone, let me see."

Kelley disconnected their call, opened the app, threw her phone to Amy. She watched as her friend read her exchanges with the man Kelley thought of as "Matt," but what if he really was *Matt*, a flesh-and-blood person who happened to think Kelley was wonderful?

"He seems great," Amy said. "If it's not Tom, can I have him?"

"Amy! It's Tom. It has to be Tom."

"So what happens now?"

"Before we started, Tom suggested we have nonsensical safe words. When I'm sure—absolutely sure—I'm supposed to send the word 'baloney' to him. And if it's him, he'll text 'mayonnaise' back. Because he eats his baloney sandwiches with mayonnaise, sad to say."

"So why haven't you texted him 'baloney' yet?"

Why indeed?

"It's . . . fun. Sexy, even. I go about my day, wondering if there will be a message for me when I check. And the messages, when they show up, are so thoughtful, and complimentary, without being gross. I've exchanged messages with a few other men on here, just playing process of elimination, and they're all dull and ordinary. I see through them right away. This one—he has to be Tom. I feel as if he sees this as a chance for him to make up for the damage he did last year. He's saying all the things I wanted and needed to hear. Yet it feels new. And it's been a long time since anything in my life felt new."

"I don't know, Kel. Sounds to me like part of you hopes this isn't Tom. How long has this been going on now?"

"Only a week."

A week of daily, more than daily exchanges. He asked so many questions, questions she couldn't recall Tom ever asking. What were you like as a little girl? What's your first memory? How do you take your coffee? What do you miss most in a pandemic?

Kissing, she had written back. Of course, she was coupled, she didn't really have to go without kissing. So why did she feel as if she did?

She worried she had been too bold, but Matt replied immediately: That's what I miss, too.

Fade In to Murder: An egotistic TV detective matches wits with Columbo after murdering his producer.

She began waking up with an all-over tingle of anticipation, knowing that a message from Matt would arrive shortly after she and Tom adjourned to their separate WFH spaces. "Catie" and "Matt" communicated only through the app. He never asked to get on the phone with her, much less to meet face-to-face. More evidence this was Tom. Then again, meeting face-to-face would be tricky in a pandemic. And if it was Tom, why hadn't he invoked the code word by now? She didn't have to go first. He could type *mayonnaise* and wait for her *baloney*.

There were some intense moments in which she suspected Tom was testing her, was trying to show her how easy it was to slip. Matt spoke of what he wanted to do with Catie—and to Catie. He claimed to be a "giver," which was not how Kelley would describe Tom. Not selfish, not selfish at all. More, like— reciprocal to a fault, as if sex were a chore chart and everybody had a job. If he did *this*, then he expected *that*. It would never occur to Tom not to give Kelley pleasure, but it also did not occur to him that it would be okay, now and then, if an evening centered exclusively on her pleasure. Whereas, on nights where she didn't feel crazy in the mood, he was fine with doing whatever got him off as quickly as possible. "I have needs," he would say.

"I have needs," he had said in couples counseling last year.

"What do you mean? We still had sex. We never stopped having sex."

"I didn't feel like you were into it. Sometimes you wouldn't even take your socks off."

"I thought that considerate. My feet are like ice." She thought, but did not say: *Ever heard the expression* knock my socks off? *You could have brought a little more enthusiasm to the task.*

Task. The word she had used for their sex life echoed in her head. She was glad she hadn't said it out loud.

The therapist interjected: "In the end, though—do you think this was really about Kelley, Tom?"

He folded his arms, shut down. But Dr. Blau was comfortable with Tom's silences, used them to advantage. He waited and Tom eventually spoke.

"It's just that—Kelley and I fell in love when we were so young. I'm not sure she even realizes the ways in which I've grown and changed. I go to work, people respect me. The company weathered a tough time, there was a rough period where it looked as if the headquarters would move to Connecticut, and Kelley wasn't supportive at all. She said she wouldn't move even if I were lucky enough to get reassigned. The other woman—"

Kelley wanted to object. It was so much more complicated than that. They had stayed in Baltimore for his job, but she had come to love the city. She didn't want to move. She had a job, she had friendships. But she didn't interrupt. She wanted to hear what Tom would say next, even if it was devastating to her.

"The other woman—I swear, we weren't together more than four or five times—she saw me as I am now. She was impressed by me. Kelley makes me feel like a little boy who tracks mud on her floors and breaks her rules. I feel like a guest in my own home."

She couldn't help herself. "I don't have rules! I'm not rigid! But order is important to me after the way I grew up—"

"Kelley"—the therapist held up a hand, cautioning her to let Tom have his say. He seldom got on a roll like this.

"I wanted to be *wanted*," Tom said. "To see desire in a woman's eyes. The best I got from Kelley as of late was forbearance. I wanted to feel new."

Kelley put her face in her hands and wept. It was too much. Maybe she had nagged him a little. Maybe their sex life had become perfunctory. But he had *cheated*. How was she supposed to recover from that? Tom had steadfastly declined to tell her anything about the other woman, and the therapist vouched for his choice, saying it wasn't a productive line of inquiry. So Kelley was left with the images that she assumed tortured all deceived spouses—her husband in bed with another woman who was younger, more beautiful, skinnier, and they were laughing at her. *Laughing.* How could her husband's affair not be about her?

But one day she found the words she never thought she could say. "I forgive you, Tom. And I'm sorry. I love you so much. It's not that I see your flaws and love you in spite of them. I love you and I know you're not perfect."

"I love you, too, Kelley. I stayed, didn't I? And when you confronted me, without a shred of evidence, I copped to it and immediately broke things off. I know you need to learn to trust me again. But I need to trust you, too."

Four months later, the governor of Maryland issued the stay-at-home advisory.

Columbo Goes to the Guillotine: A magician is beheaded during rehearsal for his guillotine trick by his old psychic mentor.

"So, any baloney yet?" Amy asked teasingly.

"Noooooo—I'm beginning to worry that it's not Tom."

"Why is that worrisome? Besides, if you think it's not Tom, all the more reason to stop messaging the guy. You don't want to lead him on."

Even with their phones and social distancing, they now wore masks when they walked, and Kelley was glad that hers hid the lower half of her face and hoped her cheeks weren't too flushed. *Too late*, she wanted to tell her friend, but their relationship, while candid, had never included explicit details about their sex lives.

Kelley herself was shocked by what could happen within the neat and orderly squares of a dating app, the words that could be said, the acts that could be simulated. She and Tom had, over the course of their long relationship, had some heated (good heated) conversations when he traveled for business, but it was nothing like this. Matt had progressed from saying what he wanted to do to her to fantasies in which he was doing those things. A subtle shift in syntax and yet Kelley was shaken (good shaken). She would go into the bathroom before bedtime, re-read the day's messages, come back out and climb into bed with Tom and, no, she wasn't wearing socks. She closed her eyes and imagined "Matt." Who, of course, was really Tom, it had to be Tom, although Tom seemed almost surprised by her sudden ardor. If Tom was writing these messages, wouldn't he be worked up, too?

But if Tom was the one writing those messages, maybe he

thought they were going to a stranger? Was he cheating on her again? Kelley knew she couldn't survive that, even if he was cheating on her with her.

"I don't know, it's such a strange, boring time. Any distraction has to be a good thing. It's not like this guy—who's probably Tom, but if he's not Tom, it's not like he's in love with me, it's not like he's waiting for the lockdown to end so we can meet face-to-face."

Amy sighed. "I'm having fun on the apps, too, right now. But sometimes I watch movies from the 1970s and '80s, when people met in bars and just went home and had sex, and it seems absolutely *wholesome*."

"I have a feeling that if we asked our moms about it, they might tell it differently." The chill, again. All those men. Not only the husbands. The boyfriends in between as well. Kelley's mother had shown no discretion, no discernment. Kelley's mother would have loved dating apps, said *Hi* to every *Hi*, gone out with anyone who asked. She had loved the attention of men.

Amy, clearly still thinking about movies from the 1970s, said: "Although in *Saturday Night Fever*, they gangbang that one girl. In fact, all the sex in that movie was horrible. Only the dancing was sexy."

"Have you ever been with more than one person at a time?" It was a way to change the subject.

"No, but I suppose it's only a matter of time. So many guys seem to want that now. It's on all their sexual bingo cards."

"I thought we agreed that 'bingo card' was a cliché that needed to be retired."

"The 2020 bingo card is a cliché. The sexual bingo card is very real. Trust me, guys come into relationships with these sexual bucket lists."

"Which is it, Amy, a bingo card or a bucket list?"

"A bucket list," Amy said. "And most of them are going to die with it unfinished."

They laughed as they made their way along the trail, masked and six feet apart, Amy pointing out flora that interested her, Kelley incapable of recognizing any of it. Maybe that was why she got poison ivy every year. *Leaves of three, let it be.*

Sex and the Married Detective: The disheveled detective gets some free advice from a world famous sex therapist.

"These later episodes just don't seem the same," Tom said. "In fact—they're kind of awful."

"There was a big gap," said Kelley. "At least ten years, I think."

"It *looks* different, too. The settings are kind of cheap-looking, a facsimile of grandeur. And that schtick at the end of the one about the director. That's not how Columbo did things. The villain is the elaborate schemer. The villain traps himself, really, in a vintage *Columbo*."

"Maybe they shouldn't have tried to keep it going. Not everything lasts."

In this episode, a sex therapist discovered that her business manager, who was also her lover, was cheating on her with her assistant. Because she was a sex therapist, her office had a lovely romantic bedroom, complete with a fireplace. (Kelley assumed there was some confusion about sex therapists and sex surrogates.) The therapist spied on her lover and her assistant through the slits in a louvered door. He removed the ribbon from his conquest's hair and she asked him to compare her to a dessert. "Bavarian chocolate cream pie," he said promptly. "Laced with rare Napoleon brandy." (A waste to use good brandy in pie, Kelley thought.) The assistant then pressed him to compare his girlfriend to a dessert. Rice pudding, he said, and they laughed, while a single tear snaked down the therapist's cheek.

The therapist later convinced her lover to play a game in which she pretended to be a high-priced call girl in a black wig—and shot him to death.

Columbo caught her, of course. Confronted by the evidence, the sex therapist confessed. She confessed to more than the crime. She admitted that she enjoyed her alter ego, "Lisa." Enjoyed the power she felt in that role. Relished recapturing her dignity. She was one of the killers that Columbo almost seemed to like. But maybe it was only pity.

"Do you want anything from the kitchen?" Kelley asked as Tom changed to MSNBC. "I'm going to make a sundae."

"Naw, I've got to watch myself." He patted his belly, which was nonexistent since he had finally started running in the afternoons, going out every day after his last Zoom meeting. Kelley realized he had been more careful about his diet as of late, too, eschewing desserts and bread.

In the kitchen, Kelley took out her phone. Matt had not written her all day. It had been a busy day, so that would track if Matt were Tom. She started to type: One more thing: B-A-L-O-N— then stopped, deleted the text, and quit the app.

She returned to the den with an apple and a glass of water.

"No sundae?" Tom asked.

"You're right, we've got to watch ourselves," she said.

"I never said anything about *you*. You look great."

"I've gained at least ten pounds."

"You look beautiful to me."

"If I were a dessert—"

"Tiramisu," he said. "So many layers."

She believed him. He still thought she was beautiful. And layered. That night, when they had sex, he was unusually tentative and tender.

Yet Kelley could not stop thinking: *Is he thinking of someone else?*

Is he thinking of Catie?

Does he talk to other women via the app?

Am I thinking of Matt?

Is someone new going to see me naked soon?

Did they laugh at me, Tom and his lover? Did they pity me?

Rest in Peace, Mrs. Columbo: The widow of a crooked real estate agent vows to exact her revenge on the two men that put him in prison.

"How do single people hook up now?" Kelley asked Amy on their next hike. "How does anyone get anything going?"

"I don't know. I'm giving up."

"You don't look like someone who's given up." Amy's brows were groomed and darkened with pencil. Her hair, now midway down her back, was pulled into a tight, high ponytail, very becoming. Her legs looked thinner than they had in early spring, her rear end tighter and higher.

"Oh, I'm doing my maintenance, flirting online. But that's just because it fills the days. What else is there to do but ride my Peloton, fiddle with various regimens? I found a great roots concealer at the Dermstore."

Kelley's hand reflexively reached for her hairline. She didn't have to dye her hair, not really, but she had relied on a colorist to give her light brown hair more variety and tones. It was looking pretty flat these days. Maybe there was a drugstore product that could spice it up. She had wanted a Peloton, but Tom had vetoed it because of the cost.

"Why the interest?" Amy said. "Are you thinking about hooking up with someone?"

"Of course not!"

"Have you invoked your safe word yet?"

"No . . . If it is Tom—and I'm sure it's Tom—well, I'm enjoying it. Is that so wrong? Our own sex life seems to be getting better all the time, so it's a win-win."

"Maybe because you're fantasizing about someone else."

"I am *not*."

"Not even a little? Fantasies aren't illegal, Kelley. Or even immoral. Do you think Tom doesn't think about anyone but— oh, hey, I'm sorry. That was thoughtless of me."

"Don't worry about it." Kelley was surprised at how hard the knowledge still hit, how any reminder of Tom's affair affected her on a physical level, almost as if someone had punched her in the stomach. It was over a year ago. She must not let her mind take her backward, to those raw, angry days. "I was just curious about how single people are managing during the pandemic."

Amy said: "Okay, so this is what I will do if I 'meet' someone and decide to have sex. There's a protocol to it. First, you have to put it on the table, right? You're going to meet face-to-face, and sex is a possibility. So you have to get tested, then quarantine yourself. Ideally, after two weeks, you'd then take a rapid test, but those are hard to find in our area."

"Sounds like you have been thinking about this."

"I was a Girl Scout. Be prepared, you know. So then you meet—"

"Where?"

"That part is tricky. I mean, I think a hotel would be safe— depending on the hotel. Oh, and you should have someone you check in with via text, before and after. But that's a safety precaution that applies to dating anyone new."

"O brave new world," Kelley said.

"You're lucky you have Tom."

"I know."

Back home, she locked herself in the bathroom and reread the message Matt had sent that morning.

Do you think we'll ever meet IRL? I'm not saying we should right now—too risky. But one day, do you think we will?

It was strange, how that question affected her even on second reading. Her knees felt wobbly, her heart jumpy. She had to sit down on the bathroom floor and put her head between her knees. After much thought, she wrote back.

Seems inevitable.

Inevitable because "Matt" was Tom, right?

Or inevitable because even if Matt wasn't Tom, she had to know. Know what? She wasn't sure. She had to know if this was Tom. She had to know if an app had, in fact, found her the perfect man and it wasn't her husband.

Whatever decision she made, the fantasy would end. But what was the fantasy? Was she fantasizing about her husband wooing her all over again through another persona? Or was she fantasizing about a new man?

Fantasies aren't illegal, Amy had said. But maybe they should be.

No Time to Die: Columbo attends his nephew's wedding and the bride disappears before the honeymoon.

"I've been thinking about the piña colada song," Amy said on their next walk.

"Why?"

"Because of your situation, of course. I Googled the song—I feel as if people should have written dissertations about it. What was wrong with people in the 1970s? Did you know that guy had another song, in which a man tries to propose to a woman on an answering machine? And she replies. On his answering machine. I mean, no one was that stupid, ever, right?"

Spring had vaulted into summer, and it was suddenly hot, even here on their hiking path, where the sun had trouble piercing the canopy of leaves. But Kelley felt as if someone had opened a door to a draft. *No one was ever that stupid.* She had been exactly that stupid, last year. She'd had no inkling that Tom would stray. Sure, she and Tom had been a little cross and irritated with each other during the early part of the year. Snappish, unkind. And then Tom had changed, become more solicitous, more considerate. He had even shocked her with unusually expensive earrings for their ten-year anniversary.

"The traditional gift for a decade is tin," he said when she opened the small velvet box. "I hope you'll accept platinum as a substitute."

Later, a lawyer she consulted in her brief period of fury had nodded. "Classic. We see that all the time. He probably bought you something to assuage his guilty conscience, because he was buying her gifts as well." And that had made Kelley sadder, that her husband's infidelity wasn't even original.

"Can we talk about your love life for a change?" Kelley asked Amy.

"I've got three men going right now."

"Three?"

"They're all quite different. One is totally appropriate—I meet him for walks sometimes. One good thing about coronavirus is every place sells go-cups now, so you can walk and drink. Another one is cerebral, in a good way. He reminds me of Tom." Kelley's expression must have looked stricken because Amy added hastily, "It's *not* Tom, I'm sure of that. He lives in the D.C. suburbs. And the third one is for sexting. I call them the Ego, the Superego, and the Id."

"How—compartmentalized."

"Marriage isn't for everyone, Kelley. I'm thirty-five, single in a pandemic, just trying to have fun."

Columbo Likes the Nightlife: Columbo investigates the apparent suicide of a tabloid reporter in the Los Angeles rave scene.

Do you want to meet?

It was similar to the question Matt had asked two weeks earlier, the one she had tried to deflect. Yet it was not the same. There was a world of difference between *Do you think we'll ever meet?* and *Do you want to meet?*

Her fingers seemed to type of their own volition. Of course I do.

Let's.

How do we make it safe?

We could just meet for a walk, the first time out.
Somewhere outdoors, like South Baltimore or Fell's Point,
where most of the bars are selling go-cups.

This sounds like an actual plan. You've been thinking about
this, haven't you?

Haven't you?

Kelley thought of the piña colada song. *Aw, it's you.* Would
she be disappointed or thrilled if Tom showed up for their date?

And then she remembered that Baltimore was known as
Smalltimore for a reason and even in a part of town where she
didn't live, it was highly likely that she would see someone she
knew.

Which wouldn't matter if this was Tom. But—who was
she kidding? She hadn't believed this was Tom for quite some
time.

I don't know.

Your profile said your ideal first date was a long walk.
Maybe you know a place?

As a matter of fact, I do.

She sent him a link to the Gwynns Falls Trail.
She closed the app and returned to the den. They had
reached their final *Columbo*. The killer was that handsome actor

from *The Americans*, the one who ended up in a relationship with his once-married costar.

"Don't forget," she said, "I'm hiking with Amy on Saturday. Like I do every Saturday."

"There they go again, overexplaining everything," Tom said.

"What?"

"Just talking to the television, babe."

"I can't believe this was the last one. Talk about going out with a whimper."

"NO, KELLEY, NO. DON'T DO this."

"I can't help myself, Ames. I think I'm in love with him." She was pacing in the backyard, on her phone.

"Use the code word first, at least. Because maybe the person you've fallen in love with is really Tom. Wouldn't that be the happiest ending? Isn't that what you wanted?"

"But if it's Tom, it ends."

"In a good way. What do you really want, Kelley? You always seemed so sure it was Tom."

What did she want? The very question felt audacious. She saw herself at twenty. It was like watching a character in a movie. A girl walks into a classroom. There's a nice-looking guy sitting behind her. It seems so random. Why that class, why that guy? Why is meeting someone in that way superior to being fixed up, or meeting online? Her parents' meeting through a classified ad, an absolutely romantic story until it ended with him skipping out when Kelley was two years old. What makes a romance romantic, the beginning or the end?

Once upon a time, a girl met a guy, who happened to be from the Chicago suburbs, as she was, although her mother's apartment in Skokie couldn't be more different than his parents' house in River Forest. They agreed on superficial things— White Sox, not the Cubs; sausage but not pepperoni on pizza; Dairy Queen was better than luxury ice creams. They agreed on big things. No children, no religion. They pretended to agree on other things. Tom's career came first. They would live in North Baltimore.

Kelley disconnected from Amy, locked herself in the bathroom, and opened the app. Her profile had been paused long ago, but anyone who had communicated still had access to it. She pulled down the photos of "Catie" and replaced them with her real face, choosing a selfie from late last year, when she was a little slimmer. But it otherwise was an unremarkable candid shot, a fair likeness. She wasn't trying to fool anyone, not anymore.

Dear Matt, she typed. One more thing: "Baloney."

His response came swiftly.

I don't understand, he wrote. Are you saying I said something false? Are we still meeting Saturday? And why did your photo change?

This is the real me. I had reasons to hide behind fake photos. Nothing sinister. It was—she cast about for a plausible reason—a safety measure.

I hope you're okay?

Oh, yes. I'll explain everything when we meet. If you still want to meet?

I do. I confess, I'm mystified, but we've talked so much, shared so much. I feel I know you and can trust you.

You can! she typed. You can!

She held her phone to her throat. She felt like a heroine in a nineteenth-century novel, clutching a man's written declaration of love. It was magic. It was science. The app had found her perfect man and now that she knew he existed, how could she not see this through?

NO OTHER CAR WAS PARKED in the lot by the tennis courts, where she and Amy usually met. Ah well. Kelley checked the app, realizing she had no other way to communicate with Matt. Good thing, as there was a message waiting.

I screwed up, entered the park at the dead end on Wetheredsville Road. Can we meet halfway? I'll start walking toward you and you start walking toward me.

There it was again, that heady feeling of being in a movie. She had to exercise all her self-control not to break into a jog, to start running toward—what was she running toward? Her future? A grievous mistake? Tom would be hurt. But he had hurt her.

And what if it was Tom? What if he had taken their mutual game and piña colada'ed it, as Amy might have said. Yes, she would want to kill him, but only because she could not bear for Matt not to exist.

She came to Wetheredsville and started heading in what she hoped was the right direction. How far had he parked? The trail was a confusing place, accessible from so many points. Was he not good with maps, did he lack a sense of direction? She began to think about all the mundane things she didn't know about Matt. Yes, they had "talked" endlessly about what they liked. She knew his preferences in food and drink—uncannily like hers—but not the manner in which he ate and drank. What if he slurped? She did not know if he was a good tipper or how he held his liquor when he had a little too much. She did not know any of his day-to-day habits. Did he pick his teeth? Leave his clothes on the bathroom floor? Never hang up his jacket? Leave cabinet doors ajar as if closing them was simply too much to ask?

Some of these were Tom's habits.

She was beginning to despair when she heard footsteps from behind her, fast and light. Maybe she had overshot his position somehow and he had figured it out, had come running to her. She turned in delight only to be surprised.

"Why are you—"

"I STILL DON'T UNDERSTAND," TOM said. "Why was Kelley in Leakin Park? That's miles from here."

"We've been hiking there on Saturdays, but she specifically told me she couldn't make it last week. I don't know, Tom. I'm as baffled as you are."

"Did she confide in you? Did she tell you what was going on?"

"No, Tom. I mean—she did mention signing up for one of the dating apps, but she said that was just a game she was playing with you."

"The game? Oh, that crazy idea of hers. We were just joking. I never even got around to signing up."

They were in Tom's backyard, which, up till a few days ago, had been Tom and Kelley's backyard. Amy looked at the plantings, the lawn furniture. Not to her taste. Kelley wasn't a gardener, though. She could barely tell a weed from a flower. The natural setting of their hikes had made no impression on her. She was so busy talking about herself and her fauxmance that she didn't register much of anything on their walks.

That was fine with Amy. Kelley's self-involvement had made it easy to create the perfect man for her.

Kelley definitely didn't notice how weak and rotted the old guardrails were, how easy it would be to go crashing through one and tumble down the rocky hill toward the stream. Especially if someone pushed you.

Of course, Amy knew better than to rely on a fall to do the job. After she pushed Kelley, she removed a pair of size 9 male hiking boots from her backpack, making her way gingerly in the too-big shoes. Kelley was unconscious, but still breathing. Amy rolled her over so her face was submerged in the water. Kelley didn't rouse or splutter, so the injury to her head must have been pretty severe. Amy then smashed Kelley's phone and tossed it downstream. The data would live on, of course. But someone had to know to look for the data.

She walked back up the hill, changed into her own shoes, and hiked to her car. She tossed the boots in a dumpster behind a bakery, drove home, and waited, knowing it was only a matter of time before Tom would call with the awful news. She was good at waiting. She had been waiting a long time for this opportunity. Since Kelley had given her access to her dating app. Maybe even before. She was no fling, no dalliance. She was tired of performing singlehood for her married friends, who treated her like an exotic creature. If it weren't for the pandemic, Tom probably would have broken up with Kelley by now in order to be with Amy. He had been miserable with Kelley, but he was such a good man he had sacrificed his own happiness to honor his marriage vows. Well, now Amy had freed him of that obligation, that albatross.

Tom held his head in his hands. "You didn't ever tell her, did you, Amy? About what happened with us last year? I know you always thought I should come clean with her, but I didn't want to wreck your friendship."

"No, I respected your wishes, Tom. Do the police have any leads?"

"Nothing they've shared with me."

Amy risked patting his shoulder. They were masked, of course. The funeral had been sad—not only because it was a Zoom event, but because Kelley had no family to mourn her. Her mother was dead and Tom didn't know how to find her father. Tom's parents were as Amy had imagined them—youthful, lean, the spark of romantic love between them still evident. One day, Tom and Amy would look much like them. One day.

For now, she would help with the garden, tell him that she was executing a vision Kelley had outlined on their hikes. She would start to bring picnic suppers over. He would open a bottle of wine, they would sit out under the stars and share drinks and confidences. Eventually, she and Tom would take their masks off, go back to doing what they had done so memorably last year, even if it had been only a handful of times. He would fall in love with her. So sad about Kelley, but hundreds of people were dying every day. What was one more body on the pile?

AFTERWORD

In the musical *Merrily We Roll Along*, lyricist Charley is asked what comes first when he works with his partner, composer Frank, the words or the music.

"Generally the contract," Charley says. It's a dig, an insult. It's also more or less how I write short stories, although my answer would be: "Generally, the *contact*." Almost every story here began with an email from a friend or acquaintance who asked if I would consider writing a story inspired by a theme, or, in the case of "Snowflake Time," featuring a particular bookshop. The only exception was "Just One More," written for this collection.

The other stories were produced over a twelve-year span, from 2007 through 2019. The world changes a lot in twelve years, and I was careful to note where language and ideas might have aged poorly. Is that "woke"? So be it. I know some people use that word as a pejorative, but I consider it a good thing.

One story in particular, "Ice," gave me pause: Should I be writing from the point of view of a young Black girl? Had I created a story in which Black people suffer so white people might live? I made two small changes to the text, but decided the story ultimately is about how Athena frees herself—not only from the pond that has held her body for so many years, but also from the fate of being a cautionary story used only to remind other children of the world's dangers. Athena does not save Mickey; she uses Mickey to save herself, to transcend, literally and figuratively, the false myth that has trapped her.

I also thought hard about Marissa in "Waco 1982" saying she's one-quarter Lebanese when she so clearly identifies as white. What is the point of that, other than to explain her "exotic" looks? I'm not sure. I am sure that Marissa does not believe she has experienced bigotry based on her ethnicity, only on her gender. I thought about making her Jewish, but that would have been a loaded choice as well. Trust me, I know. When I lived in Waco, Texas, from 1981 to 1983, I had a Star of David on my checks, a strange choice for a Presbyterian, but my grandfather was Jewish and, like Marissa, I thought I was an envelope-pusher.

I noted, but did not change, small anachronisms in the older stories. One example: Lenore, aka the "Cougar," would probably have an iPad or a similar tablet by now, and would be able to watch movies in her kitchen. However, I think she would still be upset about her son taking over her basement to manufacture meth.

And when the indefatigable Laura Cherkas pointed up similar turns of phrase in the stories, I let them stand. I don't care if the world knows I'm obsessed with eavesdropping, or that I find many rom-coms, with their insistence on pain-free breakups, darker than most crime stories.

There were some joyous discoveries—in "The Book Thing," written when my daughter was two, Carla Scout is clearly modeled on my child. The mystery series described in "Snowflake Time" not only made me laugh, it made me wonder why there is not, in fact, a series of cozies written about Christmas, Ohio. It's also dumb luck that this earlier version of Judith and Patrick Monaghan more or less aligns with their history as presented in *Lady in the Lake*. More or less.

It was also nice to be reminded that I can write stories in which no one dies. There are four in this book, although I think we can all agree that the stepfather in "Seasonal Work" is living on borrowed time. Then again, aren't we all?

Laura Lippman
Baltimore, Maryland
March 2021

CREDITS